EMMETT

L O N D O N

112 Jermyn Street

D0059521

www.emmettlondon.com

CBC

CURTIS BROWN CREATIVE

THE WRITING SCHOOL FROM THE
MAJOR LITERARY AGENCY

We have been supporting new writers for more than 10 years

With over 190 former students with publishing deals

Image© Julia Boggio

Stacey Thomas

*Author of The Revels
(HQ, Jul 23)*

'The CBC course
made me a
more intentional
writer'

Alex Hay

*Caledonia Novel Award-winning
author of The Housekeepers
(Headline, Jul 23)*

'That was the special
thing about CBC: a
sense of fellowship with
other writers'

Image© Jillian Edelstein

Imogen Crimp

*Author of A Very Nice Girl
(Bloomsbury, Feb 22)*

'Having other
people discuss
my writing in
workshops was
so useful'

Join a writing course online or in London

www.curtisbrowncreative.co.uk

GRANTA

12 Addison Avenue, London W11 4QR | email: editorial@granta.com
To subscribe visit subscribe.granta.com, or call +44 (0)1371 851873

ISSUE 163: SPRING 2023

Edinburgh International Book Festival

12–28 August 2023

The World, in Words

Come together for over 500 events featuring the best writers from around the world, in the beautiful leafy surrounds of the Edinburgh College of Art nestled in the heart of Edinburgh.

Programme launch Wed 14 June
Tickets on sale Thurs 29 June

edbookfest.co.uk | @edbookfest

CONTENTS

Subscribe to *The Drift*!

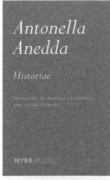
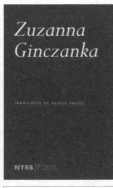

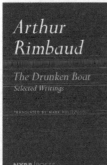
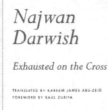
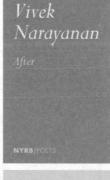

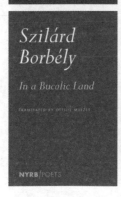
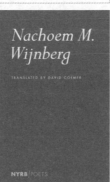

Find what you

National
Art Pass_____

weren't
looking for.

Get endless inspiration with free entry
to hundreds of museums, galleries and
historic places across the UK. Search
National Art Pass or visit artfund.org

The more you see,
the more you see.

Art Fund_

AESTHETICA
CREATIVE WRITING AWARD 2023

WIN £5000 & PUBLICATION
SUBMIT YOUR POETRY | FICTION

DEADLINE 31 AUGUST 2023

aestheticamagazine.com

Introduction

This is *Granta*'s fifth edition of the Best of Young British Novelists issue, our once in a decade list of twenty of the most promising writers under forty living in the UK. These issues have a long gestation. For over a year, editors on the *Granta* team read and discussed several hundred submissions to compile the shortlist for the judges: renowned novelists Tash Aw, Rachel Cusk and Helen Oyeyemi, and critic, essayist and lecturer Brian Dillon. The deadline for the judges' deliberations was August 2022, to give the authors ample time to write the pieces for this issue.

It soon became clear that the submitted works separated into genres, or, more loosely, trends: the historical novels, most notably *The Parisian* by Isabella Hammad and *The New Life* by Tom Crewe; speculative fiction (Sophie Mackintosh, Julia Armfield, Sarvat Hasin, Missouri Williams and Alison Rumfitt); and, perhaps most distinctly, a number of autobiographical novels about gang culture, all written in the vernacular. Graeme Armstrong (*The Young Team*), Gabriel Krauze (*Who They Was*) and Moses McKenzie (*An Olive Grove in Ends*) all made the shortlist, as did the works of Guy Gunaratne (*In Our Mad and Furious City* and *Mister, Mister*), which are more explicitly concerned with the theatre of global violence drawn onto a particular London stage (a council estate, a bus). The former three are novels of masculinity and honour, where violence (beyond its role in the commerce of drugs and robbery) is a force simultaneously tainting and purifying. The characters – mostly boys and young men – seem to be always in motion, moving through decaying environments, inventing codes and gestures, buying, selling, planning, talking. Eliza Clark's *Boy Parts* has some affinity with these worlds, with its protagonist's voice of dirty disaffection and thinly veiled disdain, but her alienation is symbolic, static, singular to the point of loneliness. Camilla Grudova's writing, too, deadpan, experimental, at times scatological, evokes some of the same atmosphere, as does Lauren Aimee Curtis's faintly distorted women (nuns) in the short novel *Dolores*, which creates a similar juxtaposition (and interrogation) of the sullied and the pure.

I t is a platitude to say that every list reflects the taste of the jurors, but this panel represented a wider range of taste than I had expected – our ideas of, and feel for, literary merit diverged quite radically. I hope the final list might be more interesting for it, containing, as it does, a wide range of voices, but still, the dividing line between the writers who made the final list and those who didn't has never felt quite so permeable. I never have much faith in lists in any case, and I think we should acknowledge that a different panel might easily have chosen a different group of novelists. Apart from the shortlisted authors mentioned above, Oyinkan Braithwaite, Claire Powell, Naoise Dolan or Kirsty Logan might have been chosen for their works of deceptive simplicity and narrative verve; Daisy Johnson, Aidan Cottrell-Boyce, Lauren John Joseph or Shola von Reinhold for their innovation and exuberance; A.K. Blakemore, Fiona Mozley, Barney Norris, James Cahill, Samuel Fisher or James Clarke for their serious and polished writing; and Vanessa Onwucmezi, Dizz Tate, Omar Robert Hamilton or Daisy Lafarge for their originality. These writers could all have been on the list, and of course there are others, too.

The judges read, and thought about language, intention, originality, characters, structure, plot and complexity. In our meetings, Rachel Cusk talked about writers' ability (or failure) to control and transcend their own material as an important criterion for inclusion on the list. We discussed authenticity of voice, particularly in relation to the works written in the vernacular. We were interested in experimental writing, but we also felt it was important to include authors who did not necessarily play with language, but whose craft and imagination made them outstanding storytellers. Tash Aw questioned how far we should privilege a text's internal sense or logic in our choices, and Brian Dillon noted the slightly caressing, watery feel of many of the novels on the shortlist, and the hard singularity of others. Helen

Oyeyemi (the judge among us perhaps most committed to fiction testing the boundaries of convention) was also interested in whether the writer succeeded in evoking curiosity in the reader – were we compelled to know what happens next?

What does the list tell us about the next generation or the state of the nation? I am hesitant to speculate, particularly since we changed the eligibility criteria for admission, dropping the requirement of a British passport in favour of those who live here and think of this country as home. Five authors on the list, including Eleanor Catton, were born abroad, and Sara Baume was born in Britain but lives in Ireland. But some common themes still emerge – these writers are millennials, the 9/11 generation. Most of them are too young to have experienced much of the brief period of hope following the end of the Cold War. They grew up affected by harsh threats and counterthreats – terror and the war on terror, the financial crash of 2008 followed by austerity and economic polarisation, radical moments followed by disillusion. There are dystopian themes in the novels we considered but affection for the local is here, too, most notably in the short stories of Thomas Morris (*We Don't Know What We're Doing*) and Saba Sams (*Send Nudes*). We noted the struggle to make meaning of hard lives (Yara Rodrigues Fowler and Natasha Brown) and the various attempts to understand the conditions of displacement or (more generally) alienation (Olivia Sudjic, Lauren Aimee Curtis, Jennifer Atkins, Anna Metcalfe). We were all excited by the more experimental texts trying to understand and explore the limits of what language and writing can do (Eley Williams, Derek Owusu, Sara Baume, Graeme Armstrong, Sarah Bernstein). Some of the writers on the list defy categorisation – Eleanor Catton's work is conceptual and imaginative, yet pacy and well plotted, mixing the historical with the contemporary, and the genres broadly termed 'literary' and 'thriller'. Finally, K Patrick's short novel *Mrs S* was a revelation. Like Maggie Nelson's *The Argonauts* (a hybrid memoir essay on queer identity), it simply and tenderly returns to the question of love: what it is, and what it feels like.

To the judges: thank you. I am grateful for your company, your commitment, your diligence and your insight. To the publishers and agents who engaged with this process, thank you. To all the *Granta* editors – Luke Neima, Rachael Allen, Josie Mitchell, Eleanor Chandler, Lucy Diver and Brodie Crellin – who took on the extra burden of reading and logistics. Chairing those editorial meetings has been a privilege and a pleasure. Most of all, thank you to all the writers, whether they were on the final list or not. Writing is a mysterious thing: marks on the page evoking images in the minds of others, but it has given me and many others the backbone of our lives, our work, our culture and our own imaginary homelands. ∎

Sigrid Rausing

THE CLOUD FACTORY

Graeme Armstrong

There's this photograph ae us at Christmas. Ma granny is wearin a wee sparkly blue cardigan wae hur hair aw done nice. A'm lyin on a chair next tae hur, wearin white trackies n a black polo shirt wae the collar up, in a total state. This look hud become semi-permanent. A stayed oot aw night wae the YOUNG MAVIS, stood ootside the Orange Hall, drinkin Buckfast oot oor nuts on ekto pills. Ma maw wis annoyed cos she didnae want ma gran tae know aboot the violence, drugs n madness. A hud awready been expelled fae Airdrie Academy n turned up regularly wae broken teeth n black eyes. Ma eld gran wisnae daft. That wis wan ae hur last wae us. Ma maw got me a card that said, CHRISTMAS IS A TIME WHEN YOU WANT YOUR PAST FORGOTTEN AND YOUR PRESENT REMEMBERED. A laughed but felt bad aboot it. Ma lovin family wur collateral damage tae aw this.

The lure ae gangs n territorial violence is unstoppable fur many young men in Scotland's former industrial heartland, North Lanarkshire. The hallmarks ae modern poverty ir aw aroon yi. Deed high streets ir filled wae graffitied shutters n tannin salons n bookies n charity shoaps n off-licences n eld pishy pubs. The prophetic message ae WELCOME TAE HELL wis spray-painted on the way intae ma high school in Thrashbush, home tae the YOUNG CRAZZY BUSH. They fight wae Rawyards wans, the YOUNG BUNDY. Yi hud us, the YOUNG MAVIS, the GYT fae Greengairs,

the WINHAW YOBBOS n the TAMLAHILL fae Gartlea. The YOUNG
PARNELL wur fae Cairnhill, the C/HALL TOI fae Chapelhall, the PLAINS
TOI, the CRUIX DERRY, the YOUNG CLARKSTON DERRY, the YOUNG REOS
fae Petersburn, the YOUNG BATS fae Calderbank n the YOUNG MOB fae
Craigneuk. Coatbrig next door wis worse, if anyhin. Doon there yi hud
the RBYT fae Redbrig at Coatbridge Sunnyside station, the ALBION
STREET FLEETO that took in the big flats at Jackson Court n Dunbeth
Park, the YOUNG DYKES fae Sikeside n Greenend, the CARNBROE TECHNO
next door n the SYT fae Shawheed. The famous LL TOI n the YOUNG
KIRK wur aw wan team fae Langloan. Their enemies ir fae Toonheed,
the PYTO. The KWOOD RA fae Kirkwood, the GYTO fae Glenboig, the
YOUNG MONKS fae Eld Monkland, the YOUNG SHAWS fae Kirkshaws n
the last before yi hut Glesga, the BAR G POSSE fae Bargeddie. The whole
place wis mapped oot n divided among young teams.

A came fae a good home, but ma father dyin when A wis a wee guy
increased ma risk tenfold. There wis nae immediate reference
point fur me aboot wit it wis tae be a Scottish man. Being mental wis
the chief virtue among these tribes. That became oor reality. A wis
in two gangs, the YOUNG MAVIS in Airdrie n the LANG EL TOI in
Langloan, Coatbrig. Violence wis par fur the course. A wis always
fightin wae cunts n took a few sore wans. There wis a pervasive
culture ae carryin blades. Ma maw found a few lockbacks A stashed
in ma room n flung them aw in the bin. We sat wae the pals ae a young
murder victim n they wur aw mad, but stull cried fur their mate.
Tano pulled oot a machete on me at the shop, then stoated away
wrecked oot his nut. Doon the lane, a wee jakey walked by the troops
n somebody geed him cheek n he whipped a knife oot his leather
jakit n said, 'Yees ir no fuckin wide noo, ir yees?' Doon the park, Div
fae the YOUNG DYKES pulled a big Kitchen Devil oot n tried tae stab
oor mate. McIntosh fae the YM grabbed it aff him n flung it doon the
drain. If he hudnae, Danger Mouse wis deed guaranteed. Del, fae
ma year in school, appeared in a party up oor way n A couldnae stop
starin at the slash mark on his face, across his eyebrow, nose n cheek.

Ferguson, oor mate, got bottled n left like a jigsaw. Two LL TOI wans took a knife oot oor mate's gaff n wur gonnae stab Mai-Tai ootside Farmfoods, he grabbed his sister's baby n held it until he jumped in a taxi. Me n Wee Joe sat in a mad dodgy gaff wae a boy who went on tae kill. Joe got stabbed three times, he wis a lucky boy. A mad cunt wis after me n said he wis gonnae git me n, withoot hesitation, A grabbed a long, pointy wan wae a wooden handle oot the cutlery drawer n carried it aboot fur a week in ma blue n yella Berghaus jakit. He never showed up in the end n A'm glad, cos at fourteen A wis probably the most dangcrous A ever wis.

Aw that wis the external violence. The internal revealed itself in the level ae substance abuse, isolation n suicide. Plenty faces we knew hung themselves n a good few died cos ae drugs. We wurnae generation heroin, but it wis aw aroon us. A seen Boydy overdose on smack n almost die right in front ae us in a gaff. He wis aw blue n strugglin fur every breath. A called an ambulance n his best pal, Walker, pulled the phone cord oot the wall while A spoke tae the operator. Life is cheap here. A saved Boydy that day, but they both died no long after. We smoked a power ae green n took diazepam n hammered white n pills n guzzled gallons ae drink. A sat wae boys who pawned their PlayStation weekly fur drugs n would sit n smoke solid hash n munch blues aw day. They never worked. Oor elder wans wur heroin addicts n would eat aboot twenty or thirty blue diazepams in wan go then drink warm, sugary tca tae melt them quicker. They hud pushed the button years back n wur coastin towards ruin. Two boys A knew took frightenin psychotic episodes. Wan recovered, wan didnae really. Ma ain addiction became so oot ae control that A barely lived on anyhin. A would turn up at ma maw's door once a week tae git bags ae messages aff hur so A wid huv suhin tae eat. Drink slowly drives yi insane in its ain insidious way. Cunts like us ended up paralytic n blackout drunk every time we went on-it, in some condition, rantin n ravin, no makin a bit ae fuckin sense, fightin or gittin lifted aff the polis. There's nae escape. Eventually, wan way or another, they aw git yi. Wit follows wis the beginnin ae the end fur me.

We hudnae long finished oor dinner when oot the blue Maria texted sayin, *Merry Christmas . . . wit yi uptay?* She wis fae Wishy n wan ae the lassies who used tae sit wae the YM. Somebody said they hud seen us kiss in a party wan night but A couldnae remember it cos A wis mad-wae-it. It ended up just me n hur left conscious in Steff's gaff after a mad wan n we sat oorselves in the kitchen n rolled joints n smoked them oot the wee square windae. We hud a pure heart-tae-heart, talkin aboot the point n pointlessness ae life here. A liked hur n thought she wis sound as. We got ready fur T in the Park the-gither n bounced on a bus wae aw the GYT wans. Eventually A asked hur aboot that kiss. She didnae answer but she geed us a look tae say it happened and that she defo remembered. A laughed n said, 'Well next time yi kiss me, make sure A'm compos mentis!' We held each other's gaze n laughed. 'Who said there'll be a next time?' she said wae another look.

Maria n me arranged tae meet that Christmas night. She left hur pals in the pub n A bounced in a taxi. It drapped me aff in hur street, wae the flats that loom above yi n gee yi vertigo. A saw a lassie walkin doon towards me smokin, wearin pinstriped shorts wae black tights, a wee waistcoat n a hat. We kissed under the fallin sleet, then walked along towards the tower. Ma mate lived on the third floor. A got chased oot the ninth years before by a cunt tryin tae stab us n took flight doon the staircase, five steps at a time. Fuck yir ankles, prioritise survival. Fear gees men wings. Maria lived away up in the heavens. We walked in through the foyer n intae the lift. If yi took the stairs, yi could look intae the hollow innards ae the buildin n see scores ae needles lyin that heroin users hud tossed oot after injectin themselves. Hur gaff wis in darkness. We bounced intae the bedroom n she shut the door behind us. Fuck knows wit we spoke aboot after, but we smoked a joint in the livin room then she crashed oot on the couch. A stood, smokin n starin at the snow settlin below fae high up in Heroin Heights. Strange how the gatherin white could make even a place like oors look almost beautiful.

The followin year, me n the troops aw stoated intae Bryce's gaff tae sit n git a smoke. His face wis funny n pale. 'Did yi hear wit happened last night?' he asked us. A felt that same concentrated dread, a free-fallin sensation, every time A heard they words. The first time wis when Tony hung himself, then when Big Mick died ae a heroin overdose. There wur others anaw. 'Maria stabbed somebody last night n killed them.' The room aw went quiet. Tryin tae process the enormity ae somebody losin their life tae violence is enough tae drive yi fuckin mad. Cunts aboot here wur desensitised tae repetitive horror. It wis normalised tae them. A felt like we wur engaged in some endless war cos that many young wans we knew hud died. Maybe that's just a trauma response n is best left inside yir ain heed. It's too sad n strange spoken aloud n other people who lived better lives don't really understand yi anyways. It never felt normal tae me.

Maria n me wur lyin in Steff's back room on a mattress wan day, years before aw that, rough as fuck fae boozin n takin pills. 'Want a Pro Plus?' she asked us. A took wan n the caffeine pill pulled me instantly intae a horrible panic attack. A went that lightheeded way n couldnae feel ma hands n ma breathin wis wrong n A wis drownin in maself again. Sensin ma anxiety, she pulled me close n kissed me n the panic went. That kiss wis the next time. She looked me right in the eye after it n A thought aboot that look aw day. We aw went fur a munch, rough as fuck, then drove intae Glesga city centre but A cannae really mind where or why. On the way back, Maria looked at an industrial chimney puffin oot smoke then laughed n called it a cloud factory. It struck me as the kinda thing yi said tae a wean . . . or maybe suhin somebody said tae hur when she wis wee n it stuck wae hur aw they years later.

The summer after that killin, A wis in a gaff party doon Airdrie n a squad ae TAMLAHILL wans bounced in. Big Daz, the former tap man fae ma eld school, wis wae them. He wis a big unit but a sound cunt n good mates wae McIntosh fae the YM. A could see wan ae the others growlin at us across the room. The atmosphere hud changed tae wan ae threat. Yi ignore they kinda bad feelins in yir gut at yir fuckin peril. A stayed when A should ae left cos a wis mad-wae-it. Wan ae them soon mentioned this TH boy's wee brur gittin done in up ma scheme years ago. 'You're a YOUNG MAVIS wan ir yi no?' he said, tryin tae start suhin.

'Aye, how?'

'Your mate bottled ma brother!'

It wis only a matter ae time.

The big cunt turned away then whipped round n whacked me a dillion. A swung the Buckfast bottle A wis hoddin hard at his face. It connected n he jumped backwards. They aw set upon me. A got bottled three times n saw the white flash fae heed trauma. The green tonic bottle smashed n wan ae them stabbed me in the back wae it while A wis lyin foetal on the floor. Big Daz pulled me aff the deck wae ma ears stull ringin like a bell n saved us. Ma nose wis aw cut tae fuck n there wur awready thick lumps n blood under ma hairline at the base ae ma skull fae takin serious blows. Before boostin, A drank a bottle ae Orange Jubilee MD 20/20 tae take the edge aff. Big Daz wis ragin at me fur bottlin his mate. A'm glad it didnae burst in his face but there's no much yi kin say if yi set aboot somecunt n they react. 'Don't go tae sleep,' the big man said tae me right after it.

'How no?' A replied.

'In case yi don't wake back up.'

The broken Buckfast bottle left a bumpy pink scar on ma back. A wis lucky. Lyin on a floor gittin done in n plugged is nae way tae die, especially no after aw ma fuckin struggle tae actually live. A wis stayin in a wee damp, ex-council flat in Tillicoultry, tryin tae study n pull maself oot this miserable life. Ma drug use intensified in the months that followed n A wis totally isolated. The wheels finally fell aff the bus on Christmas Eve.

Memories ae the past kept comin back tae me aw day. We used tae go bowlin wae ma maw n uncle, but the whole thing wis a covert operation so ma aunty could sneak presents intae ma maw's wardrobe withoot us seein. Aw that love felt a million miles away. Ma worsenin mental health hud compounded the alienation ae addiction. Trauma n drugs eventually destroy yir ability tae function n cope. A wis pacin the room, to n fro, chain-smokin n couldnae settle. This wis it, the void, the great precipice they talk aboot. A felt so alone A cannae tell yees. Ma letter box snapped later that evenin. It wis a Christmas card fae wan ae ma neighbours, a wee eld wuman. Inside it said, *Love from Betty. No 16*. That small kindness sent me intae such a spiral in ma state. A headed oot determined tae git a card tae pit through this eld wuman's door in return. It wis a desperate act n A wisnae thinkin straight. Aw the shops wur awready closed n the lights wur oot. The notion passed n A went hame, feelin worse than before. Everyhin wis a fuckin blur as A paced aboot the room, tormented by it aw. A couldnae take it any longer n wept in total crisis n despair. Until then, A hud never really prayed but A clamped ma paws the-gither n interlocked ma fingers. A said sorry fur everyhin up tae that point n if yi irnae too busy this Christmas, Big Chap, then A badly need some salvation or at least redemption. A finished ma plee n nuhin happened. Neither ceilin nor clouds parted, nae herald ae angels wae golden trumpets appeared. Anticlimax, eh? A cannae tell yees categorically that somewan is on the other end, listenin wae ear pressed against pearly gate. There's nae proof or absolutes here.

The troops wur aw dain the usual, sittin on-it n smokin a few joints in Bryce's bit. A needed tae git tae fuck oot ae that lonely gaff, so A drove ma motor doon n A sat fur a bit but only smoked a few cigarettes, stull mega oot ae sorts. Another feelin came like A hud somewhere tae be n A got tae ma feet n said, 'A needty bounce. Catch yees after.' Naebody said anyhin n A walked oot intae the night.

A chapped ma maw's door at twenty tae eleven. She wis dressed in hur nice coat fur the Watchnight Service in the church n wis surprised tae see me. 'A'm gonnae come wae yi . . . is that awright?' She told me A wis always welcome. The church is three hundred year eld, a solid grey giant at the tap ae the brae. There ir original stained-glass windaes aw roon it. Behind the pulpit, there's a massive wan showin the parable ae the Good Samaritan. He's lyin hurt n naked on the road tae Jericho after gittin done in n robbed. Yi kin see the priest in purple n the Levite in blue, both traipsin past uncarin, but the red-cloaked Samaritan is kneelin by his side n his donkey's there anaw. We sat right at the back where ma gran used tae sit. The service finished n people wished each other 'Merry Christmas' n hugged n shook hands. We walked oot intae the celd Christmas mornin n A turned tae hur n said, 'Things ir gonnae be different fae noo on.' Hur eyes wur tired. She'd heard it aw before.

'That's good, Graeme. I hope so.'

'A promise yi. Suhin's different this time.'

Drug-inspired delusion or Christmas epiphany, A cannae say fur sure but everyhin changed fae that night on. A never used drugs again n the violence wis finished tae. Suhin stirred in that wee flat that feels fundamental tae ma life noo. Maybe it wis always kinda there n just a ringin phone, never answered. The mare A sat n scrutinised it days later, A felt stupid n that kinda exposed way that speakin aboot faith sometimes makes yi feel, like if yi told any yir pals they would rip the pish oot yi n aw laugh. That feelin started tae pass. A dunno the ins n oots ae aw this either. The required leap that faith demands is complicated tae the best ae us, but ask yirself this, who really made the clouds? N when they clear, ask yirself, who put aw they fuckin stars up there? No everybody hus faith n that's sound. A don't minister tae anycunt, but A know the difference it made tae me wis life or death. That's no nuhin.

Gangs huv dominated ma life. A've spent the last decade recoverin fae them n tryin tae find the words fur it aw in ma writing. That's twenty year ae gangs in total. Their effects on yi ir far-reachin n complicated. Substances n drink ir used by many as self-medication. The aggression n hypervigilance that years ae gangs create don't just disappear. They're stull somewhere below, stored as a memory in yir very cells or expressed as violent tendencies.

Yi wur taught that being the best fighter n a violent man wis desirable. This is the unlearnin. The resultin trauma, a variety ae negative physical n mental manifestations, often becomes a burden fur partners n children tae bear. That's how aw this is cyclical; passed on tae future generations like an infernal relay baton. A'm stull healin aw these years later, but A'm stull here. Fur lots ae oor young men, gang membership wis the pinnacle ae their existence. Their future never offered anyhin startlin n they lack meaningful connection wae anybody. The constant togetherness ae gangs is replaced wae unsatiated longins fur the past n a deep loneliness. Life beyond becomes a sort ae nae man's land. Yir no welcomed wae open arms intae new friendship groups n neither dae yi belong in yir eld wans. The alienation is complete. There's this paradoxical nostalgia where even though yi suffered, yi miss it. It's no easy tae let it aw go n move on. The past is a prison yi kin git trapped in if yir no careful. Ma pals sit aboot n tell stories fae the edges we endured n say 'Mind that, man? That wis mad, eh?' Somewhere there came a crossroads point where they stopped livin n started only rememberin. These eld stories huv lost their appeal fur me. This is the end ae aw that. A don't want tae just sit n remember. A want tae live.

A look back at the picture ae me as a young man, lyin sufferin n ma wee granny smilin in hur sparkly blue cardigan. It feels bittersweet cos A've got painful regrets aboot the way a spent hur final years. A wis too numb wae drugs n drink tae process n mourn deaths in ma family properly. They passed me by, along wae everyhin else. A cannae help think aboot hur sittin by hursell, waitin on hur phone tae ring or me tae walk through the door, but it doesnae n A don't. A wis otherwise occupied then but know intimately aboot long days n solitude noo. Sometimes A huv this reoccurrin dream that she never died n A'm walkin past hur hoose n A see hur in the windae, stull sittin on hur chair, watchin the world go by, alone. A always go in tae make sure she's awright n we speak, but aboot wit A dunno, then A wake up n she's gone again. She always felt that faith wis gonnae play a part in ma life n said as much tae ma maw. Ma eld gran wisnae daft. A just wish she hud seen hur prediction come good n me back tae some kinda wholeness before she left. She gave me two pieces ae advice. 'Drink in, wits oot.' A huvnae drank fur seven year noo. This Christmas made ten year aff substances. They chaotic forces in ma life ir gone, no dormant but extinct. The second is mare difficult tae master. 'Look forwards, no back.' Aw the mistakes ae a youth lost follow yi aboot like the Ghost ae Christmas Yet tae Come if yi let them. Yi cannae change nuhin. Sometimes yi huv tae go back tae go forward. Sometimes the only way oot is through. ∎

Peninsula Press congratulates

JENNIFER ATKINS

one of *Granta's*
Best of Young British Novelists 2023

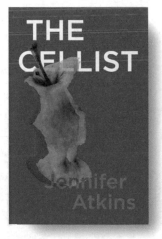

Scan the QR code below
to buy *The Cellist* and
support local bookshops

PENINSULA PRESS

A CERTAIN KING

Jennifer Atkins

O ne evening back in August I left work early and took a train to the country. It was a Friday, warm with white clouds bearing down, and the storms that had so plagued the preceding weeks seemed finally over. After arriving at a small, busy station, I found a taxi without trouble – Annie had promised there wouldn't be trouble. Earlier that month she'd invited me to come for dinner, the last weekend of the summer, for a reunion of sorts at her and Edward's bungalow. She had spoken, drolly, about the meadows and the fields in their part of the country, and the drollness with which she'd spoken didn't match the sight of the late-flourishing land I saw from the taxi window. The sight from the window didn't match anything. The canopies of the trees were dark after the rains and the fields were heavy before the harvest, and the world seemed changed, altogether rampant.

It had been a decade since we'd been at university together. I had not been surprised by Annie's insistence that we all come together, it had not surprised me that F's return would be a reason to do this, but I hadn't heard from any of them, not even F, since the winter. I'd been spending my evenings in the pool near my office, entering the changing rooms at nine each night, stripping alone and finding few other bodies in the water. I'd started swimming after F had moved to Italy, and I suppose it was for that reason I'd emailed him once to tell him how my biceps and my pecs were growing firm, how my body was feeling, in some ways, more certain. But he hadn't replied, and recently I'd become ashamed and unsure of why I'd told him those things. Except I'd had the desire for someone to know. And there was a sense of joy, waiting just out of reach, as usual.

Annie opened the front door of the bungalow in a bright yellow apron and laughed to see me standing there. I was exactly on time, she said. There was a shadow at the end of the hall that turned out to be Edward with his arms raised, ready for an embrace that he'd forgotten by the time I reached him. They took me to the back of the house and through the dining room to the patio, where three plastic chairs were arranged facing westward. They seemed excited, agitated by the cooking maybe. Lena was there already, and she smiled when she saw me, and there was some fuss over getting me a glass and then a bottle of white wine was produced before Annie and Edward went back to the kitchen.

Lena was sitting on one of the plastic chairs facing towards the unkempt garden and the meadow beyond. I wasn't sure what time F was supposed to arrive, but if she was concerned about seeing him, I gathered she wasn't going to admit it. She was leaning forwards in her chair, looking at me with her chin down. I was tanned, she remarked, and when I told her I'd spent the summer in London she started talking about a recent trip to Greece. A breeze moved through the canopies of a group of ash trees that were about twenty yards from where we sat, at the edge of the meadow that bordered the bungalow's garden. There was a thin stream, we'd been told, beneath them. There were no other houses on the horizon. Lena's face seemed strained in the diminishing light. Possibly it was strained from the story she was telling about sea urchins, how she'd gone swimming in the sea with hundreds of their sharp bodies, but I couldn't tell how she was actually feeling, what she might admit to herself.

Two years before, she'd asked to meet me after work by the Thames. At that point, I hadn't seen her since before her and F's break-up, which had been a month earlier, and I hadn't heard anything either, yet, from him in Italy. On the phone, I'd assumed she was drunk from the way she whispered and from the fact that she was calling. She never called me. I went to meet her in a pub with wood panelling where she was waiting, her fair hair tucked into a black scarf looped about her neck, drinking a glass of red wine as if she'd been there for ages. I walked in wearing my suit, holding my silly briefcase. A few eyes turned to me, and I suppose it might've looked like a liaison of some kind. But she'd never really warmed to me.

I can't remember what she said immediately in the pub, but I do remember that after a few minutes she stopped speaking and stared into the centre of the room, then looked down at her scarf as if someone else had wound it about her neck. She wanted to know if I'd heard how he'd left her. She lifted her chin. I hadn't heard, not really, only that it was why he'd moved to Bologna. Well, he'd been cruel, she said, widening her eyes, which seemed to contain some shock, still – perhaps the fact that he'd done it, or that she found herself there telling me, of all people.

He'd done it in their favourite restaurant, she said. It was an old-fashioned place in Soho where the tables were greasy, and she said he leant forwards on the table to tell her that he'd never loved her, then he carried on eating, as if nothing had happened. When she asked what he meant, he put his knife down and leant forwards again on his elbows. He stared at her without a single further movement. He didn't explain; he didn't say anything. And she realised how sharp his elbows seemed on the table. How sharp the bone of the pork chop he was eating. She became stuck on that and was speaking violently now in the pub, about sharpness.

Then she grew quieter.

'He was cruel,' she said. 'He's capable of cruelty.'

Her mouth stiffened and she looked towards me.

'Everybody is,' I replied.

'Not everyone. Not like him.'

She held my gaze from the corner of her eye.

'Are they?'

I did not know what kind of answer she expected from me, if she expected an answer to that question. How was I to know if he was crueller than other people? *How would I know?* I thought. Her eyes narrowed, and she leant her head back against the wood panelling. On the table I held her hand – I was surprised that she let me.

They'd tried to be together, Lena and F, on and off, for eight years, right up until he'd gone away. He'd rarely spoken to me about their life together, but he would mention her sometimes when we were running on the marshes. He would tell me something about her behaviour as we ran side by side, our thighs shooting out beneath us like pistons, his voice bright and forceful through the wind and exertion. He would speak as if her behaviour happened to him at some distance. At times it was like he was playing a game where I had to guess what he'd done to provoke a given reaction: when she'd abandoned him on a night bus or cut through the collars of his shirts or ripped the pages from a copy of his debut novel. I never did guess. Out in the open, I could never put these things together. I would only listen, then say how it was weird of her, and he would smile and tell me I was right about that, and we'd keep running through the mud along the train lines.

Although F and I emailed from time to time while he was in Italy, I did not tell him about my drink with Lena. I did not want to reveal what she'd told me of how he'd left her, or mention that word *cruel*, which she had spoken and then been quiet about. He and I did not speak as much as I would've liked, anyway, and I did not want to cause any issues. I could read him – that was what I'd always felt – I could read him better than other people. But he was not always readable.

When he finally emerged onto the patio, the clouds had broken at the horizon, and a harsh, orange light was falling over us. He came out of the French doors and we turned, and I saw that Lena's expression became, briefly, ugly.

'Was it bad?' he said, bending down to kiss her cheek.

'Not so bad, no.'

So they'd spoken before, I thought, more recently than I had spoken to either of them, and there was something here she hadn't mentioned to me – the journey possibly or her work. He embraced me for several seconds then stood before us, and we both had to shade our eyes to look up at him. He was just taller than me, and he was a lot taller than Lena. He was wearing a loose white shirt, navy trousers. His hair was blonder.

As we continued looking at him, he raised one eyebrow while at the same time closing the eye diagonally beneath it, a jaunty sort of action – a type of wink – and I was amazed that he might feel jaunty. Nothing about the situation felt jaunty to me, but after he'd done that, the winking thing, it was as if he'd been there first, as if I'd interrupted them. The breeze moved through the ash trees, and through his hair, and he smiled at us and then at the garden. He asked us to show him.

'What?' she said.

'The garden, anything.'

'But you don't care,' she replied, pulling her eyebrows together.

I stayed on the patio. They walked around the edge of the garden, Lena pointing out to F what Edward had pointed out to her earlier, and F, after a while, began asking questions. What would be put where, what could be grown, what would be discarded. Would they have flower beds or a vegetable patch, would they have trouble with moles, did they fancy a pond – what could they manage? For some reason it became funny. Even from a distance I knew it had become funny. Even before I heard Lena laughing. That was a trick of his. That was how he slipped inside any situation. I felt the evening swing on its hinge. The two of them were standing at the end of the garden, gazing towards the ash trees, beyond which the sun was sinking. There was the washing sound of the wind in the grasses of the meadow, which led to the low, brown undulation of the fields beyond it.

For dinner we came inside and ate two broad, grey fish. The French doors remained open to the patio, and I'd been encouraged to take the head of the table, which meant Lena and F were together, with

JENNIFER ATKINS

their backs to the darkening garden. They didn't speak to each other directly apart from some shy, polite comments. He had a high colour to his cheeks, an impatient manner. Annie was coming back and forth from the kitchen with plates and glasses, and Edward was talking about rolling his ankle.

'So now *everything* scares me,' he said.

From the table we could see through the doorway into the kitchen, and every time Annie leant down to check inside the oven, the dimples on the backs of her knees were revealed as the skirt of her satin dress lifted. Edward kept looking up at the sound of the oven door to appraise her bared legs before turning back to wipe his lips with his napkin. Annie looked younger than when I'd last seen her. Edward seemed restless since they'd moved to the country.

And why are you so restless and why is she so elegant? I wanted to ask him. *And what do you see when her back is turned, what do you think of?*

Annie placed a bowl of potatoes in front of me.

'How's your flat?' she said to Lena.

'It keeps cool.' She seemed to consider this. 'The garden door's right by my bed, so I've been sleeping with it open.'

'That's not how I pictured it,' F said.

'Should you sleep with the door open?'

Lena didn't reply to Annie but seemed on the verge of asking F how he did picture it, yet then she didn't. She looked away from him, pulling her lips together, and I recalled her doing the same when we were at the pub, as if she were trying to do the opposite of speaking.

Edward began talking about all the people we knew who'd got married, who had lives he found curious or banal, homes he found beautiful or ugly. We became loud discussing these people while we ate, and I saw that sometimes F would glance at Lena and rather than look back, she'd run her tongue over her teeth and check her bun, which was fastened at the midpoint of her head. If they shifted, the tablecloth moved, and I could see their feet were very close together.

34

What I had expected, I suppose, was some evidence that evening of the same anger she had shown in the pub. It did not seem at all obvious what she was feeling, sitting beside F at the table. In some ways she seemed happy. I didn't think she was happy; I thought she was in love, but I didn't know what that told me, if it told me anything. I didn't know what love should look like.

Once we finished eating, F, who had been speaking vaguely about his second book, pushed his plate away from him and started talking about the town where he'd been living in Italy, just outside Bologna. The white wine had run out, so Edward offered us red, and the bottle was passed around the table as F told us briefly about the history of the town, and I recalled looking its name up online after he'd gone there, scrolling through the photos of its old streets, of its churches. He said it was maze-like, but at the town's centre was a large, open square, and this was where he'd rented his apartment, in a building with many other apartments above and below it. He would sit up writing his book most nights, because that was when he could write the most, and every night he would hear the woman who lived below fighting with her lover.

'She was German,' he said, 'but the guy was Italian, so that's how they spoke to each other.'

'And you could understand them?' Lena said.

'I could.'

He brought his wine glass to his lips but then put it down again without drinking.

The fight, he continued, would go on as if unendingly. The floors were thin, so he could pick out certain words easily enough: when the woman called her lover a cunt, when she called him a piece of shit or a dirty monster. It was a strange music to write against, he said, and there were some nights that he would find her words starting to impregnate his text, translated back from Italian into his own language.

He saw the woman leave for work at nine each morning. She would walk across the square with her hair plaited, her green trainers flashing across the paving stones, a rucksack worn high against her suit jacket. At first he didn't look for her in the evenings, but one day he noticed her on the other side of the square just before seven. She was sat on a bench beneath a cherry tree, gazing across the square to the apartment building. She had her rucksack beside her on the bench and laid across her lap was a bunch of flowers. He watched her for some time from the window before she got up and slowly walked across the square.

'After that I watched for her most evenings,' he said, 'and every night it was the same: she arrived at the bench about six forty-five, sat there for half an hour with some expensive-looking flowers, then slowly made her way into the building. And an hour later the argument would start again.'

He wasn't sure about the flowers. He couldn't work out who the flowers were for, or where they'd come from, or why she sat there for so long before entering the building, or where she put the flowers – how many vases she must have had. Or why she looked so calm in those moments before entering the building, sitting with her flowers on the bench, her rucksack beside her. And why the argument started, and what she was trying to say, and why he, her lover, could never solve things.

F began noting down the arguments to try and work out what they were about. He tried to apply logic to get to the root of the issue, using a dictionary for any words that were outside of his knowledge, of which there were some: slang words beyond the reach of his Italian, bits of German. As he did this each night, it struck him there was something devotional about the arguments. He began picturing them down there in her flat, surrounded by the lavish flowers, engaging each other in a fight that felt lavish in its own way, in its own fixedness. F paid a lot of attention to the man when he saw him, entering or leaving the building with her – a tall, thickset man with eyebrows that arched in a way that was surprisingly feminine. He didn't live there, yet the arguments were always between the two of them. F was sure about that. They were to do with privacy, or closeness. *Intimità*. That was the word he heard them use most often.

One day F's bath overflowed, and he had to go down to the woman below, to warn her and apologise. He knocked on the door with some agitation. He was eager to see the inside of her apartment, to see all the flowers, the sight of this struggle. He wondered if he might even have let the bath overflow on purpose.

When the woman opened the door she was wearing a simple white dress, her dark hair plaited to the sides of her head, her face bare of any make-up and her feet bare and her arms bare. He explained the issue and she frowned slightly before leading him through the apartment to her own bathroom, where the water was coming through the ceiling. F shrugged, apologising as best he could in Italian. As he was apologising, he looked around the tiny flat, which, like his, was a studio, and to his surprise he saw no flowers. Not even one, not even a dead bunch, drooping in a vase somewhere. The room was ugly. The furniture was entirely grey and breaking. There was nothing on the walls but one long mirror. He looked at the woman in the white dress with her bare face, her bare apartment, and he left, making excuses.

The non-existent flowers troubled him for days after. A handyman came to fix his floor and her ceiling, and he had to provide some money for the damage, but he couldn't face going down to her again. He read through the notes he'd made on the arguments, trying to see if there was anything about flowers in them. He went out to the back courtyard, where the bins were, to see if he could find the flowers disposed of in some corner. But he couldn't find anything.

He questioned, for a long time, what had made him fearful in the woman's apartment. He believed that was the right word to use for how he'd felt. There was something terrifying about the lack of beauty in that space. Something terrifying in the banality. Once the work on the floor and ceiling was complete, he decided he was going to do something. He went to the florist and bought a large bouquet of red peonies. They were the same flowers he'd seen her with the previous night, sitting on the bench. He felt they were what he had to offer, so she'd know someone had been watching over her. And he wanted to know there were *some* flowers in that apartment at least. He offered them to her when she returned home that evening. He knocked on the door and said he was sorry. He was sorry about everything. He spoke in German. He'd looked up the words beforehand. F trailed off at that point in his story, and he drank some water.

'But what did she say?' Annie asked from across the table. The sun had set by this point. The room was dark at the edges.

'She didn't say anything.' He put his glass down. 'She shut the door in my face.'

Edward, Annie and I laughed at this. But Lena didn't laugh.

'What did you do with the flowers?' she said.

She was staring at F with an expression I couldn't place.

'I gave them to her. She didn't want them, but before she closed the door, I managed it. I wanted her to have them.'

Lena was looking at him intently, and the intentness seemed to take him aback.

'But that's horrible,' she said.

Edward laughed, shortly, then stopped himself and looked towards me. Three tapered candles were burning in the middle of the table, and their flames wavered. We were, briefly, silenced. I felt she was wrong: the story hadn't been horrible. There'd been nothing horrible anywhere in it. But it felt impossible to say so.

'Who did she buy her flowers for?' Edward said eventually.

F was staring at Lena. I knew he wanted to ask what she meant, but there seemed to be something stopping him. Perhaps we were stopping him. Perhaps not. He turned to Edward. He didn't know, he replied. He didn't know anything about it. Lena didn't say anything more but drank her wine and when the edge of the tablecloth rose – F had shifted suddenly in his chair – I saw her feet were no longer towards him, and her body was slack and unmoving.

I felt F had intended the story to be humorous, and certainly Annie, Edward and I had found it that way, but F's satisfaction seemed disrupted by Lena. He sat back in his chair and put his hands palm down on the table. As we spoke about other things, the recent elections, the fires burning on the moors, a maths paper Edward had published, I watched Lena. Her manner seemed altered, and I wondered. She hadn't been calm before. I sensed she was calm, or something like calm – something as contained as that – now.

There was a growing weight to our continued conversation. When Edward rose from the table to get more wine I went to the bathroom, and I was glad to find it cool in there after the close heat of the dining room. I washed my hands and noted the flush of my neck in the mirror. There was a long, frosted window beside the sink, beyond which lay darkness, and the road I'd come from.

In the weeks that had followed our meeting, I had kept close the story that Lena had told me in the pub, her and F's story, closer than I'd expected. I hadn't told anyone else. But the story, its proximity for those few weeks, had transformed the usual things I did: the hours I spent in the office, the empty lengths I swam on my own, the new shape of my body in the mirror. It was like being roused from a stupor. I had considered the sharpness of F, and the way Lena's eyes had widened and narrowed in the pub, and I'd felt something fine and especially hard beneath the surface of life, and I'd wondered if this was what the world felt like to them. If there was something real and deliberate beyond the mere appearance of things, which was accessible to some and not to others. Something that existed for them, which I had only caught a glimpse of. And I'd wanted to know what might happen.

F had told me once there had been a time when, without exchanging any words on the subject, Lena had begun to dress him in the mornings. He would lie on his unmade bed where she'd place every item of clothing on his body. He'd told me flippantly, but it was something that had stayed with me, and in the pub, as she'd spoken of cruelty, this was the image that had come to me: his body over the tangled covers, her hands passing across his skin in circular motions, arranging fabric, pulling zippers, closing buttons. The image was one of devotion. I didn't know how true the image was. It came to me as a piece of truth might.

Dessert was plum tart presented on green plates, and when I came back Annie was passing these around the table, and we made space for them among the old plates that we still hadn't cleared because we couldn't be bothered. We messed around with the plates for a while before settling. The candles had burnt low on the table, and the sound of the wind in the ash trees had grown louder, so that from time to time the commotion would fill the room as if it was coming from us.

'Maybe you'll just meet someone at a conference one day,' Annie was saying to me.

We were eating the tart and it was sweet and sharp, and Annie had been asking about my love life in a gentle voice, as people tended to, as if my solitude was soft, as if it hadn't toughened. The patio doors banged gently behind the table.

'I heard a story once,' Lena said, interrupting. 'About flowers. It wasn't the same, but it was similar.'

She said these words cautiously. The rest of us were busy eating, and the sound of our forks on the plates filled the silence.

'A woman I was working with in South London, Clara. She had this issue with her partner. He was possessive.'

She looked around at us.

'Is it okay?' Annie said. 'Are the plums sweet enough?'

The plums were sweet enough, we said. They were delicious.

'Although it's not really a story about him,' Lena continued, 'the partner. It's about a colleague – a man we both worked with.'

She looked upwards and I thought she wouldn't keep speaking. I thought this because of the way she'd been cautious, and the sense I had that the others didn't want to hear the story, even though I did. I believed we might start talking about the sweet plums again instead, except then Lena did keep speaking.

She said Clara used to come in every morning complaining about this boyfriend. She would outline in detail the argument they'd had the night before, which was usually a fight about her behaviour; everything Clara did was taken as a symbol by this boyfriend, so that everything bore scrutiny, and the thing she found most annoying was the sheer number of hours they spent talking about her, how boring it became to look at herself with such intensity.

'This was during a winter,' Lena said, 'years ago now. But that was when she started talking to me and our other colleague about it.'

There seemed to be a new thing each day with the boyfriend, and at first these things were banal, like how much make-up Clara put on, what she was eating, if it seemed like she was trying to lose weight, if her clothes had changed. Her boyfriend's paranoia centred, obviously, around whether she was interested in other men. Then one day she got sent some flowers, Lena said. They were horrible: fierce-looking roses, with red faces as tight as navels, and the stems tied together by plastic ribbon that made a screeching sound whenever she moved them. They were addressed to Clara, but there was no note attached, and her boyfriend was unmanageable after that. And then the next evening the same thing happened – yet more flowers, and then the evening after that it was chocolates.

'It started becoming a regular thing,' Lena said, 'just endless tacky presents and no clue who was behind them. Well, obviously her boyfriend was convinced she had some other man on the side who was announcing himself, and even I became convinced she must be seeing someone because who would be spending so much money, who would care that much?'

We had all finished eating the tart by then, and although we were listening reluctantly, I felt we were listening.

Lena looked at her hands on the table, looked hard at the nails.

'It was our colleague. He told me about it in the kitchen one day. He said he couldn't stop. It had become a compulsion. When she'd started talking to us about the fights, he'd decided to send her something to see what happened. He was very upset, I remember, while we were speaking, but he kept doing it. He said it felt so intimate.'

She took her hair down and it ran over her shoulders.

'That's ridiculous,' I said.

She turned and stared at me, and I remembered her face in the pub, drinking wine, leaning against the wood panelling with her eyes narrowed. I remembered the stillness of her hand when I'd held it, the fine and brittle things I'd become aware of. She continued staring at me in the dining room, her eyes not narrowed now but perfectly open, and they seemed to be bearing the weight of that word I'd just spoken, as if it was a word I'd directed at *her*.

'Clara broke up with her boyfriend, and that was probably for the best, so maybe it wasn't a bad thing,' she continued. 'But I don't think that's why my other colleague did it.' She cleared her throat. 'He was lonely, I guess. And it made him happy, to feel close to her.'

She drank a lot of wine from her glass and kept holding the glass afterwards.

'Who knows why people do things,' F said.

'But she didn't understand. She thought she was going mad. It was devilish – she thought she was going mad with everything.'

At this her voice had grown piqued.

'Devilish,' F replied, 'is an odd word for it.'

She looked around at us, and her face was pink now, like a small, determined animal, very dark pink, almost like the horrible roses she'd described, and she kept looking at us and I looked back at her as best I could, but it was as if our looking at her was only a let-down. I felt something pressing from her, like the night outside the patio doors, the sound of the wind in the canopies. It was a commotion. I wanted to ask her more about this story, but when I glanced at Annie and Edward they were looking away from Lena, as if something about her in that moment was too trying.

'He had these punishments for her,' she said, quieter now. 'Her boyfriend. He would make her go and buy seventy red apples, and he'd keep them on the kitchen counter even after they were rotting. Or he'd forbid her from looking directly at him, so she could only look at him from a right angle.'

Edward leant forwards and blew out the end of a candle.

'It was meant to be ridiculous,' she added, 'so no one would believe it.'

She set her glass down on the table, and the patio doors moved in the breeze, and on the breeze I could smell the jasmine growing on the back wall of the bungalow.

Flowers for herself, I thought, without knowing the reason.

There were old dishes all over the table in front of us, and red crescents on the tablecloth from the bottom of our wine glasses. Remnants of food were on the plates, but instead of clearing them we had simply pushed everything into the centre of the table, and we sat around this mass looking at the remaining candles burning lower.

Annie got more plates from the kitchen and started giving out the last bits of the tart without asking if we wanted them. She used new plates, so she didn't have to deal with the old, and no one protested, and once the second skinnier pieces were handed out, and we were eating the plums, Edward told us about a woman he'd seen walking through the nearest village in long, black riding boots.

'You know the ones that go all the way to the thigh?' he said. 'Except they were too big for her, like a man's boots, and really well polished.'

I watched Lena, who was not eating her tart but staring down at it, and F, who looked, just once, at her.

'It was funny,' Edward continued. 'She had to walk with her toes pointing out because the boots were just enormous, and they rubbed together, so there was this terrible sound of the leather, and all this exertion on her face, but she couldn't get anywhere.'

He glanced around at us with his hand on the edge of the table. There seemed to me something unfathomable about it. Unfathomable about the idea of the boots and the woman and her motives. Perhaps it seemed the same to everyone else because nobody laughed, and we were all quiet.

I *had* met a woman at a conference, once. In the winter I'd been seeing a woman called Beth, briefly, after meeting her at a conference in Glasgow. We went for coffee a few times, at a bright and homely cafe near her flat in Clerkenwell, and each time we sat talking for hours and left with a promise to meet again, and I would think about her as I worked or swam or cooked my dinner. She was quiet but forceful, and I always wanted to see her.

After the last time we met, she told me we should meet again that week, but when I got in touch, she never responded. She didn't reply to any of my messages, and soon enough I stopped messaging. I was under no illusions about myself.

That was in January. We spent our last meeting discussing rare weather phenomena, and a month later F emailed out of the blue to say there was a dust cloud over Italy. The cloud originated above the Sahara, and it was moving across Europe to England, and he asked me to inform him when it got there. I did notice that day the sky was redder. It was a strange atmosphere. The clouds turned red from the dust of a desert. When it rained, the water looked muddy. I walked through that rain on my way to the office, and again on my way to the pool. When I got into the empty changing room there was orange residue on my shoes, on the leather.

I thought of her all day. Orange marks on the pavements outside, brown water rising in the gutters. I suppose it shouldn't be surprising that things as light as dust can travel. That the things of the earth unsettle. That evening I sent F a reply about the marks on my shoes and the muddy water, and I considered telling him about Beth. I considered asking him why it had stopped, and what I was meant to have done, where the fine and deliberate part of life was, why I couldn't find it. I considered what to say for a long time, if he would understand what I was saying, but in the end I didn't. I didn't tell him. I lay in bed masturbating until the last of my pleasure felt petty and vicious, and then I did nothing.

The dirty plates were before us in the dining room, and there were so many now and the last of the candles were nearly out. Edward said we should go into the meadow to get out of sight of the plates. We should hide in the meadow. He said the grass was soft and tall and the flowers would be gone before we knew it. We should go, he said, getting up, even though it would be dark with the sky full of clouds, and the flowers and the grass invisible.

We left the room and the table and the leftover food, as he said, and outside the air was thick despite the breeze that was still coming. Our feet made no sound on the lawn, and we could hear nothing except the wind in the trees and our laughter. I was still hungry to be with them. We crossed over seamlessly from the garden to the meadow, and the lights from the bungalow disappeared as the ground sloped, and I was surprised by how the grass felt against my fingers. The grass was sharp rather than soft, and after a while we stopped laughing. Perhaps we were exhausted. Perhaps we no longer found it funny. The lights from the bungalow went and I couldn't see the others, but I kept feeling my way towards the sound of their bodies. We were in the middle of the grass. It was so dark that we could've been anywhere. And if the night was beautiful, or if the night was empty, I could no longer tell the difference. ■

THE HAIR BABY

Sara Baume

Alannah, sitting on her mother's bed in the lotus position. It is morning, raining. She feels unwell – queasy, leaden – but does not complain. All over the printed duvet cover there are flamingos in bandanas, facing right, facing left. Alannah's mother is putting out items on the bed, arranging them around her daughter's folded legs, wordlessly. Three piles of clothes, four magazines, two pill bottles, a phone charger, a stack of cotton knickers. Alannah is embarrassed by the sight of her mother's frayed and faded underwear. A few wispy strands of elastic have come loose from the pair on the top of the stack. The waistband is torn. She looks away. Down to the carpet, where a wheelie suitcase is lying on its back with its mouth thrown open. Up to the curtains, which are still drawn even though it is light. She hears cars passing, an electric scooter hurtling across the uneven footpath. She hears the mechanical front door of their apartment building followed by the dog that barks, sadly, every time it clunks.

Alannah, bowed and folded, surrounded by pink birds, haloed by the yellow ceiling lamp. She has limp brown hair and wide-spaced eyes and a weak chin. She is ten. She has been ten for a month and she does not like it. She carries the weight of her extra digit like a chain-mail vest. She hunches her shoulders as if recoiling from the cold metal.

Her mother is twenty-nine. Alannah calls her by her name, Maia, except for when she is upset, and forgets, and calls her Mum. Maia has blonde hair with the sides shaved and a tattoo of a man's name across the notch at the base of her throat, *Reuben*. Maia and Alannah live together in the apartment with Reuben, who also has tattoos but hides them beneath an ironed white shirt every weekday morning and leaves at precisely eight to drive Maia's car to work. Reuben is not Alannah's father, though he has been around for years. Alannah can remember back when Reuben and Maia were kind to each other. Nowadays she hears them quietly shouting in their bedroom at night.

This morning Alannah and Maia are leaving the apartment and going on a journey without telling Reuben and Alannah is both worried about where the journey will take them and pleased that she does not have to go to school.

Alannah, standing in the daylight and the rain on the footpath. Maia stands beside her, just a few centimetres taller. The main door of the apartment building clunks behind them and the sad dog barks. Maia says they are going to stay in a holiday home that belongs to one of her friends from work. Cathy, she says, who had cancer last year. It's in a nice place, she says. A nice place in the countryside, by the sea. The wheels of the big suitcase clatter as they walk in the direction of the bus station. Maia yanks it through the shallow puddles and the splashes spot her soft shoes. At the end of the street Alannah looks over her shoulder and up to the balcony of their apartment on the third floor. She sees the sunflowers she grew in pots in the summer, their heads hung. She sees a fat gull land on the balcony railing, eyeing up their dry hearts.

Alannah, on the bus. There is a faint smell of nappies and vanilla. There are no two free seats together by the time she and her mother board. Maia sits beside a teenager who has his coat balled into a pillow against the glass. Alannah goes a few seats further back and chooses an old man in a basketball cap who smiles at her. He has a walking stick between his knees and his lumpy fingers knotted over the handle. He is archaic to Alannah. He speaks in a barely decipherable language, repeating himself. He tells her an elaborate story about how he once plucked a hair from a horse's tail. He lets go of the stick to flap his hands; his eyes shine. If she ever finds a hair from a horse's tail, snagged in a gate, a hedge – he tells Alannah – she has to put it in a glass jar of water, the biggest she can find, and screw the lid on, as tight as she can, and wait for three weeks, and see what happens.

What happens? Alannah says.

But the old man just cracks a black-toothed smile and repeats himself. She is relieved when he reaches his stop. She moves into the vacant window seat. Outside she can see fields and sometimes trees and sometimes the coastline rising in and out of sight. There are grey birds in a flock as fine as smoke. There is a hollow building with light pouring out through the empty windowpanes. The rain has stopped. People get off and on the bus and then only off.

Alannah, on the asphalt beside a solitary petrol pump, waiting for the door of the bus's luggage compartment to open. Maia is explaining that there aren't any taxis and so Cathy's neighbour is going to pick them up. As soon as the bus pulls away they see a large man bounding towards them. He has a beard, a woolly jumper. He reminds Alannah of the sort of dog that looks ferocious at a distance and then runs up with its tail wagging. He is Michael, he says. He has the key for them. Do they need anything in the shop? Alannah focuses on the pattern of his jumper as he talks. There are reindeers and snowmen in white against a jagged landscape of Christmas trees. Michael scoops up the wheelie suitcase and throws it into the back of his jeep. In the back of his jeep there are two sacks of cow nuts, a mallet and an orange rope, long and loose and twisted. In the shop he talks loudly to the woman behind the counter while Alannah follows her mother down one side of the only aisle and then back up the other. Maia picks out a loaf of bread, two cans of tuna, a block of cheese, a bottle of wine. Alannah picks out a big bar of chocolate and a bag of popcorn kernels. At the counter they can hear Michael roaring with laughter.

Alannah, in the front seat of the jeep, squashed between Maia and the passenger window with the shopping at their feet. There's a cardboard lemon and a grubby face mask dangling from the rear-view mirror. Michael pops his phone into a holder on the dashboard and hangs one arm out the opposite window. The road is narrow and the unruly bracken whacks his elbow. His phone is strangely small. It rings twice during the journey between the village and the holiday home. The ringtone is unlike any Alannah has heard before. It seems antiquated, a sequence of sharp notes, tunelessly tumbling. Michael has to pull his elbow in to answer it, and then in the middle of a sentence he lifts the phone away from his ear to wave at a man on the road. He beeps the horn. He pauses the jeep at the mouth of a narrow, rutted path and the engine idles as he points out a sandy beach that has appeared miraculously at the edge of the fields.

You'd walk down here easy, Michael says.

He points out his own house as they pass. It's a beige bungalow with arches and columns. There's a derelict farmhouse out the back and a swing set on the front lawn. A sheepdog rushes out to chase the jeep. Alannah sees that it has one black eye and one blue eye.

My two-headed dog, Michael says, and lets out his roaring laugh.

Alannah, outside the holiday home, beneath a sickly palm tree. She had imagined a cottage, but this is a substantial farmhouse, brilliant white and square.

If you need anything at all now, Michael says.

Maia thanks him for the tenth time and dabs the number of his phone into hers. She smiles her purse-lipped smile, as if she is posing for a photograph. The holiday home is bigger and cleaner than any house Alannah has ever seen. All over the place there are nautical-themed souvenirs that look brand new. There are green glass buoys in rope nets on the walls and model ships on the windowsills. In the kitchen there are fish-shaped fridge magnets and shell-shaped ashtrays. There is more food than they had expected – posh muesli, a jar of olives stuffed with anchovies, a biscuit tin with an unopened packet of Viennese whirls inside, a big bottle of rock shandy. There are three different guest bedrooms but Maia says it would be polite to take the one with two single beds so that they make as little impression as possible. She dumps the wheelie suitcase on the red shag rug between the beds and flings it open.

Alannah, on the narrow, rutted path down to the sandy beach, a few paces behind her mother. Maia is carrying a towel that she took from the hot press of the holiday home, rolled up under one arm. There are clumps of tall-stemmed yellow flowers lining the path and they make Alannah think of the balcony and the apartment and she can't believe that everything is still there as they left it and Reuben has not even arrived home from work. The path down to the beach meets a band of stones slippery from the morning rain, and then sand. Alannah and Maia walk slowly to the end of the beach and back again. They find a fish head, a poo with a ribbon of tissue paper stuck in it. The way the weed lies on the sand is strange. It has layered up into loose sheets, blanched and crumpled like old, pale skin. There are three plastic bags beneath the ring buoy, bulging with rubbish. There are two deep holes above the tideline; it is not clear whether they have been made by an animal or a man. There are hardly any gulls, less than in the city. Alannah and Maia sit down in the sand. They look out to sea and Alannah tells her mother the story that the old man on the bus told her.

What do you think happens? she says.

I don't know, Maia says. I guess it swells up and comes alive or something.

Alannah, on the sand, in the lotus position, the damp soaking through her leggings. The sun comes in and out. Low waves roll and break. They have been at the beach for almost an hour and nobody else has arrived. Maia stands up and declares that she is going for a swim. Alannah watches, embarrassed, as her mother strips to her underwear. She looks back towards the road and sees that the only houses overlooking the beach are the holiday home and Michael's

SARA BAUME

bungalow and Michael's ruin. She turns back as Maia sinks into the dark water, bit by bit, until she is only a head moving rhythmically, getting smaller. Alannah looks down to her runners. All the tiny perforations of their breathable fabric have been filled in by grains of sand. She finds a skinny, pointed stick and starts to prick the fabric. When she looks up again there are two heads. One has Maia's blonde bun; the other is sleek and perfectly rounded, like a full, black moon rising from the surface of the water. At first Alannah just stares. Then she sees the black moon swivel and show its snout. A seal. She untwines her legs and pushes herself onto her feet and as she does a second seal appears.

MUUUUUMAIAAAAA!

Maia is already swimming back and so she cannot see the seals behind her.

SEEEEEAAAAAAALS!

Maia glances over her shoulder and the speed of her strokes accelerate; the rhythm becomes jagged and panicked. From the shore Alannah sees two more heads pop up. The first two are decisively following the swimmer, disappearing and reappearing at intervals. Now a fifth. Maia finds the seabed with her feet and runs the last few metres in slow motion. She spills onto the shore, heaving for air but pretending to be calm.

It's OK! she shouts to Alannah. Everything's FINE, everything's OK!

For the first time Alannah notices the shape of her mother's belly. A neat bulge as if she has swallowed a whole, small bowl.

Alannah, queasy and leaden, watching from the shore as the seals gather together and swim away. Maia unrolled her towel and sat down on it without drying herself. She has drawn her knees up to her chest and she is hugging them and crying, savagely, running out of air and choking. Spit and snot gush down her face and dangle from her chin. Alannah slumps to the sand and starts pricking at her runners again. Maia has done this once before, when she was six. They were in the car, driving out of the city on a trip to visit Alannah's grandparents.

There had been a crash on the dual carriageway and by the time Maia noticed the tailback it was too late to turn around. They got stuck in an enormous traffic jam. The cars could only inch along and there was nothing but traffic for as far as they could see. At first Maia had been optimistic.

We're just lucky that we aren't the ones in the accident, she said.

They played I spy even though there was not much to spy on the dual carriageway. The tail lamps and street lights. A featureless concrete barrier that stretched forever. The clouds. Almost two hours had passed when Alannah noticed that Maia had started to quietly cry, and then to cry loudly, to cough and gag, to enter a kind of trance of crying. She seemed to have forgotten that they were the lucky ones. She seemed to have forgotten that she was driving and Alannah had to remind her when to inch ahead in time with the car in front. She needed the toilet – that day in the traffic – and afterwards she regretted telling her mother. She imagined this was the reason why Maia had started to cry. After two and a half hours they had finally been diverted off the dual carriageway. Then Maia had to navigate an unfamiliar commuter town. She made an emergency stop in the grounds of a luxury hotel and Alannah climbed into an extravagant hydrangea bush to crouch down and piss.

Alannah knows that Maia will eventually stop crying and she does. She stands up and shakes the sand and white weed out of the towel and puts her dry clothes back on over her wet underwear and together they walk back along the path from the beach and then up the road to the holiday home.

Alannah, on a high stool at the breakfast bar, legs swinging. She watches as her mother prepares popcorn on the gas cooker, in a saucepan with olive oil and the lid on, tossing and shaking. Maia finds a set of fluted glasses and serves the wine and rock shandy. Alannah sips and listens to the rustling, pinging saucepan and feels at ease for the first time all day. They eat tuna melts for dinner. They leave a mess in the pristine kitchen, cheese drips in the grill pan, black crumbs. Maia doesn't seem to care any more about making no impression on the holiday home. They dump their plates in the sink and bring the big bar of chocolate through to the living room. Maia spends a long time fiddling with the remote control and eventually settles on a documentary about reincarnation. They have missed the first half and the second half is about a boy called James from Louisiana who has clear memories of being a fighter pilot who was killed at Iwo Jima. Maia is very quiet until the programme ends and then, without shifting her eyes from the screen she says:

When you were little, Alannah, three or four, you used to say things like that, but just normal stuff, like we'd be in the car and you'd say that you used to drive a car too. You'd say, 'When I was big I did this; when I was big I did that,' and I would just think it was something you'd invented or picked up from playschool or TV. Do you remember?

Alannah doesn't. She shakes her head.

Maybe they were dreams.

Her mother is looking right at her now.

There were dreams too, but you would never describe them to me. You would wake up screaming, thrashing the air. It would happen maybe once a week, then maybe just once every couple of weeks. Then it stopped.

Alannah shakes her head again.

I don't remember, she says. I never remember my dreams.

They are both quiet again, Maia channel-hopping, the chocolate gone. Suddenly Alannah says:

Maia, why am I here?

And Maia puts down the remote control and gets up and starts to move clumsily around the big room, straightening the sofa cushions and pulling the curtains, one hand laid protectively over the little bowl of her stomach.

You're here, she says, because of a decision I made years ago when I was only a baby myself. A decision I made but that you're going to have to live with for a whole, long, complicated life, sometimes happy, sometimes sad.

She looks like she has more to say. She looks like she might go back into her trance of crying and so Alannah pipes up:

No, no, she says. I just meant here, here in the holiday home.

Alannah, out on the gravel driveway beneath the night sky. She had suggested they go and look for stars but she had not expected there would be so much cloud. She had thought of clouds as strictly daylight entities and stars as things that appeared dependably each night, searing through every sort of atmospheric obstruction, piercing through space. The well-kept garden of the holiday home is spooky in the dark. There's no wall; the lawn melts into the untended landscape. Alannah knows the fields are there and she knows the ocean is there but she cannot see either of them. The wind has intensified. The palm tree rattles. Its fallen, dried-up leaves shimmy across the grass like snakes. Alannah and her mother stand beneath the lamp above the front door searching for the obscured stars. Then they lock up and go to bed.

Alannah, lying with her eyes closed in the dark guest bedroom of the holiday home. It takes her a long time to become drowsy even though she is tired. She holds her body very still and tries to think of nothing. When this doesn't work she starts to count backwards from five hundred. Around three hundred she falls into a shallow sleep and dreams about a glass jar with a baby horse inside and a long hair snaking out from the centre of its belly and tangling around its neck. The jar is full of water and the horse must be tiny because Alannah is holding it, or perhaps Alannah is a giant and the jar is giant-sized and only the horse is normal. Then she drops the jar, the hair, the horse baby and wakes with a gasp at the moment that it would have smashed.

There is no shattering glass in the guest bedroom of the holiday home, no big splash. There is no sound except for her mother breathing. Outside there is only the rattling palm. Alannah is used to the night noise of the apartment block where she has lived most of her life. She thinks about what she would be hearing now if she was at home – the passing cars, the groaning lift, one of the neighbours having a night shower. She substitutes remembered sounds into the oppressive silence of the countryside and this is why it takes her a couple of seconds to register the footsteps.

There is the sound of footsteps on the gravel outside. A crunch, crunch, crunch – as if the person is deliberately treading carefully. Alannah sits up. She hears a click, a soft thunk, like a door opening and closing towards the back of the holiday home, the kitchen door. Maia's bed is by the window. The red shag rug separates them. Alannah slides onto the floor and crawls, laboriously, around the suitcase, across the rug. Maia's hair fans out over the pillow. The duvet lies across her chest. It is printed all over with anchors; they point towards her head like crossbows. His name is there in the notch of her exposed throat, in cursive script, *Reuben*. Maia wakes and starts to say something but Alannah presses a finger to her lips. She points downstairs. They talk to each other with the wideness of their eyes. They smell each other's fear like dogs. They listen. The steps are less defined now. Instead there is the occasional sound of a person brushing off unfamiliar furniture in the dark, the squeak of a hinge, the creak of a stair. Maia snatches her phone from the windowsill, her hands trembling. Alannah can see the screen and her mother's fingers bungling across it, swiping, dabbing. She selects Michael's number, selects the green circle with the symbol of the phone receiver.

Alannah, listening in the dark. She feels the blood rushing out of her head and hitting her heart. In the second that it takes for the call to engage, she parts a crack in the curtain. Down on the driveway, the two-headed dog is sitting calmly, its blue eye shining through the dark. Out in the hallway, Alannah hears the antiquated ringtone. A few sharp notes, tumbling, tumbling, and then silence. ∎

Tramp Press is proud to congratulate

SARA BAUME

for being selected as one of

Granta's Best of Young British Novelists 2023

handiwork

SARA BAUME

a line made by walking

SARA BAUME

seven steeples

SARA BAUME

spill simmer falter wither

Sara Baume

A DYING TONGUE

Sarah Bernstein

W hat needs explaining was that, and it was a funny thing, a very funny thing, I did not speak the language. It was not for lack of trying, for I had been enrolled in a programme of daily language tuition for several months prior to my relocation, tuition I continued remotely upon my arrival in the place my brother called home. I was studious. I was meticulous. For whatever reason it would not stick. I had never had a problem with language acquisition up to that point, in childhood I had spoken four languages, at least two of which I had lost in the passage of time, all the same I pursued in a haphazard manner my studies of foreign languages at university, picking up German and Italian with ease, in fact the facility with which I read and wrote, not to mention conversed, in these languages after barely a month's attendance at weekly classes floored my instructors of German and Italian, in no small part because of a certain vacant quality I had always had. The teachers lavished me with praise, holding me up as an example in front of my classmates, who despised me with good reason, in the first place because I appeared to relish the attention, taking every opportunity to answer the questions the teachers posed to us, delivering sentences with multiple clauses to showcase my linguistic virtuosity, revelling in every single syllable as it rolled off my tongue and into the space of the classroom in which

I sat, together with my classmates, who observed the spectacle with silent loathing, suspecting I had prior knowledge of the languages and was in point of fact a cheat. But the mother tongue of the locals foiled me, as it did not foil my brother, who had long mastered the language, who even as a child loathed any sign of weakness, who always sided with the victors, whatever their stripe. For a long time it did not occur to me that my brother had come to the town for just this reason, not an overwriting of history so much as a realignment of himself with the powerful, the crowning achievement in a lifelong pursuit of dominance.

But here again I go too far. Let me confine myself to my own motives. With regards to the problem of language, it was not the weather of the place that hindered me, for I liked the cold, had been born in the wintertime, and as a child had often lain down in the snow, in my snowsuit, and looked up at the white sky for hours, for hours. The situation in this northern country town seemed to me to offer a robust life, a hale life, a life of people with smooth and youthful skin, a much healthier lifestyle, in short, than I had been accustomed to, and my brother, prior to his illness, had been exactly this sort of vigorous person, could be found, at any given time, running a marathon or energetically and in a team rowing a skiff on rough seas. I, on the other hand, had been a dedicated and lifelong smoker, I loved nothing more than a smoke, it's true, from the age of fourteen I could be found smoking on street corners and doorsteps, in alleyways and in stairwells, and yet I was a stationary smoker, never moved while smoking, hated the sensation of smoking while walking, and I walked plenty – if I had a second, not quite equal, love, it was walking; I spent entire days walking from one end of the city I lived in to the other and back again, travelling by foot from tram terminus to tram terminus, bus station to bus station, municipal park to industrial park, and back again, always back again. I felt these were pleasures that ought not to be mixed, I had always wanted to be good and so, as a kind of offering of gratitude for my new life, I gave up smoking, which was just as well, for I had enough to be getting on with, as it turned out.

At first, I stayed away from the town in the valley, supplementing my brother's stores of dry goods with vegetables from the overgrown kitchen garden. I got to know my immediate surroundings. I explored the house, inside and out. I stood under the pines on the long drive, under the stand of alders by the creek, by the birch trees at the edge of the forest. I felt the cold ground of the kitchen garden give beneath me as I knelt down, so many hours spent weeding, mending the fences and darning the netting that cradled the winter crops. I untangled the tender leafy greens from the viny plants that had grown around them, wondering about the lives of cabbages, their hearts and their vitality. They did not know, how could they, the care and attention with which I applied myself to them, and I loved them for that, the essential mystery of their being, no exposition possible, no question of knowing or being known. The beautiful, the unthinkable cabbages! The kales too and the mustard greens, even the garlic, having survived the winter, throwing out its slender stalks. Do you understand what I am saying? Beauty is something to be eaten: it is a food. I endeavoured to learn from staying in place. I studied under the plants, under the earthworms, I felt the texture of the earth in which all these organisms lived changing with the seasons. How might a person, a people, take root? Roots and rootlessness, the preservation of what little remains of the past, such were the thoughts that blew through me on any given morning, standing very still in the porch, or in the garden in my bare feet, feeling suddenly: that sound, that rushing, it is the wind, it is the trees!

Sitting one afternoon on a rock by the creek that bordered my brother's property to one side, I observed the water running under the melting ice, carving out patterns, and then the ice itself, in its incalculable shades of white and grey and blue, how long and lovely and terrible the springtime, how unbelievable to be alive. If I could be anything, I thought, sitting on my rock, eating a granola bar, I would be that ice, with its multitudes, always in the process of transformation. It was not long before I took to immersing myself, of course I did, in the creek where it pooled at a bend, breaking up the clear layers of ice with my walking stick, treading slowly into its dark waters, deeper and deeper, feeling on the brink of something, sinking, I thought, not knowing what else to call it. Another way of putting this is I began to take note of the rhythms of the place, and even, from the distance, of the town.

There was, for instance, the strange behaviour of the dogs. Three times a day, at daybreak, at noon and at sunset, in all corners of the township however far-flung, every canine, as if mobilised by some mysterious force, stood to attention and howled in one long, unbroken, collective howl. And there were other peculiar occurrences, some more alarming than others, but I will get to them in time. The people, for their part, so far as I could tell, had closed, white faces. They had, I am sure, characters of their own, interests of their own, but such things were difficult to discern from a distance. Nevertheless, I continued to observe them just as they, I know, observed me. Patterns became apparent, days of work and rest, feast days, market days, days set aside for religious devotion. I began to love the town in the valley, which seemed, from my vantage point in my brother's house on the hill, so tidy, so well ordered. I began to love the people, whose history I knew was so entwined with mine, whose ancestors had lived side by side with mine, had worked with them, broken bread with them, lived under the same sky, suffered the same cold, the same blight, the same floods, the same kinds of catastrophes, for a time, for a time. For all things come to an end, yes, as the lives of my forebears had come to an end, life itself and life as they knew it, never knowing, never understanding why or wherefore, only that a feeling, running under the seams for centuries, had broken to the surface. How then could I not love these people, who represented the closest thing to an inheritance I could be said to have? I wondered how they would receive me. Of course I had heard stories of other such meetings, of spitting and stones, of defacements and assaults, but these people, I felt, were different, they were serious, devout. Above all, I sensed, they understood the importance of perceiving things without using their names, they understood that names were secret, they were sacred.

The time eventually came when I was required to leave the seclusion of the house and the woods and go into town for provisions. I knew that, whether or not I intended it, I would be presenting myself in public as the representative of my brother, as the one person, absent his wife and children, looking after his affairs. I could show no sign of weakness. I would do him proud. I dressed with care in one of the many loose, linen garments I had acquired over the years, a long coat against the weather, and set out on foot down the road, a single paved track that led down into the valley. At the centre of the town, there was a church, there was nothing sinister in that, and around the church, a churchyard. I had always had a feeling for churches, especially country churches such as this one seemed to be, surrounded by trees, planted perhaps at the time of the church's construction, the church and trees growing together over the years, over the centuries, over the long and unbroken life of this town. I imagined the scrubbed wood benches, the kneeling on flagstones, the spareness of it all, I admired churches greatly, yes, and yet I confess I had never set foot in one, had then as now a superstitious fear of crossing the threshold, passing up the chance to see inside some of the world's most famous churches and cathedrals on tours in my youth. But still, I liked to look out the window of my room on the second floor of my brother's house, down into the valley, and see the church spire rising out of the trees, it felt like, as indeed it was, a meeting point – of life, of the spirit, of some kind of organising principle I had tried in vain my whole life long to live up to. There was so much one had to live up to, so many good deeds one had no reasonable expectation of carrying out, because of one's resources, because of one's will, and they would loom over the whole of one's life, these specific failures, representing metonymically as it were the profound spiritual failure of one's life, the community always holding one to account. In the Church it was different. In the Church, I felt, one began from the principle of original sin, one's guilt assumed from the get-go. From childhood I felt always on some precipice, reaching for a state of grace ever unattainable to me, always on the point of falling. I tried yoga, I tried harmonising with

Mother Earth, but only scraps of it took with me. Perhaps I liked looking at the church spire because I saw in it the possibility of a life of obedience where one's sins had been acknowledged and already redeemed. Such were my thoughts as I walked into town that first time, crossing the road to get a closer look at the crocuses emerging in the churchyard, smiling up at the church itself, still there after all these years, never succumbing to fire or flood, to natural disaster or man-made catastrophe, a place whose doors were kept immemorially unlocked, to which confidence gathered, bringing the people along with it. In truth and as it happened a building further away from God one could scarcely imagine.

Driving the town's economy, my brother had given me to understand, was, or at least had been, a trade in tombstones, in which he himself naturally had a hand. The quarries still brought up stone for this purpose, a dwindling number of carvers still carved it, and the finished stones were sent to mark the resting places of the dead all across the country. Much of the land in the township was owned by this quarrying company, but there remained a small community-run farm for the growing of fruit and vegetables and the rearing of various animals, including cattle and sheep. Perhaps, my brother said one evening, I might find some small, harmless way to become involved in the endeavour, make an effort to assimilate into the local community, take part for once in the things happening around me. There was a rota sheet in the shop, he explained, where one could sign up for such tasks as milking, feeding, walking, shearing, grading, carding, spinning, lambing, cleaning, digging, weeding, strimming, mowing, tilling, sowing, seeding, walling, liming, scraping, watering, erecting, dismantling, soldering, separating, hitching, unhitching, mucking out and transporting to slaughter. My brother had not specified which of the aforementioned I might be qualified to undertake, nor did he provide any advice with regards to the particulars of how to go about communicating my intention, my difficulty in learning the common speech was still painful to him, he was ashamed and even offended, owing it to some wilfulness on my part.

The single track that ran from my brother's house became, down in the valley, the town's main street, and where it intersected with one of the few subsidiary avenues, one could find the shop, a kind of general goods store. It stood on a paved lot, empty but for a lone petrol pump, a low wooden building lined with windows, over the entrance of which hung a neon sign in cursive script giving the name of the place. Underneath this was a second sign, striped yellow and white, that read: CAFÉ. For, I noticed, peering through a window, one half of the space had indeed been given over to a number of booths, to a counter with a row of stools, where people sat eating such fare as one might expect to see in a roadside diner of this kind, admitting of course certain regional variations, such as the type of berry used in the pie, the thickness of the chips, the type of toast served alongside the plate of eggs, the brand of cherry cola, and so on and so forth. The far-reaching and long-lasting influence of mid-century American road culture might be cited here, though it hardly needs explaining at this point in history, cultural imperialism, military imperialism, the long march of the American diner, its rise and fall, its rise again in the present age of nostalgia, when one finds oneself yearning for a landline, for a rotary dial, for the hard edges of a VHS cassette, for the smell of the video store on a Friday night, for the commercial life of another era when one knew slightly less, for one's personal golden age, yes, yes. From the outside, the shop, and especially the diner appeared like a haven from the age of anxiety, not to say terror, in which one lived. I wanted so badly to be able to sit alone in one of the booths and drink a cup of coffee that would be refilled periodically by a server, smoke a cigarette perhaps, have a slice of pie. It would be a long time, I reflected, before I could gather the courage to sit in the diner on my own, I would first have to brave the aisles of the shop, the counter where, no doubt, the shopkeeper presided over her till.

That first time I entered the shop I was in an extreme state of agitation, I so wanted to make a good impression on the shopkeeper and yet knew there was no hope of my doing so, for we could not communicate other than by pointing and nodding as a result of my continuing failure to learn her mother tongue, and although it was common in the country for people to speak English, I could not count on anyone being willing to use it. Thus, the anticipated difficulty was twofold: first, in the failure more generally of my own expression which, when not plagued by aphasia – receptive or expressive – or dysphasia, of the same orders, when not affected by aphonia, by a stutter or a lisp, by the loss of control of my vocal cords and sometimes the muscles in my face, was, at the best of times, ambiguous and even obscure. Second was the problem of comprehension on the part of the listener, taking into account the language divide, the listener's incapacity or unwillingness, their degree of hearing loss – congenital, selective, injury-induced or as a natural result of ageing – and a number of factors besides. And so each time someone might try to speak to me, to place me, to find out where I came from, though they would already and without a doubt have the information second-hand from my brother who as I said spoke fluently, having mastered the regional accent and even the local idiom, his difference was barely perceptible, his proximity to the dominant culture within a hair's breadth, I felt a renewed sense of shame and failure for being unable to do the same, for providing further evidence of the arrogance of English speakers, the way they contrived, by virtue of their tongue, to bring destruction with them wherever they went in the world, and I was sorry for the townspeople who, I knew, must, with the passage of time, only grow to resent this failure. And so as I stood in silence before the counter in the town shop on that first visit, in a state of heightened confusion, attempting to count out the currency that was still unfamiliar to me, and doing so with what must have seemed to any onlooker like deliberate and obstructive slowness, I groped for something to rescue the situation. My eyes alighted on a piece of lined yellow paper where other people had signed their names in hand-drawn boxes, names I could not read. I knew, or at least felt, that this must be the rota sheet for the community farm. My gaze roved to the single empty space, and before I could stop myself, I grasped the pen lying on the counter, a bolder action than I was accustomed to taking, and wrote in my name. As I did so, I told myself that it behoved me, after all, to give up my free time to this community initiative, to do something to show my gratitude for the beautiful place in which I lived, for my life which had proceeded up to that point without any major tragedy or disaster, no serious injury, no debilitating illness, no poverty or homelessness, no addiction or sudden psychological break, no love lost having never been gained, no kidnapping or attempted murder, no extortion or blackmail, no assault that had been reported, investigated and brought to trial, no genocide or exile in my generation, I had been fortunate, yes, luckier than most, I ought to do my part, to serve the community, to pay what I owed. I replaced the pen in its holder and ventured a look at the shopkeeper. Her mouth was in a thin, grim line and she had one hand under the counter, reaching, I thought wildly, for a weapon of some kind, yes, I thought, my time had come and I deserved it, for although on the one hand I felt I was expected to perform community service; on the other, I had come forward without first having been asked, without knowing the details of the project or the ways of doing things into which the townspeople had without a doubt been inculcated since childhood and which I would struggle to master despite all my best intentions and sincere efforts. I had always been awkward, if not completely inept, and I realised with horror that in signing my name to this rota sheet, ostensibly to offer my assistance, I had in fact placed a burden on the townspeople to teach me how to do things, to explain by gesture and with difficulty their ways of being, the local practice of animal husbandry, to give up their own limited time only so that I could feel good about myself, about my participation in society. It would be no bad thing, I had long felt, for someone to put me out of my misery, in any case it was too late to rectify my error, I could not now remove my name, not so soon and not under the watchful and suspicious eye of the shopkeeper. I stood for a moment, holding my breath, waiting for the shopkeeper to raise her hand from beneath the counter, which she did, and it was empty, and so she must therefore, I reasoned, have pressed some kind of security alarm hidden cunningly beneath the counter, to summon guards or the local police force, to release the large black dog I had seen kennelled behind the shop. I looked around, fully expecting to see a group of men, a group of women, a pack of dogs, coming through the front door, through the door leading to the storeroom, but nothing happened, no one came. When my gaze fell once again upon the shopkeeper, she did not seem to be smiling, no, not quite, but she took the coins and bills from my hand and counted out what she felt was the correct amount for the items I had placed on the counter in what seemed like some distant past. She held the door open for me as I left, I had purchased more things than would fit into my tote, out of guilt, out of terror, and I was required to carry in my hands certain items like a punnet of strawberries grown in the town's polytunnel, a bottle of milk from one of the local cows, a box of eggs from the chickens. The shopkeeper did not chivvy me out, and yet the door closed swiftly behind me so that I found myself suddenly and once again in the car park. I felt a motiveless sorrow. ■

Congratulations

to Sarah Bernstein, Eleanor Catton and
Anna Metcalfe, three of *Granta*'s
Best of Young British Novelists.

'Sarah Bernstein
manages to combine
cool, perfectly
weighted prose with
an extraordinary
emotional sensibility'
Fiona Mozley

'Eleanor Catton's
storytelling is deft
and irresistible in this
merciless whirlpool
of a book'
**Kiran Millwood
Hargrave**

'*Chrysalis* announces
Anna Metcalfe as
a distinctive and
daring fresh literary
voice'
Sharlene Teo

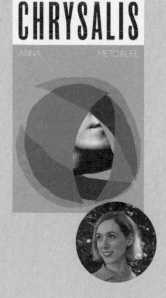

GRANTA

UNIVERSALITY

Natasha Brown

A gold bar is deceptively heavy. Four hundred troy ounces, about 12.5 kg, of ultra-high-purity gold formed into an ingot – a sort of slender brick crossed with a pyramid. Holding one such bar on a chilly September evening last year, thirty-year-old Jake marvelled at its density; how the unyielding sides and edges felt awkward, yet somehow natural, in his hands. Behind him, from the main building of a Queensbury farm, music and coloured lights throbbed against the night sky – a so-called illegal rave, roughly one hundred youngsters partying in defiance of the UK government's lockdown restrictions. Jake didn't look back towards the noise pumping from the farmhouse where he'd spent most of his fraught 2020. He wasn't even looking at the gold, not really.

The bar in Jake's possession was a 'London Good Delivery' – literally the gold standard of gold bullion – worth over half a million dollars. An obscene concept; Jake couldn't quite believe it was possible to hold so much 'value' within his two hands. Let alone to wield it. Again and again. Again. Until his target had finally stopped moving. But it had happened, hadn't it? Yes, it had happened. He couldn't stop himself from staring at the proof. The motionless body lying at his feet.

At some point that night, or perhaps as daylight crept in at the edge of the horizon, Jake managed to stop looking and start thinking.

He decided to run.

In the weeks following Jake's disappearance, the Queensbury and Bradford local papers reported on the events of that night: an illegal rave, the resulting three hospitalisations, significant property damage and an ongoing police investigation. The story was soon forgotten, however, and national focus remained on the Covid-19 pandemic and the government's strategy heading into the challenging winter months. Yet unravelling the events leading to this strange and unsettling night is well worth the trouble; a modern parable lies beneath, exposing the fraying fabric of British society, worn thin by late capitalism's relentless abrasion. The missing gold bar is a connecting node – between an amoral banker, an iconoclastic columnist and a radical anarchist movement.

'Of course I want it back – it's my gold.'

Richard Spencer has not forgotten the events of that night. Indeed as the legal owner of the farm, he thinks of little else. 'I want my life back!' he complains, bitterly. The first time I meet Spencer, he sits across from me, his elbows propped against the dull aluminium top of our outdoor dining table. He chose the place – an earnestly ironic American-style diner in Covent Garden. The menu lists an £11.50 avo 'n' cream cheese bagel. Spencer wears a deep blue Ted Baker shirt, starchy but unironed, with the sleeves rolled to mid-forearm, lending a disembodied, theatrical effect to his expressive hands and wrists. He's garrulous, keen to detail the many ways his life has been turned into 'an absolute shitshow'.

An overly indulgent, even selfish, comment, perhaps. After all, since the Covid-19 pandemic swept across the globe in 2020, many people have suffered badly, losing their lives and loved ones. Spencer is alive and well. His loved ones are safe – though possibly not reciprocally loving, at this moment. But Spencer has lost something significant: his status. Back in 2019, all the excessive fruits of late capitalism were his. He owned multiple homes, farming land, investments and cars; he had a household staff, a pretty wife, plus a much younger girlfriend. As a high-powered stockbroker at a major investment bank, he enjoyed obscene power, influence and wealth. He had everything.

Now, stripped of all that, he has become the man across from me: a grounded giant, cut off from his castle in the sky.

Spencer's gold-thieving, beanstalk-chopping 'Jack' is Jake from the farm, whom Spencer suspects of running off with the gold after allegedly committing the assault. 'Of course he bloody took it with him,' Spencer says, certain of his own version of events, despite having never met Jake.

In fact, Spencer knows virtually nothing about the man he blames for his ruin. Spencer invited Jake to the farm as 'a favour to Lenny', a woman he'd met in the building. 'Her friend needed a place to quarantine for a few days,' he says simply. Spencer doesn't know much about Lenny either. She was a neighbour of his – one of the few to remain in their Kensington apartment block during the lockdown, a time when most residents retreated to secondary homes. Does he know her surname? 'No.' Age? 'Um, mature.' What did he actually know about this woman, when he decided to hand her the keys to his farm? 'Well,' he hesitates. 'I knew her pretty well, in a sense . . .' he trails off.

Reluctantly, Spencer will admit to his philandering. He is separated from his wife, Claire, who remains in the family home raising their three-year-old daughter Rosie alone. 'Not exactly alone,' he's keen to point out. 'They have the nanny four days a week. And it's not like Claire has a job.' Claire and Spencer split in 2019 over his tryst with a colleague fifteen years his junior.

'Typical. He would say that.' Claire opens the large front door to her Cobham home one-handed when I stop by days later – her left arm is wrapped around a shyly curious toddler. We sit down at the kitchen breakfast bar with a pot of filter coffee between us. Little Rosie lies on the soft-play mat in the corner, kitted out in stripy leggings, a builder's hard hat and a glittery tutu, mumbling as she forces plastic trucks to collide. 'I'm a designer,' Claire says. Since Rosie's birth in 2018, Claire has taken on part-time freelance work for a handful of clients. Before that, she worked at a boutique branding agency, after reading Art History at Oxford, where she met Spencer. The pair married soon after graduation, living in London apartments until deciding to move to the suburbs and start a family.

Claire is sanguine about their separation, 'People change, don't they?' Their suburban house had never really felt like Spencer's home – 'He stayed in the city most nights. His hours were so long, it made sense.' Spencer had spent weeknights in his Kensington pied-à-terre until after Rosie's birth when, increasingly, he began to spend weekends away from his family, too. 'I'm not stupid,' Claire says of the unspoken affairs, 'I know what goes on.'

A few years earlier, in 2015, Spencer's father had died after a prolonged illness. 'That was the beginning of his farm obsession,' according to Claire. Every weekend Spencer would attend auctions or travel to remote towns to view land plots and properties. A late effort, perhaps triggered by grief, to emulate his father – a 'man's man' who had built a successful construction company from the ground up. 'His dad never quite understood him,' Claire says. 'But Rich idolised the guy.' Eventually, Spencer bought an old hilltop farm in Queensbury, a quiet West Yorkshire village. Claire didn't think much of the property. 'It's a complete wreck,' she doesn't mince her words, 'a rubbish heap on a big hill in an awful little town. No one with any sense would touch it.'

Claire's dismissal of the farm hit personally. I grew up in Queensbury, a stone's throw from the Alderton farm. I walked past it almost daily as a child; occasional summer afternoons spent 'mucking in' with the Alderton family as a teenager were a part of my upbringing. Fresh produce was a staple at our dinner table. Nothing at the supermarket can beat the warm, frothy taste of unpasteurised cow's milk, ladled fresh from the milker's bucket. Though economically disadvantaged, and unapologetically working class, the town provided a wonderful backdrop for my childhood. It has value. But somehow, our country's towns and industries have become the playthings of London's elite. The Alderton farm fell into hard times in the wake of the 2008 financial crisis, when the government subsidies that had buoyed the farm's modest revenues dried up. The remaining livestock was sold off and the family boarded up the outbuildings. But living in the main house, without income from an operational farm, proved untenable. 'We lost everything,' Mrs Alderton says. 'It had been in our family for generations.' The Aldertons searched for new owners who would continue to run it as a community-minded farm, but there was little interest. 'We ended up selling to property developers, we had no choice.' No investment or redevelopment in the area took place, however, though the farm changed hands a few more times. The abandoned plot became a familiar pockmark atop the town's hill. Until, in 2016, Richard Spencer snapped up the property at auction.

'He has a weird "prepper" fantasy. He thinks he can survive the end of the world there or something.' Claire is doubtful, 'I've never seen him do so much as water the garden.' Spencer went on to renovate the farm's main building, fashioning a safe refuge for when society inevitably collapsed – possibly galvanised by his part in the '08 crash, and the societal fragility each subsequent economic shockwave revealed. When a global catastrophe finally did arrive by way of a novel coronavirus, however, Spencer clung to London's familiar comforts: restaurants, his housekeeper, and same-day deliveries from Mr Porter. He remained in his Kensington apartment, and the renovated farm stood empty.

Until Jake arrived.

There are currently no suspects in the police investigation. On the night of the rave, local police issued over thirty fixed-penalty notices for lockdown breaches. As the venue owner, Spencer also received a £10,000 fine. Most attendees fled before police arrived, and interviews with the few arrested proved fruitless – the majority lived outside Queensbury and knew little of the farm. One unidentified person of interest was found unconscious and admitted to a local hospital, having suffered a blunt force trauma to his head. Initial news reports noted 'evidence of squatters at the property', along with an apparent 'small-scale marijuana growing effort'. Spencer has been questioned, though police declined to provide details of his statement, citing an ongoing investigation. There is presently no search, however, for a missing gold bar – or Jake, for that matter. A police spokesperson gave a terse dismissal: 'Primarily this is a drugs offence, as well as a serious lockdown breach. Not a wild goose chase for a pot of gold.'

Mixed metaphors aside, the investigation appears to have petered out. Until the hospitalised John Doe regains full consciousness, much of the goings-on at the farm will likely remain unknown. Today, the boundaries of the farm are still cordoned off by police tape, a striking reminder to the town's residents.

'I hate to see it come to this,' Mrs Alderton tells me via a telephone call. 'Drugs, violence and who knows what else? That was our home.' The Aldertons believe the farm's new owner Richard Spencer had an active role in the criminality. 'It's big business,' says Mr Alderton, a comment his wife relays to me enthusiastically. Spencer's months-long renovation of the farm's main house, which then stood empty, had already sparked speculation among local residents. 'Something's not right there,' Mrs Alderton surmised. 'Men like that don't spend their money for nothing.'

'I'm making a stock,' says historian and lecturer Rodger Walters, an explanation of sorts for the kitchen chaos surrounding him. A chicken carcass is splayed open on a Pyrex dish beside a large, propped-up cookbook, and surrounded by an impressive amount of root vegetables, some half chopped, others caked in mud. He directs me through the conservatory to a garden where his partner, columnist Miriam Leonard, sits with a tumbler of whisky, in spite of the biting cold.

It would not be unfair to say that Leonard, who goes by Lenny, exists in spite of pretty much everything. 'A rare dissenting voice in this perplexing time of media polarisation and moral orthodoxy, Leonard is one of the few souls brave enough to say the unsayable,' proclaimed the introduction to her 2018 book *No Mo' Woke*, a lightly edited selection of her newspaper columns spanning a twenty-plus-year career. Publishers, it seemed, had noticed that what Lenny said was actually quite sayable, and suspected it would also be rather profitable to print in book form. Lenny accepted a 'sizeable' advance in 2016 for a two-book deal, and began the work of repackaging her various columns into a single cohesive volume, her magnum opus, framed with an impassioned polemic detailing the imminent threat of 'woke culture and anti-white sentiment'.

'Problem is,' Lenny reflects, 'the book just didn't sell.' Apparently, the people who weren't embarrassed to place *No Mo' Woke* on their shelves didn't, by and large, actually have bookcases. Early indicators had been positive, the book garnered rave, collegial reviews from across the papers – *The Times* hailed it 'a breath of fresh air' and even the firmly left-wing *Guardian* newspaper managed cautious praise, albeit with a passing swipe at the 'unfortunate' title. 'Actually, the title was genius,' Lenny grins. She has a point. The title maximised upset and grievance, but was impossible to criticise without coming off as, well, woke. Even now, two years post publication, #NoMoWoke remains a popular hashtag on social media.

Lenny's editor Rob Neeson – 'a thirty-five-year-old with ridiculous glasses' – advised her to find a fresh take for the second book. 'Something "less Shriver, more Cohen" – that's what he actually said. Like I don't know how to write my own sodding column.' Lenny is entitled to some indignation. She's the seventeenth most influential columnist in the UK, according to the market research company YouGov. After punching her way out of the women's and lifestyle sections in the nineties, Lenny has established herself as a fixture in the opinion pages of Britain's right-leaning papers. Despite her oft-stated anti social media stance, in recent years Lenny has monitored Twitter fastidiously, always ready to pen a scorching opinion piece about the latest online brouhaha. She boils her sentences down to high-sucrose sweeties and calibrates her tone for maximum engagement. And newspaper editors know it; a piece of hers is guaranteed to attract clicks and social shares.

The book, however, was a reach for something grander. Lenny had grown disillusioned with newspaper work, 'in the end, it felt cheap.

I became an attack dog.' To Lenny, commentary should serve a higher purpose than mere punditry. 'We're not in the business of changing minds. I have to understand my readers' suspicions . . . their deepest fears. It's my job to inform those concerns by offering up the relevant *facts*.' She argues that her bruising brand of journalism helps readers to contextualise and interpret events. 'I zoom out,' she spreads her hands wide apart in demonstration, 'and reveal how all these trees come together as a forest.'

Back to those trees. Who is Jake, I ask Lenny. And how did he end up on Spencer's farm? I'd found Rodger simply enough from the electoral roll. He'd happily answered that he did, in fact, know a 'Lenny' when I called his extension at the university. But after a couple of hours' conversation in the bitter cold, I'm no closer to any answers about Jake or the farm. Instead of acknowledging my question, Lenny invites me inside for dinner. It's a generous interpretation of London's Tier 3 lockdown rules, but I accept, hopeful that the warmth, wine and food will encourage openness.

In November 2011, Indiya popped open a brand-new Quechua '2 Seconds' tent in London's Paternoster Square. In her rucksack, she'd packed marker pens, baby wipes and a water-purifying straw, all in preparation for the Occupy Wall Street protest. Barely nineteen years old, she accompanied her housemates from Central Saint Martins art school to join the ninety-nine per cent in an unprecedented uprising. 'It opened my eyes to the power of the people,' Indiya says of the experience. I find her sitting beside the now semi-conscious, semi-identified John Doe at the Bradford Royal Infirmary, the nearest hospital to the Alderton farm.

'His name is Pegasus,' Indiya says, reaching over the motionless man to rearrange his blankets, before smoothing his wayward hair. 'He's a visionary.'

Almost entirely unresponsive, Pegasus stares ahead with wide-open eyes. 'He's in a minimally conscious state,' Indiya says. 'It's a good sign – he's getting better.' Pegasus had spent a worrying forty hours unconscious after police transported him to the hospital without identification. Claiming no knowledge of how Pegasus was injured, Indiya instead speaks of the 'chaos' as officers arrived at the farm. 'Everyone was running around, the music was so loud, it was impossible to know what was going on.' She spent days searching for Pegasus in the aftermath, before finally locating him here at the hospital.

Indiya is tall, six foot exactly, with mouse-brown hair styled in long dreadlocks, loosely tied back. Her organic cotton face mask bobs as she speaks. Wearing an oversized waxed jacket with heavy boots, leggings and a cropped T-shirt that occasionally flashes her pale midriff, she looks like a revolutionary hippy from central casting. 'Occupy changed everything for me,' she says. Indiya had camped at the protest on and off for about three weeks, until her parents intervened – 'They only cared about me graduating, not, like, the large-scale inequality in the world.' To her parents' relief, Indiya did graduate in 2014, though she remained in close contact with the motley characters she'd met during the occupation, especially Pegasus. 'He's a magnetic force,' she says of her injured compatriot. 'He has this way of drawing people together.'

Though Indiya occasionally undertakes work in video game design, she's mostly eschewed the traditional rat race, choosing instead to experiment with various communal living arrangements. Some were relatively formal, with leases or co-op agreements in place; others, less so. 'I'm a hard core Marxist,' Indiya tells me solemnly. In the years since Occupy, she's committed to several other sociopolitical causes and is currently active within an Extinction Rebellion cell. 'Activism,' she explains, 'is crucial. It's now or never.'

In that spirit, Pegasus led a small group of activists to the farm last July. Together, they aimed to create a new 'self-sustaining community'. Christening themselves as the Universalists, the group considered their takeover of the farm to be political activism, rather than squatting. 'It's an unused property,' Indiya says. 'There's so many buildings like that in the UK. All these spaces – empty. It's criminally wasteful, when so many people need homes.' The Universalists viewed the farm as an opportunity; it was a chance to realise their specific vision for communal living.

Today, that dream is officially over. After visiting hours, Indiya cycles back to the Alderton farm. A heavy padlock and chain secure the doors to the farm's main building, a charming two-storey stone house, punctuated with square lead windows, set atop a gently sloping hill. Bulging bin bags and a few suitcases are piled up in a heap out front, along with some mismatched furniture. There's a Billy bookcase, a couple of worn armchairs, and what looks like the parts for a substantial sound system. Stray lengths of police tape flap about in the breeze as three young men load the bagged-up items into a small truck parked outside.

'We were building something here,' Indiya says in a wistful tone. Though only 'about a dozen' people had lived full-time at the farm, Pegasus believed the Universalists were ready to expand. The main building was almost at capacity, Indiya says, but the group had plans to convert an outbuilding into functional accommodation. 'It wasn't a rave – it was an open evening. We were opening our doors to potential new members, growing the movement.' Covid, it seems, was not a good enough reason to postpone such growth. 'The virus spread *because* of unbridled capitalism. Because of globalisation, and the profit-driven destruction of natural ecosystems. What we were doing here –' she gestures around at the sad aftermath – 'what we're building is the solution. Of course it couldn't wait!'

'Everyone pitches in. Everyone gets a say.' Indiya lists the rules of their burgeoning micro-society. 'Everyone is treated equally. We decide everything by a vote' – though Pegasus, as the group's de facto leader, held the power to adjudicate disagreements. This, Indiya insists, was an important improvement on her past commune experiences. 'Sometimes pure consensus isn't possible,' she says, 'and you just need a way to make a decision and move forwards.' As the community matures with time, the need for such ideological compromise would reduce, Indiya believes. Though she concedes that most of her other communal living experiments had ended before reaching such a point – either by petering out or collapsing spectacularly.

'But it's different here,' says Tim, twenty-nine, who had lived in a south London squat for two years before joining the Universalists. 'A farm offers possibilities that a city building just can't. We could have become self-sufficient here, living off of the land in conjunction with nature, rather than against it.' Tim, who refuses to give his surname (citing his objections to 'the patriarchal concept'), wears tortoiseshell glasses and affects the mumbling grandiosity of a grad student. 'Humans are small-community nomadic animals,' he says, arguing that simpler models of living are needed to counter climate change and other pressing issues. 'We're not meant for living in densely populated areas, or eating tomatoes year-round,' he adds.

Although the Universalists had no official hierarchy or fixed responsibilities, leaders began to emerge. Tim, who had previous experience with his parents' allotment, took charge of the farming effort. After sowing seeds late in the season, the group managed to grow a few vegetables. 'Kale, chard, sprouts – we even had carrots and turnips in the harvest,' recalls Tim. Despite his dominion over farming, Tim claims no involvement with the cannabis plants. 'Of course I'm not against it in theory,' he insists, explaining that the group's efforts were focused on establishing a sustainable food supply. 'We're serious about self-sufficiency,' he says. 'That's why we're doing this. It isn't a jolly.'

In fact, the Universalists eschewed many of the luxuries and conveniences Spencer had installed at the farm, keeping the electricity mostly off and attempting to survive entirely on chopped wood and solar power. 'Humans need to get back in tune with the land,' explains Pete Wright, thirty-eight, a bicycle mechanic from Durham. With his manicured beard, neat chequered shirt and deep blue jeans, Wright is the odd man out in this crowd. He looks positively conformist, aside from a messy topknot. He's more hipster than anarchist. But a few years back, when Pegasus chanced upon Wright's bike shop, the pair 'ended up talking for hours'. To Wright, what Pegasus said made a lot of sense. 'He really got me. More than politics, or protesting, or any of that noise. He just understood exactly what I'd been thinking,' says Wright. 'He talked about how we could live differently' – outside of the forces of capitalism and consumerism. Or 'a bullshit-free life', as Wright calls it. Soon after meeting Pegasus, Wright gave up his cycle shop job and moved into the same London squat as Tim.

'Quite the lifestyle change!' Wright laughs.

'You broke free, brother,' says Rob Martin, approvingly. Describing Wright's encounter with Pegasus as an 'awakening', Martin is keen to share the anti-capitalist gospel further. 'Wage slavery. That's what the system thrives on. The credit crunch totally exposed it. Occupy was just the start, we're still carrying on that work.' Martin was a fifteen-year-old school student at the time of the 2011 protests. Undeterred by its underwhelming end, he makes an enthusiastic case for Occupy's enduring legacy: 'Bernie Sanders, Jeremy Corbyn and obviously BLM. All of those movements came from what we started back then.' Martin has not had any first-hand experience with Black Lives Matter activism, explaining that he feels 'the environment is humanity's most pressing issue right now'. Still, he's sympathetic to many of BLM's stated aims, despite some concerns about the group's divisive rhetoric. 'Their demands are to the benefit of all of us, all humans,' he says. 'But focusing on race puts people off the message. What we need now is unity.'

'That's why we're called the Universalists,' Martin goes on. 'We want change – we want progress – but for *everyone.*'

'We're open to everyone,' Indiya agrees. That said, the Universalists are a noticeably homogenous group: young, middle-class and white. 'This lifestyle takes a leap of faith,' Indiya explains. Intentional living requires a step away from the 'activism myopia' that can ('understandably!' she stresses) afflict marginalised groups. 'But we would welcome anyone with open arms,' she says. 'This is just the beginning. We'll get there.'

Once the last bag is loaded, Indiya leads the group to a large barn and forces the door open. Inside, the wooden ceiling is four or five metres high. Strips of dusty light stream down through the gaps between the slats. Remnants of stalls, feeding troughs and milking equipment line the walls, untouched by renovation. During the weekly 'community meetings' held in this barn, the Universalists debated all aspects of their fledgling community, from the group's mission statement to squabbles over the washing-up. Today, the four Universalists remaining have reconvened to discuss an urgent problem: Jake.

When the group last met here on the afternoon before the rave, they voted to expel Jake from their community. Pegasus informed Jake of the decision, telling him to leave by morning. There's confusion about exactly what happened next, as the gathering spiralled into a rambunctious party, ending with the arrival of police officers (responding to multiple noise complaints from nearby residents). Among the Universalists, the prevailing belief is that Jake, who took the news of his eviction badly, attacked Pegasus in a drunken rage.

'I would really like to see him face some restorative justice,' begins Tim. 'But as we don't have any way to achieve that, perhaps we should defer to the authorities.' Although the group initially refused to cooperate with the police investigation, Tim now proposes sharing information on Jake's whereabouts with police – an idea that's met with muted agreement. In the ensuing discussion, Jake is blamed for a plethora of misdeeds: shirking his work duties, growing the cannabis that landed the group in legal trouble and, most seriously, the assault on Pegasus. 'But remember –' Indiya interjects carefully – 'Jake found this place for us. He invited us here. Even if he didn't become a constructive member of our community, that counts for something. Surely.'

Her words hang in the air.

After the tense meeting, Indiya splits away from the others, tracing a slow path along the perimeter of the farmhouse. In her quasi-militant attire, she doesn't look wholly out of place trudging through the mud. Everything is packed away now, ready for the long drive back to London. Spencer's farm will sit unoccupied once again. At the back of the building Indiya pauses, her expression inscrutable as she stares down at the town below. ∎

DOUBTFUL SOUND

Eleanor Catton

Eight months after my divorce from Dominic, I saw a woman he had led me to believe was dead. Her name was Kayla Kimrey, and she had worked as a cleaner at Dominic's firm until – so he had told me – she had overdosed on fentanyl sometime towards the end of 2018. I knew nothing else about her life, and if I asked any further questions about the circumstances of her death, then either Dominic didn't have the answers, or I've since forgotten what they were. I am sure I would have said that I was sorry – she couldn't have been more than thirty-five – and I expect that Dominic probably quoted some statistic off his phone about chemical withdrawal or per-capita prescription volumes or the relative potency of fentanyl to other drugs; nothing about the conversation struck me as peculiar, at any rate, and after it, I scarcely thought of Kayla Kimrey until the day I saw her lining up to board the boat to Doubtful Sound.

She looked oddly younger than when I'd seen her last. Her hair was up in a high ponytail, seeming straighter and blonder than I remembered, and showing off multiple piercings in each ear. Had her ears been pierced like that when she had worked at Marbus? No matter: there was no question in my mind that it was her. She was wearing a hard-shell jacket that was zipped up past her chin, and as she shuffled forward in the queue, she kept ducking her face into her collar and pressing her mouth tight against the windproof panel, extending and then retracting her jaw in a compulsive motion I had seen her make before. I was on board already, standing at the shoreside railing with a mug of milky coffee in my hand, and I had a sudden urge to throw it at her – not to hurt her, not even to provoke her, really; just to do something that no one would be able to predict. I imagined it exploding at her feet, imagined people shrieking, shouting, leaping back, imagined Kayla whipping round in shock and disbelief until she raised her head and noticed me above her, empty-handed, looking down.

Instead, I turned around and shut my eyes and tried to regulate my breathing. I felt a strange exhilaration: a sense of inward precipice, a rush of air. Since my divorce I have discovered that it is very difficult to explain to people that your ex-husband is a pathological narcissist without coming off like a pathological narcissist yourself; but here was proof, concrete proof, at last, that I wasn't crazy, that I wasn't paranoid, or sick, or playing games, that it was *him*, that *he* was the liar, that *he* was the manipulator, that *he* was the one who'd gaslit *me*, for years, through deceptions and petty cruelties purposely designed to be so trivial, and so obscure, and so inconsequential to anybody's happiness but mine, that I would seem hysterical even to perceive them. Like telling me a cleaner at his firm was dead – for no reason, probably, beyond the expectation that I'd repeat the lie at some workplace barbecue in months or years to come, and nobody would have any idea what I was talking about, and I'd appeal to him to back me up, and he would feign bewilderment, assuring me that Kayla Kimrey was very much alive and well, and asking me how much I'd had to drink, and denying any memory of ever mentioning her name to me except in passing, and soon everybody would be laughing nervously, and I'd be feeling every bit the raving lunatic that he was painting me to be, and later we would fight, for hours, over whether he'd embarrassed me or I'd embarrassed him, and he'd be stony cold, and I'd be sobbing, and he'd be saying I had sabotaged his self-esteem, and did I realise how insane I'd sounded and how utterly humiliated he had been, in front of his workmates, in front of his boss, and steadily my confidence would weaken to the point that I'd apologise for contradicting him in public, whereupon he'd tell me that I wasn't sorry, I was only playing yet another game, drawing attention to his insecurities, making him feel like a child, mocking him, bringing him down, and by now it would be long past midnight, and I'd be visibly exhausted, but he'd refuse to let me go to bed until our disagreement was resolved, which of course it never would be, because he'd lied, because he always lied, because he was a liar, and every time I yawned or closed my eyes he'd pinch my leg and say that I was only acting, that I was only pretending to be tired as a way to hurt him even more, that I was phoney, that I was twisted, that I was pathetic, that I had no backbone, that I sickened him, until finally, maligned, belittled, enervated, trembling mad, I'd snap – which of course was what he'd planned for all along. In fights with Dominic, I was always first to hit below the belt. He knew it, and he counted on it. Whatever nasty things I said or did to him, he could then hold over me forever after, demanding ransom in whatever form of payment that he chose.

But I was in New Zealand to put all of this behind me.

My eyes were still shut tight. I breathed. I gripped the mug. I felt the deck beneath my feet. I told myself what I should do. I should wait till the last of Kayla's group had boarded, then slip off the boat before she noticed me, muttering quietly that I had taken ill. I should return to the ticket office, where I should tell the staff that I wanted to exchange my ticket for a different day when I was feeling better, and as soon as the replacement ticket had been sorted out, I should ask if somebody would drive me back to my hotel. Then, without further ado, I should leave, not watching as the boat cast off and motored down the river and towards the lake, not wondering what on earth she was doing here, in New Zealand, on a package tour, not permitting any further thought of her at all.

I opened my eyes again. I knew that Dominic had cheated on me. I couldn't tell you when, or with whom, or how many times, but I was certain that he had. At the top of every list of narcissistic traits is the fact that narcissists tend to be promiscuous, and I couldn't count how many times he'd come home late, and sometimes very late, never saying where he'd been, but always showering before he came to bed. It killed me that I had never caught him, especially since he fitted the profile in every other way. When I'd first started joining support groups and discussion boards for people trapped in bad relationships, I'd been astonished by how much of other victims' testimonials I recognised. Isolate, confuse, self-alienate, deprive of sleep and other basic liberties, assault, incite to violence, disproportionately punish, withhold affection and reward: had it not been for these online communities, I might never have understood that these are very common methods of control. And it wasn't just the patterns that I recognised. It wasn't just the fights, the silence in between the fights, the debilitating vigilance, the shame, the misery, the period of helpless dread, and then the fight again; it was the actual lines of dialogue. Sometimes, reading these accounts online, it was as though I was reading an exact transcription of a fight I'd had with Dominic. It was as though there'd been another person in the room.

I turned again to get a second look at her. She was halfway up the gangway now, eyes still cast down, mouth and chin still buried in her collar. From the space around her, I guessed that she was travelling alone: there was an Asian family in the line ahead of her, and a couple in their sixties immediately behind. What was she doing here – a night-shift service worker from Grand Rapids, Michigan, vacationing halfway across the planet, day-tripping out to see a fjord? Doubtful Sound was one of the remotest corners of the country. It was miles from any major settlement, disconnected from any major road. To get there, as I knew already from the tour brochure, you had to cross Lake Manapouri, then disembark to where a fleet of coaches had been shipped into the wilderness to ferry you across a mountain pass. On the other side, a second boat was waiting to take you out into the silent fjord and back again. All up, the trip would take you seven hours. After you had left the wharf and crossed the lake and traversed the distant pass, after you had reached the sound itself, that was it. You were committed. There was nowhere else to go.

There was nowhere else for her to go.

She slid an arm out of her backpack and pulled it round to take a pair of sunglasses out of the front pocket. I watched her put them on. It had never even crossed my mind before that he had slept with her, and God knows I'd suspected almost everybody else; the first few times I'd laid eyes on her, in fact, were from the Marbus parking lot, parked up in the shadows, trying to glimpse him at his office window, or at any other window – while Kayla went from room to room, emptying wastebaskets, wiping down computer screens, dusting blinds, periodically dipping her chin and pressing her mouth into the drawstring of her hoodie in just the way that she was doing now.

She stepped on board, and the couple behind her followed. I didn't move. She passed into the cabin and out of my line of sight. The crew pulled up the gangway and cast off the mooring ropes. The engine juddered, and we were on our way. ■

You won't want to miss a word.

UNDER THE FIG TREE
Time to go...One Last Coffee
Rita And Anna M Wright

Paperback | 978-1-6655-9283-3 | **£16.95**
Ebook | 978-1-6655-9282-6 | **£2.99**
Audiobook | 978-1-6655-9723-4 | **£9.99**

www.authorhouse.co.uk

They say that time heals all wounds. But as Rita Wright reveals in this searingly honest memoir, recovery is rarely so simple. As *Under the Fig Tree* unfolds, she traces the stories and memories of her late daughter Anna, who tragically committed suicide at the age of 37. In honoring her passing, Rita faces painful truths about the demons that plague us all, and comes out the other end offering a new light to her readers. Loss can leave us with terrible scars. But through compassion, clarity, and care, *Under the Fig Tree* assures us there's hope for healing yet.

SHE'S ALWAYS HUNGRY

Eliza Clark

Thou shalt have a fishy
On a little dishy
Thou shalt have a fishy
When the boat comes in

'Play it again, and I'll gut you,' said our Mary's Samuel. He had his knife in my face, and he tried to slam the lid of the piano down upon my fingers. I pulled back my hands before they were crushed, like a hermit crab beneath a shoe.

The pub was lively tonight, but I did not feel lively. All the men were crammed into this small space – the pub had once been a cottage like any other in the village, and was not built to house us all. I was dragged along. I did not want to drink or play darts, or weep over lost brothers. So I played the piano. I played the only song I knew.

'Mary Mountjoy's Sammy doesn't want his fishy,' said Violet Fisher's Daniel.

'Our Kitty's John has played that flaming song fifty flaming times, and I won't hear it again,' said our Mary's Sam.

'But it's the only one I know,' I said. I did not care for my cousin, who was rough and quick to anger. He did not care for me, because I was meek and mild – a mother's pet.

'Then let someone who can play properly have it,' he said. Our Mary's Sam pulled me up and away from the piano by the collar of my shirt. 'Where's Rosie Andrews' John?'

Rosie Andrews' John got up from his table with his pint and mean smirk. He played piano well, but he loved to prod a sharp stick into a soft spot. He opened the lid of the piano, and keeping his eyes to our Mary's Sam, he played, and sang loudly.

Come here my little Jacky
Now I've smoked my baccy
Let's have a bit of cracky
Till the boat comes in

'*Dance to thy Nanny,*' sang Rosie Andrews' John. '*Sing to thy Mammy,*' he was laughing, and the rest of the pub joined. We all laughed at our Mary's Samuel. Our Mary's Samuel went red as guts, and stomped to the door like he was leaving, knife still drawn. Then, at the sound of a snigger, he turned around and put his knife in Rosie Andrews' John's back.

So Betty Hardy's David smashed a glass on his head, and he fell to the floor. We tied his hands and took him to the Mothers. We dragged him through the village, past all the little cottages. Some of our good women looked out from their windows and doors. They shook their heads but did not ask what we were up to. Men's nonsense, they knew.

All the cottages were arranged in circles around the Mothers' longhouse – our Mary's Sammy was spared no dignity on his journey. We rapped on the door, and were greeted by Mother Perch – who was unmoved, and unimpressed. She ushered us inside with a click of her tongue.

'I told you,' she said to the Mothers. 'We should shut that pub when the sea's rough. A rough sea –'

'Wets a man's brain, we know,' clucked our Mother Mountjoy, as she scooped up our Mary's Samuel.

Mother White tended to Rosie Andrews' John's back, while Mother Andrews saw to our Mary's Samuel. She called our Mother Mountjoy to see to him. He was still unconscious and the top of his head was wet with blood. He was balled up on the wooden floor, twitching. Mother Andrews and our Mother Mountjoy moved him to a rug.

Mothers Hardy and Perch spoke in hushed tones – I could tell they were arguing about the pub. They did not like the fights the alcohol brought, and they did not trust a space with no woman there to keep things under control. But it seemed that it was good for us; the men seemed happier when we had a place to be in covenant with one another. I did not trust the pub.

Our Mother snapped her fingers in front of my face and scolded me for eavesdropping.

'Why did you have to wind up our Sammy, so?' our Mother asked me.

'I didn't know he was getting annoyed, Mother. I can only play the one song.'

'I'd think hearing any song enough times would drive a man mad,' said Mother Fisher. She was the oldest Mother. She was also the smallest and her hair was the longest and whitest. Violet Fisher's Daniel spoke up for me.

'If I can, Mother . . . and Mother Mountjoy – your Kitty's John really only played the song a few times – then it was Rosie Andrews' John that pushed him over the edge.'

We looked over to Rosie Andrews' John, and he nodded.

'I was winding him up, I'll admit to that. But not so much I deserved a knife.' We all nodded, all of the men. 'With all due respect, I think it was your Mary's Sammy who was in the wrong,' he hissed while Mother White worked the little knife from his shoulder. 'In my opinion, anyway.'

The Mothers looked at one another. They made faces at each other, and they made gestures with their hands. Mother White shrugged, and Mother Perch clicked her tongue. None of them seemed happy with one another. I got the sense they wanted us, the men, to leave.

Our Mother sighed. She bent down to our Mary's Sam, and picked a small piece of glass from his hair. He was still knocked out, still bleeding.

'Well, we'd best get my Mary. And –' she looked over to Mother Andrews – 'best fetch your Rosie, too.'

They sent me to fetch Rosie Andrews and our Mary. I got them together and explained what had happened. I was worried they would be angry at me once I told them I'd been playing the song too much. But they said I had no need to worry, nothing to apologise for.

Then they apologised to one another on behalf of their sons. Our Mary said her Sammy's got a vile temper, and Rosie Andrews said her John's a little wind-up merchant and might well have deserved it. I led them to the longhouse and thought about how wise the women were. They forgave each other and they even forgave each other's men. They always thought the best of each other; they always assumed the best of each other.

At the longhouse, our Mother asked our Mary how our Sammy had been lately. Had he been irritable, or distracted? Did he seem distant? Hadn't he gone under a few weeks prior? Hadn't he fallen in the sea?

Our Mary looked worried.

'Should we get him deaf?' she asked.

'We haven't gotten a man deaf since my Daniel sixty years hence. It didn't work. It didn't contain anything, it just drove him mad,' said Mother Fisher.

'Then what?' our Mary asked.

'We shouldn't talk about this in front of the men,' said Mother Fisher.

Mother Hardy took me and Rosie Andrews' John outside. She admired the stitching on Rosie Andrews' John's back, then told us to be good, and slapped us both on the wrist.

I didn't know why they'd want to get a man deaf, but I knew my place and did not ask questions. If the Mothers wanted us to know something, they'd tell us. That was good enough for me. I was one of the best boys – people were always telling my Mammy that – and I built and protected that reputation. As much as I earned it, I was good by nature, too.

Despite my youth, the other men looked to me as a peacemaker. Some even said I could have come just from my Mother alone, with no man's blood or seed inside to spoil me. I was told the man who had fathered me was meek and gentle; I was well bred. I was told that he had long since gone to the sea and that his name was also John; but I can't remember which Mother he belonged to – so he is as good as lost to me.

The Mothers told us we would not see our Mary's Samuel for several days, so Mammy sent me to get fish for our Mary, and her Brogan and Melinda.

I went out on the boat with a net, and Rosie Andrews' John came out to help. It was a gentle day, but our Brogan told me to be careful and not to go out too far on the water.

'Don't feel the need to overfish for us. If the weather turns, come back,' she said. 'I'll be here on the shore with a line.'

'Thank you,' I told her.

'And the same goes for you, Rosie's John.'

We got on a little boat, and we watched our Brogan set up her fishing pole as we paddled out. We watched her get smaller, and smaller, as we floated further into sea. We did as we were told and did not go out too far. We set out the net and hauled up fish.

Rosie Andrews' John asked me if I knew what was wrong with Mary Mountjoy's Samuel.

'If the Mothers needed us to know –'

'They'd tell us. I know that. But we're out of their earshot for the time. So what do you know? Or what do you think if you don't know nothing?'

'I don't know anything I'm not supposed to know.'

'Well do you want me to tell you what I know? Because I know things. My Mammy's brother told me, you know, our Maggie's Gerald.'

Maggie Andrews' Gerald had a high status among men, on account of the fact he had lived to be over sixty before the sea took him. Maggie Andrews' Gerald was one of the best men – he was a mentor and helper to many of us. He was gentle. And because of his nature and his long life he was often privy to secrets that many men would not live to hear.

I did not say anything. My curiosity fought with my desire to be pure of any knowledge I had not been given by our Mothers. Men's knowledge had done so little for this place, and for the world outside of here.

'There's something in the water here that takes the men,' he said.

'We all know the water takes men. We all get taken by the water eventually.'

'Not the sea. Something *in* the water. Something what calls out to us, and drives us mad, and takes us.'

'We've all heard tell of finwives luring fishermen from their women, and they're just children's stories.'

'*No*,' said Rosie Andrews' John. 'You're not listening to me. Because this isn't some finwife or siren story. It's not some folk tale. It's in your head. It gets in your head and brings you down with it. Maybe to make you a slave –'

'Sounds an awful lot like a finwife story.'

'– maybe to eat you. We don't know. Our Maggie's Gerald said that we'd lost a lot of men that way – some women, too. Sometimes, getting bred helped rid the afflicted. But any babe born by a man or woman with that thing inside their head came out wrong – with gills.'

'I've never seen a baby with gills.'

'They put them in the water. They swim away.'

I winced when he talked about breeding. I tried not to think about it. Men who thought too much about getting bred became strange and disrespectful with their eyes. They tried to lure our women into secret trysts that their Mothers did not know about. I looked over to our Brogan on the rock. I could see only the shape of her, and not her pole. I think she was reeling in a fish.

'I feel sorry for your Rosie Andrews, you know. Because that is one of the most wet-brained things I've ever been told. I think if my son was coming out with such a salty mess as that, I'd send him out

to sea with a net and hope he got stuck in it,' I said. Rosie Andrews'
John glared at me.

'I heard you reeled in something funny last week, *John*,' he hissed.
'I heard you was on the water alone, and you reeled in something *dead*
funny.'

I smacked him, so he punched me hard in the arm. I lost my
balance, and I fell from the boat.

I had fallen from much bigger boats into much rougher seas, so
I did not panic. I tried to let myself float upward, but my ankle was
caught in our net. And while I was under, I heard it whisper to me. I
heard it clear as day, as if there were no water there to catch the words.
I heard my catch of the day, calling to me from where I was keeping it.

john john john john john john john john

A chorus. Rosie Andrews' John pulled me up, and when I surfaced,
I could here our Brogan shouting from the rock.

We came back to the shore with a boat full of fish, and our Brogan
slapped our wrists. She sent Rosie Andrews' John home and had me
warm up by the fire while she gutted fish. Our Melinda deboned
them, and our Mary salted them. They had me take the fish out to
their smokehouse, where I hung them up to dry.

'Our Mary said you fell in the water,' said Mammy. At home,
she was writing at her desk. I'm not sure what she was writing
– she helped organise the stores for winter, so maybe something to
do with that. She always told me these things did not concern me, so
I did not ask. She rose from the desk and smelled me. 'Too much fish
stink on you for my liking,' she said. She sent me to the bath with a
little bottle of lavender oil.

I could not be bothered to warm the water, so I sat in the bath
behind the cottage in cold water pumped straight from the tap. I
dripped in the lavender oil, and hoped it would kill the smell of fish
and seawater. I thought about my catch of the day. And I thought
about wet-brained Rosie Andrews' John, and I thought about his
stupid story. And I found myself unable to draw a line in my head

between the two: between my catch of the day and Rosie Andrews' John's story.

My catch of the day could not be some siren because it did not speak. It did not look like a man or a woman so it could not be finfolk. It did not even have a mouth.

I was quiet at dinner and Mammy was worried. She asked me if I was nervous about my first big fishing trip – if I was worried about getting taken out on the big boat at this time of year. And I told her that I was. So she told me that all men must go to the sea eventually, and she smiled.

'But I'll hope you'll live to spring,' she said. 'Might be a breeding season.' I twisted my face, and she patted my arm affectionately. 'The Mothers said I might be able to claim a granddaughter,' she said. 'If you sire more than one.'

'Yes Mammy,' I said. I poked at the potatoes she had made with my fork.

'You're such a good boy,' she said.

After Mammy went to bed, I went to see my catch. I did not want to string it up in our smokehouse, because I didn't want to smoke it. I could not keep it in the cellar, because Mammy's down there all the time, so I took it to an old fisher's shack.

We have them all over the coast; little shacks with a cot and some preserves inside. They're useful if you're night fishing or lost and on your own. Sometimes you open a shack, and pull out a wheezing, half-drowned man; sometimes you find still-dressed bones, and you have to check his clothes to see if his mother's name is sewn into them.

The old shack – where I left my catch – was tucked alongside the cliffs that bordered our land; the place where the sandy beach gave way to jagged, slippery rocks. The shack was rusty, with a hole in the roof. There was no mattress on the cot, and no preserves left inside. I knew of it (as did a handful of others) as a place to hide secrets. Stolen objects, stolen kisses – I had never used it before – but a girl cousin (I forget which) took me here once as a little boy. She showed me a small knife she had stashed here, then grabbed my arm and cut it. My skin parted like butter.

I could hear the sea, and I could hear my own name. Both became louder as I walked towards my catch. *John john john john john john* and the crash of waves. Upon the door of the shack was a hastily scrawled sign, one I had written and hung myself.

KEEP OUT – UNSAFE STRUCTURE

I entered. And tangled in a net atop the bare frame of the cot was my catch of the day.

I would not call it a merman or a mermaid. I would not call it a siren or a selkie, or finfolk or bucca, because it did not seem human enough to be any of those. But it was too human to simply be some enormous fish. It had a person's torso. It was small: more womanly at the waist and breast, but masculine at the shoulders. It had arms which looked to me like the legs of goats or horses. I would not say that it had hands – but it did have fingers.

It had a long, slippery tail – more like an eel's than something a fish would have because it was slick and serpentine and frilled. It didn't have fins or scales, it was totally hairless and moist and spongey to the touch. The entire body was slick with mucus and smooth – again, like a worm or an eel.

I have already said that it had no mouth. It also had no nose. Instead, it had gills ribbing its neck and where its jaw would be if it had a mouth. Most of its head was dominated by two huge, black eyes. They were clear, jellyfish domes over deep black pits. They were delicate, and endless; they shimmered and glittered in light like the moon on the water.

When I first pulled it up into my boat, I was afraid. And then I was not, because I knew that this was *my* catch. My thing. I was to keep it forever and admire it. I thought about butchering it and eating it, so it could be within me forever. I thought about making its bones into little trinkets. Then I did not think that any more – like a door had slammed closed on the thought. Instead, I thought the creature itself could be my slippery trinket, living and breathing and in my arms.

I thought about untangling it from the net, but I was too frightened it would leave me. I rowed it to the shack, and I fastened the net to the bed frame.

'Hello,' I said. I dropped down to its level and inspected it. The net was beginning to cut into its flesh. I touched its tail. It now felt dry to the touch. 'I think I can hear you.'

lovely john hungry john john john hungry john hungry john

'You're hungry?' I asked. And it flexed its tail. 'What do you eat?'

the sea eat the sea the things the sea in the sea suck suck suck the sea in the sea eat eat eat eat eat in sea

I decided to bring it a basin to sit in, one I'd fill with seawater. There was an old tin bath in our cellar – one I'd used as a boy and grown out of. I would take that and bring it tomorrow.

no no tomorrow sea now in the sea the eat in the sea eat eat

So I did not wait till the next day. I brought the bath, and filled it with seawater. I dragged it into the shack and proceeded to untangle the catch from its net. I picked it up from the floor like a bride and lowered it into the water. It shuddered, and the water turned pink. I petted its tail; it became slicker and slicker the more I touched it.

good sea good touch sing song sing song sing song

I sang to it. *Thou shalt have a fishy on a little dishy. Thou shalt have a fishy when the boat comes in.* It swayed when I sang. It shuddered. If it had hands to clap, I imagine it would.

I left at sunrise.

The men take the biggest boats out for the pre-winter fishing trip. I had never been on one before – I was too young. It was a trip to catch as much fish as we could to hang and smoke and dry for our winter stores. It was dangerous, and we sometimes lost as many as ten men.

In November we made the trip, and the women spent the rest of the month gutting and drying the fish. In January, the pregnant women who had ascended to the midwife's hall the previous summer would come down from the hill with new babies. They would be presented with extra provisions, containing the biggest and best catches.

We had to prepare for the trip, and the women had to manage our preparations. Mother Mountjoy was overseeing our work. We were stocking the boat. We needed provisions like clean water, lemons, dried fish and fruit. But also tools, rope, nets, harpoons, knives. I was hauling a barrel of fish that was too big for my small body. I was yawning and swaying on my feet. Mother Mountjoy came to me and stroked her hands through my hair.

'Sleep badly, pet?' she asked. I nodded. She had me rest. I sat with her and watched the other men continue with their tasks. I saw an Andrew – I think he was Bess Perch's Andrew – crack open the barrel of lemons he was dragging, and begin to eat them like apples.

'I'm starving,' he said. And then a few more men followed suit. They opened their barrels and began to eat. Mother Mountjoy whistled, and more men came to control their hungry brothers. Their mouths were smeared with fish bits and fruit pulp.

'Take them to the longhouse,' she said. 'Take them away.'

Many of the men looked frightened and confused, but Mother was calm. She told them to go back to work, and not to worry. I was worried.

'Little pet,' she asked, 'have you heard tell of any strange catches lately? Any especially big fish?'

'No Mother,' I said. I had to restrain myself from clapping my hand over my mouth, because I had never lied to our Mother. I wanted to tell her the truth, and then I did not.

'Have you heard anything strange? Has anyone seen anything odd?' She took my hand. Her skin was crinkled and papery.

'No Mother, nothing strange since our Mary's Samuel at the pub.' She sighed.

'No. A good boy like you wouldn't know nothing. I'll have to find a bad man to ask, won't I?'

'Yes Mother.'

'Yes, I will.'

She did not send me back to work. She held my hand. She was my great-grandmother. She told me I was her favourite boy – she had twenty-five great-grandchildren, and ten of us were boys, and I was her best one. I wanted to cry, and I wanted to tell her the truth. But then I did not. And then I felt fine.

The men began to sing as they worked.

Dance for thy Nanny
Sing for thy Mammy
Dance for thy Nanny
When the boat comes in

When next I saw my catch, its voice was clearer inside my head. No longer a collection of words – a vague sense of something being said – I heard a woman speaking, clearly and in full sentences.

Hello John I heard, *Hello hello hello John I would like a change of seawater PLEASE THANK YOU John*

So I brought it a change of water, and I listened to the things it told me. I was not able to contemplate its new voice – why it had changed.

You are a good and nice boy for bringing me new water how good it is to be a nice good boy are there other good nice boys here could they come and say hello could they be a friend to me could they bring me new water more you could bring them or I could bring them I could bring the boys or you could bring the boys but nice good boys your good women cannot hear me only your good men so I would like to see them and I would like you to sing me the song about the fishy and the dishy thank you PLEASE thank please you

When it spoke to me, I could not hear my own thoughts. I could not feel myself, only the catch of the day. I sank into what it was telling me. I closed my eyes, and I heard its voice, and I came back to myself and found that the catch was splashing happily in new water, and I could hear my own voice singing it the song. Our song, now.

I noticed that the catch now had a mouth: a long slit along its face. And its arms had changed – the joints were more like elbows than knees. Its fingers were not as long; it seemed to be growing palms.

I was weak I was sick but you are making me better good nice boy I get stronger more pretty for you john like a pretty pretty yes a pretty for john and a good touch for the CATCH OF THE DAY.

I began to pet its tail. Her tail.

S he continued to change. Each night I came back to something slightly more human. Her eyes were smaller, her skin was less slippery and softer. Full lips formed around the slit of her mouth, but she did not speak to me with it because it did not seem to open. An ersatz nose formed at the centre of her face – a little point. After a week, the catch of the day began to resemble a woman. A human woman, with silvery skin, and big black eyes.

I think you're the best boy here, John. I think you're the best boy. ■

Faber congratulates Thomas Morris and Eliza Clark, selected for Granta's Best of Young British Novelists 2023

Thomas Morris

Editor-at-Large at *The Stinging Fly* His new collection of short stories *Open Up* publishes August 2023

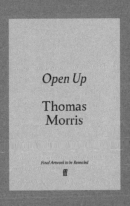

Open Up

Thomas Morris

Final Artwork to be Revealed

ff

Eliza Clark

The acclaimed author of *Boy Parts* Her new novel *Penance* publishes July 2023

faber

Chaïm Soutine, *Le Garçon d'étage*, c.1927
Musée de l'Orangerie

THE ROOM-SERVICE WAITER

Tom Crewe

They found him where he had always been, living quietly on the rue Fournier. It was August. The man sitting across from Charles was a curator at the Louvre called Monsieur DuPont. He wore large rubbed spectacles and smoked seven cigarettes during the time he was in the house. His hair had sparks of grey in it – new ones leapt out when he turned his head in the sunlight bearing through the window. The cigarette smoke, ascending, was gold-tinged; Charles was reminded of misty mornings when he was a child in Normandy, how the sun would glow behind the mist, and the cows sidle through like gods.

He told M. DuPont about these mornings. He was aware he did this often now, telling people things they hadn't asked to know. (He was getting old, past sixty.) In response, M. DuPont asked polite questions about his childhood – it suited his purpose, Charles realised, because it led him up to the hotel: when had Charles come to Paris? How had he got the job at Le Meurice? Did he remember his first meeting with the artist, Soutine?

M. DuPont was on his third cigarette. The room was a misty morning in Normandy. Charles was in a back corridor, a tray in his hands, cups shuddering, a streak of cold coffee running to the rim.

Did he remember the first meeting? He remembered the room. The smell of paint. His voice? Hard to say; he wasn't good with voices, he'd never been able to do impressions. He couldn't put his finger on the first time, no. Did he remember how he'd been asked? How many times, roughly, they had seen each other before then? It couldn't have been often, because Charles wasn't used to him yet, and you did get used to guests if they stayed long enough. Monsieur Soutine had asked very straightforwardly, man to man, like making any sort of deal; except Charles was young, he hadn't bartered the price up, but simply accepted what was offered. He would have done it for nothing, he suspected, knowing himself as he was then. It was exciting, having your portrait painted – it would be exciting now, still. He'd been flattered; he'd showed off about it to his pals, not too much or it might have started to seem funny, one man painting another in his hotel room. In fact, Charles remembered M. Soutine making a point of saying that he wanted him with his clothes on, in his uniform – that the uniform was the important part. He'd supposed that was true when he'd seen the picture, though he made no claims to be a judge.

M. Soutine was quiet when he was painting. Concentrating of course. Smoked a lot – like you, M. DuPont, Charles said to him, smiling. Sang a bit, can't remember what, not singing properly anyhow, sort of mumbling to a tune, out the corner of his mouth. There was the smell of the paint. The sound – he'd got used to the different sounds, the brush sliding this way or that, fast or slow, bigger or smaller amounts. He'd liked guessing, seeing him choose one colour or another: what it was for, where it was going to end up. He got it wrong both ways. He'd guess the red would be for doing his waistcoat, and then it would go too high or too low; later he saw red on his ears, and on his hands.

The pose? He'd been asked to put his hands firmly on his hips – it was the way he used to stand, after bringing the food or the wine up: 'Anything more, sir?' Looking round the room, trying to spot a problem he could solve without being asked, or discern some desire he could satisfy before it was spoken. With his hands on his hips. On the lookout.

He'd liked the job: being a waiter. Had liked the hotel, taken pride in it, fussed over it; swiftly removed any marks he found, picked bits off the floor, straightened the picture frames. It pleased him. Naturally the hotel wasn't as comfortable for staff as it was for guests – the back corridors and rooms were nothing like the rest of it. But the truth was that you spent the majority of your time in the nice parts, more time than most guests, so it wasn't crazy to think it belonged to you more. And if it belonged to you, it was worth looking after.

Still, it wasn't a job for a married man. And that's what he'd been from the 19th of May, 1928.

He'd met Josephine at the hotel. She was a chambermaid. He was angling for her already when he'd let himself be painted by M. Soutine. He'd stood there, listening to the brush on the canvas, sniffing the paint, hands on his hips, thinking of her, surveying the future. Asking himself: what's to be done? Wondering what problem he could solve, what desire he might be the answer to. They were both curious, later, about what had happened to his portrait. Josephine always said she'd like to see it, see him as he was then, thinking of her, scheming to catch her. This was when they were first married, when they had just opened their shop selling satchels on the rue Joubert; when all their memories were of falling in love and not of everything that came after, experience piling up like dirty laundry.

After his sixth cigarette, M. DuPont produced a photograph of the painting. He hadn't done so earlier, he said, because he wanted to be absolutely certain he had the right man. Even though he could tell as soon as Charles opened the door.

M. DuPont laid the photograph delicately on the coffee table. Charles laughed and his eyes unexpectedly filled with tears, so that the colours in the picture ran. When he blinked them away it became familiar again. He'd not seen it since it was painted, in 1927, more than forty years ago. He realised how much he had forgotten. How strong and bright the colours were: a greeny-blue behind, segments of red waistcoat on his big white shirt. And what a strange shape he'd made of him! His head and his ears stretched and rolled like dough, his arms out in great hoops. But it was undoubtedly him, as M. DuPont said. He recognised his old face.

'It's wonderful,' he breathed.

'Truly,' said M. DuPont. 'Did you think so at the time?'

'Yes,' Charles said. 'I thought I was very wonderful.'

When M. DuPont had gone, Charles opened the window and looked out onto the street. The shadows lying across it had a warm sleepy look. There were a few regulars sitting outside the bar. A car came past and he smelled the exhaust. He fancied a drink. Turning back into the room, he stared at the photograph left for him on the coffee table. There was to be an exhibition. There were lots of pictures like his, apparently – of waiters, pastry cooks, valets, bellboys. He'd known he wasn't the only person at Le Meurice who'd been painted, but he hadn't realised how many hotels M. Soutine visited. He was very highly esteemed as an artist now.

Charles took his wallet from his bedroom, and then went into the hall and got his jacket off the peg. He hadn't needed to be told that M. Soutine had died; he'd learned it from a newspaper during the war or just after, when lots of people were dying and it hadn't seemed so important, only a shame. He must have thought about his portrait then, but merely as something from his own life. It had stopped existing in a real sense; he'd not imagined it being anywhere in particular. Now he knew that it was on its third owner already. They called it 'The Room-Service Waiter'. Strange to think: that for all these years, even with the hotel long behind him, he'd been waiting on someone. And – as he walked out into the rue Fournier with a thirst in his throat – that M. Soutine had gone on being dead, all the way up to now.

I t was spring before the invitation to the exhibition opening arrived. Charles was delighted to see it – he hadn't forgotten about it, not at all. Soon after, M. DuPont telephoned and asked if Charles would mind being interviewed by a newspaper. The interviewer was a woman journalist, only a little younger than Charles, very pleasant and interested and knowledgeable about M. Soutine's life. He told her everything he'd told M. DuPont – about the smell of paint, and the sounds of the brushes, and his pose, and how M. Soutine used to sing in that mumbling way, with a cigarette jogging at the corner of his mouth. And then he added the only other significant detail he'd remembered since the summer: that when the time for each session was up, M. Soutine would make one last stroke or touch on his canvas, look at Charles and at the picture, and quietly say 'Bravo'. At first Charles imagined he was saying it to him – a thank you, for having kept so still – but eventually he realised M. Soutine was saying it to himself.

The journalist liked this anecdote. So did Charles. It had returned to him unbidden one day when he was in his shop. (And yet it was somehow still the case that he could not remember M. Soutine's voice; could hear it, and not hear it. He had begun to wonder whether anyone's voice existed in his memory, or whether memory supplied only words.) Charles said 'Bravo' now whenever he achieved anything – like buying milk before he ran out, or catching something before it hit the floor. The incongruity made him smile. He was like the valet to a famous man, repeating his master's little phrases in the dusty corners of his own life.

On the night of the opening, Charles dressed in his best suit. It was true, he thought again, looking in the mirror, that he was recognisably the same man as in the painting, even if in reality his head was a normal shape and size. He did not look so bad for his age. He still had his hair, and it had kept its colour. He tweaked his red tie. His fingers were still nimble.

When he entered the gallery rooms, he could see M. DuPont standing at a distance. There was a huge number of people, far more than Charles was expecting. The noise was deafening, similar to a crowd walking down to a football game. The pictures hung back against the walls like policemen, discreetly keeping an eye on things. Charles could see at once that they were all by M. Soutine. Accepting wine from a waiter, he began to look for himself, moving through the crowd and from the first room into the second – unnoticed by M. DuPont, who was gesturing knowledgeably with a cigarette.

And then there he was, the Room-Service Waiter, hands on hips. Once more Charles's eyes filled with tears; this time, one escaped down his cheek and he had to catch it with his sleeve. It made a great difference, seeing the painting rather than the photograph. It was very real. Charles was very real, he and M. Soutine both. It was a part of their past, very private, that people were looking at. He wished, suddenly, that Josephine was here. It was a part of her past she had never seen. It occurred to him that he could have invited her. He had been allowed to bring a guest and had brought no one. He had become lonely in his mind, he knew: he no longer encountered other people even in his thoughts.

A young waiter came up and refilled his glass. While he poured, Charles caught his eye and pointed. 'That's me.'

The waiter finished pouring and looked at the picture, then back at Charles, smiling. 'That is superb,' he said. 'You have scarcely changed, Monsieur. How old were you then?'

'Twenty-four.'

'That is only two years older than I am now.'

The waiter asked whether the painter was here this evening and Charles replied that he'd been dead a long time. 'What did he die of?' the young man asked.

'The war,' Charles said. He made a half movement and took a drink, looking at his picture. 'Well, it was hard not just for Jews. Many people died. It is a long time ago, thank God.'

The waiter's face was sad, touched with confusion. 'Yes, Monsieur. What was he like?'

Charles told him about M. Soutine saying 'Bravo' to himself. The waiter grinned and looked relieved. He pointed into the room with the neck of his bottle. 'He was right to say it, wasn't he, Monsieur?' Charles laughed and agreed that he was. The waiter filled his glass again before he went off.

Charles stayed standing in front of his picture until he had nearly finished his wine. He decided he would go over to M. DuPont. As he tried to locate him in the throng, waiting behind people, and for groups to notice him and let him through, he paid attention to the paintings. There were the others like his own, that he knew to expect, of hotel staff in their uniforms – garish and misshapen, but smart and pleased with themselves, as he looked pleased with himself. There were also some paintings of meat, strung up – slashes of red and white on blue backgrounds. One carcass looked a little like a waiter, hung upside down without a head. Charles shook his head now; it was wonderful to have spent time in the company of this great man, but also dreadful, to have thought so little of it, of him, for so long. He didn't remember asking M. Soutine a single question, unless it was how much he was going to pay him. And he could not remember his voice.

At last he found M. DuPont, still smoking and gesticulating, with a ring of people listening to him. Charles was sufficiently confident to tap him on the shoulder while he was speaking; he turned and his face scattered into a smile beneath his spectacles.

'Ah! Monsieur Bisset! You are here!' He kissed Charles on his cheeks and introduced him to the ring of people. 'This man was painted by Soutine!' The ring responded enthusiastically, constricting and asking questions: addressing some to M. DuPont that Charles could have answered, and others to Charles that were fit only for M. DuPont. M. DuPont led them over to Charles's portrait, and they all exclaimed over it. The young waiter from before topped up everyone's glasses, smiling comprehendingly. Charles told them how it had been – about the smell and the sounds, about his pose and the cigarette and the singing. He almost forgot about 'Bravo' but finished with it at the end. They all laughed. 'It is a wonderful detail,' M. DuPont said. 'The sort of detail that really lives.' Then, spying someone across the room, he grasped Charles's arm. 'Here is a former colleague of yours, and another subject of Soutine. I did not want to spoil the surprise of this reunion.'

Charles failed to recognise the man he was reunited with. He was ugly, short and grossly fat – his underchin swelled out and dropped to his collar like a big fleshy napkin. They shook hands, but regarded each other blankly. M. DuPont looked disappointed. 'Don't you remember each other?' He glanced between them. 'Monsieur Renard was a bellboy at Le Meurice. And Monsieur Bisset was a room-service waiter.'

'What is your first name?' Charles asked the man. He found his ugliness oppressive – the tight, swollen face with the eyes pushed in.

'Alexandre,' the man replied. 'And yours?'

Charles told him, but there was no answering flicker. By means of a few more groping questions it was established that they had crossed over at the hotel probably for only a month or two. Once this was understood they relaxed. They could not have been expected to remember each other. The past was full of blame and it was a relief when it could be avoided.

The three of them went to look at Alexandre's portrait. In it he was of course dressed in red from head to foot, being a bellboy (Charles wondered what came first, the uniforms or M. Soutine's interest in the colour), but otherwise it was inconceivable that the person depicted was the same one standing here. The boy in the painting, with his little black moustache, was rasher-thin, with a spindly neck.

'There's not a trace of him in you!' Charles said. He'd had another glass of wine.

Alexandre laughed. 'It's nice to be reminded,' he said, 'of when I had a neck.'

Laughing too, Charles asked Alexandre what he could recollect of M. Soutine, telling him before he could answer about 'Bravo'. Alexandre pursed up his big face to think and said he didn't remember M. Soutine saying that. 'What about him singing, with his cigarette in his mouth?' Charles asked. Yes, Alexandre remembered that. He remembered also that M. Soutine had a habit of tapping his foot on the floor, quite hard – it had stayed with him because he used to worry about the guests in the room below. Now it was Charles's turn to think and shake his head. He remembered the sound of brushstrokes, but not a tapping foot.

Their glasses charged, they began to discuss the hotel, some of its characters and what had happened to them. M. DuPont left. After a while, Charles thought to ask whether Alexandre remembered a chambermaid, Josephine. Pretty, with red hair.

'I remember her,' Alexandre said. 'She was the nicest of the lot.'

'I married her,' Charles said. He could not help blushing.

'I remember her going away to be married,' Alexandre said. 'So I must remember you after all.'

'Come and see my picture!' Charles almost shouted in response. He was growing excitedly proud of it, as if it were his son and it was his wedding day.

They walked across – it was easier now that so many people had left. Charles found he was lurching, but no matter. They stood in front of his picture. 'I do remember you,' Alexandre said. 'It is bizarre: now I see both of you, I realise you have hardly changed, and yet, before, I'd have sworn we'd never met.'

Charles was grinning, though sad that he still could not recall Alexandre from the old days. But then Alexandre had got so fat, and shaved off his moustache.

'You were very handsome, very dapper,' Alexandre said, still looking at Charles's picture. 'We younger lads envied you.'

They carried on talking and drinking. Alexandre said that he worked for the Post Office, and Charles told Alexandre about his shop – how he first got into the trade when a friend was offloading some leather found in the river, still wrapped up and hardly damaged. Finally, Alexandre said he had to go. Charles was very drunk. They embraced and he felt the fat on Alexandre's back rise up in pouches under the pressure of his braces. 'You look terrible, you know,' he said to him without malice as they came apart.

Alexandre's eyes fled further into his face. 'I know, I know,' he said, waving his hands in repudiation of himself.

'This,' Charles said, taking Alexandre's underchin in his hand and wagging it from side to side, 'this is far too much.'

Alexandre stepped out of Charles's grip. 'Yes,' he said, wincing. 'I have disappointed myself. It is hard to explain –' Abruptly he extended his hand, rather formally. 'It was nice seeing you again.'

The room was almost empty. Charles watched Alexandre amble slowly through it and into the next one, like a cow crossing a field. A man had begun to sweep the floor and the lights were brighter. M. Soutine's pictures seemed stunned, to be left alone.

Charles went back to examining his portrait. As he looked, he began to cry, and this time he let the tears wend over his lips and onto his tongue. After a few minutes he stopped and felt much better. Then he staggered out. By the cloakroom he found M. DuPont and embraced him fervently, planting great salty kisses on his cheeks. 'You have changed my life,' he told him, crying again, '– changed it utterly.'

He hailed a cab and sang loudly all the way home with the window down, drinking up the cool night air and admiring the yellow lamplight. When he got in he made himself a sandwich and sat down at the kitchen table to eat it. He was immensely happy. It recurred to him, in his benevolence, that he should have asked Josephine. He had not seen her in thirty years, though she had informed him each time she changed her address. They were only married for ten, living here on the rue Fournier. There were no children, which Charles had blamed her for, but afterwards she had two from her second husband, so he presumed it was his fault after all.

He finished his sandwich and found some paper. He wrote a letter to Josephine, telling her about M. DuPont and the picture. He would be honoured if she were to go with him one day to see it, as they had always wanted to. People said he was hardly changed! He was sure she would think that he was. I hope you will say yes to this invitation, he concluded: I would so much like to see you again. Forgive me, Charles.

He sealed the letter in an envelope and left it on the table. Then he walked into his bedroom and stood swaying in front of the mirror. He smoothed his hair and tightened his tie and put his hands on his hips. 'Bravo,' he said quietly to the empty room. 'Bravo.' ∎

Ready, set, read.

Cari Moses
Judith Tyler Hills

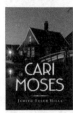

A grieving woman takes a baby in, unaware that this incident will attract a serial killer, national authorities, and the breakdown of her life.

£21.95 paperback
978-1-6655-8831-7
also available in hardcover, ebook & audiobook
www.authorhouse.co.uk

Power Of Nisa
Ms Nidhi Gogia (Agarwal)

This collection of 16 different short stories based on the lives of 16 women in modern India sheds light on the various stigmas that are still barriers for women in the 21st century.

£16.95 paperback
978-1-7283-7498-7
also available in ebook
www.authorhouse.co.uk

Prince of Thorns
Book 1 of the Luciferian Chronicles
Reda Issa

A volume of verse that poetically examines a young prince's journey to Beirut to learn the truth about his father's death and hopefully reunite the people with the monarchy.

£10.95 paperback
978-1-6655-9112-6
also available in ebook
www.authorhouse.co.uk

Fun Poems for Your Child
Feeding your Child's Imagination
Jenny Carey

This book of fun poems is written with children in mind, and is designed to stimulate their imagination, curiosity and development.

£12.99 paperback
978-1-6641-1486-9
also available in ebook & audiobook
www.xlibrispublishing.co.uk

Champaign No Pain
Dirk De Bock

Champaign No Pain shares Dirk De Bock's poetry collection with themes ranging from love and hate, peace and violence, quiet times, wild times and so much more.

£8.99 paperback
978-1-6641-1700-6
also available in ebook
www.xlibrispublishing.co.uk

Hangin' Tough
Boxing Fan, Big-Fight Analyst, Tactician & Historian
Jawed Akrim

Prepare to be shocked, amazed, and even horrified as you take a walk on the wilder side of boxing history with this collection of essays and stories.

£18.95 paperback
978-1-6655-8505-7
also available in ebook & audiobook
www.authorhouse.co.uk

---

authorHOUSE·   Xlibris

STRANGERS AT THE PORT

Lauren Aimee Curtis

I knew no history. I had little concept of time beyond the harvest seasons, the changing weather. When I stood on the fishing dock as a child and looked out at the other islands in the archipelago, I was not thinking of battleships or explorers or sea monsters from mythologies. I was not thinking about what came before or what lay beyond.

What can I tell you about my young life on the island? It is shrouded in the mystery of childhood itself. I try to picture myself age ten, for that is the time when the 'trouble' – as you call it – began. But I don't have an image of this girl. I can't see her from the outside. There are no photographs. Besides, I don't trust them.

I could tell you that my only true friend on the island, apart from my older sister, Giovanna, was a donkey with weepy eyes and long lashes, a white patch of fur on his belly I took pleasure in scratching. A rusted bell hung around his neck. He had a bung leg. We called him Shuffles. *What is the significance of this donkey*, I imagine you asking. Nothing, nothing. Except to say that when he was deemed useless we cared for him. Fed him apples. Tied scarves around his head. A big bow between the ears. I remember thinking I would marry him when the time came. I remember thinking this as if it were the most normal thought in the world.

Do you see what I am trying to say? Our world was very small. When I was ten and Giovanna was twelve, we had never left our island, not even for the others in the archipelago. We knew the islands surrounding us not by their proper names but by what they resembled: a turtle, a dog lying down, a mountain, a jagged crown. Those islands were black or grey or brown depending on the position of the sun. Ours was emerald green.

Every morning, Giovanna and I went down to the fishing dock to watch the water. We could tell if rain was coming by where the clouds hung in the sky (this, we learned from the fishermen). From May to September, it hardly rained at all. The cisterns on our roofs went dry, and the smell of dead fish – thick in the summer – wafted through the circular hole above the door of our bungalow, even when our mother stuffed it with rags.

Although we lived at the bottom of the island in a small fishing village, we still felt we were better than the people who lived on the opposite side of the island by the port. The port people were ignoble, Mother told us, because they cavorted with the sailors, and they were not ashamed to live near the rubbish heap. Besides, the port was ugly. The port was not a well-regarded place. Even where we lived – in the damp, narrow alleyways above the fishing dock – had more prestige than the port! Between the two villages was a large valley with vineyards planted all over the slopes. Two mountains – our two sleeping volcanoes – stood on either side. On our island, the higher you lived, the richer you were. Still, our little village was respected. In the evenings, everyone gathered in our square. Most nights, we saw amber specks fizzling against the black sky coming from the volcano on the island opposite. Little spurts of lava that shot up rhythmically. A constant, hazy glow. We knew those amber specks meant danger for the people on that island, but we were on the green island, and so we cared little.

You must understand: from birth we had been told that our island was rich in resources. We had no need to worry – the shipmaster would take care of us all.

He was the only person who routinely left and returned. Left not just for the other islands in the archipelago, but for unknowable places beyond. He brought back gifts. He had a gold cane with a goose-head handle, and he took it with him on his walks around the square. The way that he moved – slowly, gracefully – signalled his difference to the rest of us. He did not stumble. He rarely yelled. If I close my eyes, I can see him standing at the balustrade at the edge of our square looking out at the sea below. His long beard is neatly combed and turning grey at the tips. His lips are hidden underneath his thick moustache. He is walking past the baker's shop and raising his cane. Now the baker's daughter is running out.

He was a king to us. A god. At the very least, our protector. Really, he was a trader in exports who commandeered an impressive fleet.

All of us in the village, whenever we saw him, would make a little gesture as he passed us. Mother bowed her head, so Giovanna and I did the same. The fishermen only ever spoke to him with eyes averted and their hands clasped firmly behind their backs. The older widows fussed over him. Often, they tried to kiss his hand. Once, the baker's son saluted him, and we – all of us in the square – had to wait until the shipmaster was out of sight to let out our laughter. Our bellies sore from holding it in. It was the baker's daughter, though, who embarrassed us most with her confusing gestures. Whenever she held out the bread, she squatted before him – an awkward curtsy – and we had to look away.

There was another embarrassing woman in our village. A widow, like Mother, who went about in an evening gown that was torn and yellowing. This woman refused to wear black. She had no tact, Mother told us, because she wore her hair in the manner of the shipmaster's wife. Uncovered, that is, and twirled into two shapes that looked like snail shells, pinned at the nape of her neck. She lived alone, and although she tried to hide it, she spent her nights in the grotto near the port where the other drunks met. To get there, you had to wait until the tide was low and climb along the rocks. People talked about a secret path, a way to get there from the lighthouse above, but none of us ever found it.

There was a rumour about the woman leaving the grotto one night and throwing herself into the sea. Apparently, she had to be fished out. When she came to, she told the rest of the drunks that she had merely wanted to wash her dress. She clambered over the rocks and left the wet gown on the roof of her bungalow to dry. We knew this, because the baker had seen it there.

This woman – still so large in my mind – does not appear in your book, Professor. I woke up this morning with the thought that I could write to you. That I could tell you some of the things you missed.

According to your version of events, an insect pest arrived on our island hidden in some bits of wood and destroyed all of our vines. Excuse me for saying, but you seem obsessed with the aphid! Forty pages on its breeding cycle, its microscopic body, its way of burying itself into the roots – imperceptible to our eyes. When you explain its method of sucking the life from our vines, I detect a certain relish. You appear like a young, excitable boy at a science fair presenting his hypothesis.

There is no mention of the shipmaster in your book, nothing about our village. There is nothing about the men who arrived on our island in the spring before the vines began to die. You must not realise what an event it was. We did not know they were coming. No one had told us about the new law. We were not expecting a ship of prisoners in the archipelago. Professor, when I was a child, I did not know what a prison was.

That spring, I was ten years old, wearing a dress made of muslin cloth and a red woollen cloak, holding on to Mother's hand as we walked down the hill to the market by the port. We saw an unfamiliar ship in the distance – saw the white trail it left in the water as it approached our island. By the time we reached the market, the ship had docked. The gangplank dropped and the men came walking out. I counted twelve. Everyone stopped to watch. We did not know they were prisoners. We only saw a group of strangers. They were both young and old, with beards roughly clipped, wearing grey tunics. Some of them were paler, but most had our hue – that is, olive-skinned, as they say today, though I don't understand what an olive has to do with it. One of the men stood out for his honey-coloured hair, the tufts on his cheeks that glinted in the sun, but the rest looked similar to the men on our island. Later, Mother said that they looked nothing like our men.

In her memory of their arrival, it was always raining. But the sun was out, I remember – the first feeling of warmth on the skin after a long winter, though the wind was cold and brisk. The men stood on the dock with their tunics fluttering and their faces tilted towards the sun. Two guards wearing jackets with bright buckles and large black hats emerged from the belly of the ship. They jostled the men into the back of the shipmaster's largest carriage. The mules were whipped. The carriage travelled in the direction of Mount Fern and we followed it. Half our village were trailing behind, looking up at the men while they stared back at us. One of them even blew us kisses! I saw his head bobbing above the crowd.

When we reached the valley, the carriage stopped outside the shipmaster's house. We kept our distance and hid behind the trees. We did not talk to each other for fear that the shipmaster would hear us. He was waiting outside his gates when we arrived. He spoke to the guards and then motioned for his driver to continue up the mountain. This time we were unable to follow. The shipmaster was looking at the trees where we were hiding. He held his gaze. Little ripples. My skin felt prickly from his stare. One by one, we came out from our hiding spots and walked silently back to the market.

That evening, everyone was in the square pretending to look busy. Really, we were waiting for the shipmaster. Waiting for him, on his evening walk, to tell us who these men were and what they were doing on our island.

Giovanna was with me and Mother and she was jealous. She had not been at the port when the men arrived. We were standing near the path that led up to the forest, waiting for the shipmaster to appear among the trees. Meanwhile, the baker's daughter was doing laps around the square, talking to anyone who would listen to her about the men. She was telling us she did not need any more amorous advances; the shipmaster's sons were enough to deal with.

An hour passed. The sky and the sea turned orange, then pink, a reddish purple. Wind came hurtling around the cliffs. All of the women in the square stopped fanning themselves. We were silent. Listening for footsteps when all we could hear were cicadas, the wind whistling, the rocks being dragged into the sea on the beach below. Mother went inside the church with the others to pray, but the wooden doors flew open while they were kneeling, extinguishing their lit candles. A bad omen, we thought.

Night came. It was cold and dark and no one had thought to bring lanterns. We were not expecting to be out for so long. At the entrance to the church, our priest was sweeping sand out the door. He was telling us it was time to go home. He went inside to ring the bells. We heard them chime nine times.

The shipmaster never came to the square that evening, and rarely did he miss his evening walk. His absence was not only unusual, it felt threatening. As you can imagine, Professor, it only inflamed our curiosity about the men.

As far back as I could remember, there had been no new inhabitants on our island. No visitors, apart from the sailors, who only stayed a day or so and even then, we rarely saw them. They kept to the port side and spent their nights in the grotto. Only once had I seen a sailor close up. I was at the market with Mother and wandered off. The tide was low. I saw a body splayed out over the rocks – his back arched. His face was bloated and his pale tongue was sticking out. He had drowned. I know that now. At the time, Mother told me he was sleeping.

We knew that the men were staying on our island, but we did not know why. In those first days, their presence was not properly explained.

They were being kept on Mount Fern, sleeping among ruins that none of us would go near because a child had died there and it was thought to be a place that brought bad luck. We heard they were working in the shipmaster's fields on the port side. But the baker's wife said she had seen them walking through the forest that bordered on our square. At this, she was indignant.

About a week after they arrived, Giovanna and I came upon the men bathing in an inlet at the edge of our village. They looked nervous as they waded into the waist-deep water, holding their privates as they crouched down to splash their armpits, faces and backs. Not one of them put their head underneath. We thought perhaps they could not swim. We were lying on our bellies on the cliff above, watching them, loose rocks scattered around us. Without saying a word, Giovanna picked one up and threw it off the edge. It broke the water below and the men looked up. Days later, we returned at the hour we knew they would be bathing, both of us gathering rocks along the way.

Do I feel some shame in writing this? Yes. But we were frightened of them. Unsettled by what the adults around us said. If we threw rocks at them, it was because we feared them. But we also found their presence oddly thrilling. The other islands in the archipelago had their active volcanoes; now we had the men.

We overheard the women in our village warning Mother not to walk alone at night. They told her to listen for the trumpet each evening, telling the men to return to Mount Fern, where they would be counted by one of the shipmaster's sons.

Have I mentioned his sons? He had nine. Some of them were smaller than us, but the older ones carried rifles. It was not unusual to come across them in the square, racing one another around the benches or straddling the mermaid statue that stood near the church. Sometimes we heard shots echoing through the forest when they were hunting rabbits in the valley above. They dressed differently from the sons of the fishermen in our village – wearing long trousers that covered their ankles and shirts made from fine linen. Whenever the shipmaster was away from our island, they would knock on the drunk widow's window at all hours, singing songs about taking an ugly wife or a woman with a bosom so big that she had to walk with a stick. As a group, they were intimidating. There were so many of them! This was, according to Mother, the real reason why the shipmaster's wife rarely left her house. *Nine sons would break any woman,* is what Mother often said. The youngest was five and had an especially large head. Mother said it would have been his ears that hurt the shipmaster's wife the most, pointy as they were, like wings.

Our mother slept with a grimace – her mouth folded downwards – and sometimes a word, seemingly foreign, would shoot out of her mouth, so that Giovanna and I had to rub her back to wake her. The three of us shared one bed. Our father died when I was young, and as a child I had trouble picturing him. He always ended up looking a little bit like the shipmaster, only wearing the calico pants and red cloak of a fisherman. This secret image – treasure of all treasures – was ruined by my sister. *You wouldn't have any memories of him,* is what Giovanna said. But I did have memories! Of hairy hands filling a pipe with tobacco, the smell of smoke and brine on his wiry beard, a voice – soft and low – singing to us in the early evening. *None of that is real,* Giovanna would tell me, smiling triumphantly.

All my life, my sister never let me forget that she had been a second mother to me. I was late to walk and talk. According to Giovanna, I used to point to my open mouth and she would know to feed me. It was her, and not Mother – Giovanna said – who taught me how to speak. *Mother always slept,* Giovanna would say. *I was the one who wrapped blankets around you!*

I was a docile child. Fearful. Obedient. All the things my sister was not.

We lived off the pity of our neighbours, who gave us fish, and the shipmaster, who was our true benefactor. Every week, one of his sons would appear at our door holding a pot of something warm from their cook or a few coins. Mother would take the coins and put them in the leather pouch she wore tied around her neck, while Giovanna and I watched from the bed.

But that spring, the sons stopped visiting. It happened abruptly. The shipmaster no longer took his evening walks in our square and his sons no longer knocked on our door. Mother said the shipmaster must be avoiding any questions we had about the men. She took herself to bed. Mother could sleep for hours if she wanted. Nobody could sleep like Mother. She told us that she knew how to sleep standing up. She had taught herself when she used to wake early and wait on the dock with the other wives for the fishermen to return. ■

IVOR

Camilla Grudova

'The days passed.'
– Alfred Hitchcock, *Downhill*, 1927

We are all second, third or even fifth sons. We were sent to Wakeley Boarding School aged eight for Year Five and stayed on until Year Twenty. We didn't count how many years that was, or fully comprehend how much time constituted a year; we were just excited to go off to boarding school like our fathers and older brothers, to leave the nursery. We were disappointed not to go to the same school as our fathers and eldest brothers, but so were our sisters, who were not sent to school at all. We were given a brochure from Wakeley: there was an illustration of a beautiful, dark-haired boy playing rugby on the cover. Our nannies packed up our teddies and toys, photos of our families, shortbread and chocolate. Some of our nannies wept; we did not know why: we assumed we would see them again soon.

Wakeley was in the middle of the countryside. Which county, we couldn't say. Some of us remembered our fathers saying they were taking us to Derbyshire, others to Somerset, though a senior student with a passion for nature said based on the studies he did of animals and flora on the school grounds we were in Dumfries and Galloway,

Scotland. The land surrounding the school was beautiful and hilly; the grounds so extensive we had no need to go beyond them. There was a stable with horses, a swimming pool, tennis courts, a library, a graveyard, a chapel and several dormitories each with its own housemaster and tutors. We had advanced lessons: every year for biology, a zoo donated an elephant fetus for us to dissect and for months the specimens lay in tanks and jars of formaldehyde in our classroom like wrinkled old raincoats. There was a big grey computer that could do sums. Languages we could study ranged from Arabic to Russian.

As younger boys, we had to do tuck shop runs for the seniors in our house who had their own rooms, a mark of their status. Chocolate bars, haemorrhoid cream, newspapers, boiled sweets, Gentleman's Relish, malted milk, cigarettes. One senior would cane us if his newspaper was wet. We didn't like the seniors and didn't understand how they could look like our fathers and grandfathers yet were still boys at school wearing the same striped ties and caps as us. The headmaster told us they were special boys who had a lot to learn before going out into the world and that boys who entered the world too soon missed school and their friends terribly. We half forgot about these older students unless doing chores for them. We had our own classes, games, celebrations, clubs – the Cheese Club, the Ancient Rome Club, the French Club. The older boys blended into the antique furniture of our houses, red-faced and dusty like velvet armchairs or spindly and brown like side tables.

As we got older and became seniors ourselves, we were dependent on those tuck shop excursions, those moments of forced tenderness from the younger boys. We recognised the disappointment of a damp newspaper, pages stuck together, but as new, young boys we did not understand.

The main chore we had to do for the seniors was make toast and cut it into little pieces for them. We saw house tutors tie bibs around their necks for each meal and accompany them to the bathroom or push their wheelchairs throughout the halls of Wakeley, cut their toenails in the evening and insert their false teeth in the morning. Our teachers told us it was gracious to help the elderly. We had to ignore the sounds of them soiling themselves in the halls, or when they pinched our bottoms, weeping as they did so, their own backsides sagging like abandoned bowls of porridge.

The boys in the fourteenth form, who resembled our teachers and our half-forgotten fathers, were still hearty and athletic. They didn't need our help and they ignored us completely. They had their own clubrooms where they drank and argued. Occasionally one would come into our dorms at night very drunk and the tutors had to chase them off using brooms and smiles. Sometimes they were so quiet that none of us, not even the tutors, heard them, and we would wake up in seething, mysterious pain to find one of them sleeping beside us, hulking and stinking.

Everyone competed to prepare toast for Ivor, a head boy and senior. He didn't look like any of the other seniors: he was still beautiful, he was still captain of the rugby team, played lacrosse, swam, sang and took part in all sorts of games.

He never asked for anything from the tuck shop but we brought him presents anyway. We learned that he liked rhubarb and custard sweets and disliked the newspapers – he never read them and rolled the pages into balls he threw at other boys, sometimes filled with flour so that those he hit were left with white faces like clowns.

Ivor was the only one we served toast whole to, he didn't need it quartered.

For breakfast, Ivor had toast with anchovy paste, a beef sausage split down the middle and filled with marmalade, and a cup of tea with neither milk nor sugar.

He ate heartily of whatever was on offer for lunch and supper: steak pie with stew, boiled fish, roast, kedgeree, wellington, rarebit, ham, puddings, and in later years, lasagne and curry, chips, baked potatoes and chilli.

Ivor had dark curly hair that never went grey, red lips, flushed cheeks and a pallor so powdery some of us thought he wore make-up.

The so-called 'make-up' did not come off or run in the shower or bath, nor did he sweat when he played sports.

When he was playing a rugby game, a few of us snuck into his room and ransacked it looking for make-up or hair dye, but we didn't find any. In the drawers of his desk and under his mattress we found only old playing cards and a purple wrapper from a chocolate bar.

On his desk was an unopened Kendal Mint Cake, three *Rupert Annuals* and his Greek books, a cup full of pens, a tin of rusty pen nibs and a jar of blue ink, a paper bag of stale penny sweets shaped like bottles and babies. He only wrote with dark blue ink and we imitated him. Most of the teachers could not tell the difference between dark blue and black, but we could.

Above his desk he had a picture of the Queen. When the Queen died, the image was replaced by a picture of the King, then later another king, and then a queen again. No one knew where the old pictures ended up. They were always in the same frame.

He had piles of sports things: a pig's bladder football, wooden tennis rackets and lacrosse sticks made with sheep intestine webbing, yellowing cricket pads. On his bed was a dirty teddy bear with a crooked face named Bombozine. In between Bombozine's legs were badly sewn stitches holding a hole together. There were milk stains on the legs, the fur stiff and bunched together.

He had a small taxidermy crocodile, mounted on his wall, and a wooden African mask. These items were a source of wonder to us.

When we first arrived at Wakeley we copied the way Ivor did everything until his habits came naturally to us. His way of pushing back his hair when reading, or humming as he tied his shoes, the way he wrapped his wool scarf around his neck and used words like 'ripping' and 'first rate' and the Scots word 'blether'. We soon called him Ivy. Some of us bought red lipstick from the tuck shop and wore it as we got older and our natural boyish colours faded.

The toilets at Wakeley were unreliable, with cracked wooden seats, and rarely flushed properly. We would often judge each other's defecations by size and shape. Once, a boy using the bathroom after Ivor discovered a perfectly white piece of faeces, like crushed wet chalk. It smelled of nothing. He said it reminded him of a cloud. Like most of us, Ivor did not like to take baths or shower because the water was lukewarm. Our hair was greasy, our bottoms as dirty and cracked as those of stray cats. We rolled in mud on the grounds and spilled mashed potatoes, snot and puddings on our uniforms.

Every term a man would come to inspect everyone's hair for lice. He had a black comb which he kept in a jar of blue liquid and carefully brushed each boy's head, wearing a pair of magnifying spectacles. He was very tall and thin with a pot belly. His own head was shaven, except for a white wisp over one ear. He complained to the headmaster if he found too much dandruff, saying the boys needed to have their hair washed more often.

Though Ivor's hair always appeared to be clean and well brushed, he had the most bugs in his hair. Each time the inspector came he would find fleas, bedbugs, ticks, little white worms, dozens of eggs, and Ivor would be prescribed a foul-smelling pink shampoo we never saw him use. The inspector seemed to enjoy combing through Ivor's hair; almost every strand of hair was covered in black insects.

The man squeezed the bugs between his fingers then dropped them on the towel positioned beneath his inspecting stool where the boys sat. A boy, Clive, who was more infatuated with Ivor than most, grabbed one of the bugs that was still alive; he cradled it in his hands and brought it to his room where he put it in an old cigar box he had stolen from a senior. Unoriginally, he named it Ivor.

Clive fed the bug bits of sweets and cake and drops of his own blood by pricking his finger with the tip of his fountain pen. It grew very fat and soon became the size of a guinea pig. He got a bigger box to put it in. It gave off a sickly sweet smell from the food Clive gave it. It was round and brown in colour, with bits of black, as shiny as the polished wooden floors in our dorms, the ridges in its shell resembling the cracks between the boards. It had six furry legs and a pair of pincers.

He had read in a magazine about flea circuses and tried to teach the creature tricks. Clive trained it to jump through a ring and climb a set of steps he made from toy blocks and erasers.

'Please don't tell Ivor or any of the teachers about my darling pet,' he begged us, and we didn't, as there seemed something disgusting about Clive's care of the bug and we didn't want to be associated with it, though we still went into his bedroom to watch it do tricks, and to stroke its hard back. Pets were not allowed, except one headmaster had for a time a vizsla named Brutus whom we all loved although he would often pin us to the ground and hump us because he wasn't fixed.

One morning Clive didn't come down to breakfast. The housemaster went to wake him. Clive was lying in bed, underneath the covers, the bug where his face should have been. The housemaster knocked it off with an iron poker. Where the bug had sat was a sort of bloody indent of what it had eaten of Clive's face. It had taken a big bite out of his head like an oozy pudding. The housemaster killed the bug using the coal poker. The housekeepers burned the bug and buried Clive. The sheets were stained with blood that couldn't be washed out: Wakeley was mean with money (many families stopped paying tuition but Wakeley never threw a boy out) so every fortnight a new boy was given Clive's old bloody sheets, faded to a brown. Some were so scared of sleeping on it they jumped into another boy's bed. Others said that Clive's housemaster didn't kill the bug at all and it was still wandering the pipes and halls of Wakeley and would eat our feet. All of us started to wear our leather rugby shoes to bed and did so for the rest of our lives though we were not sure how long a bug lived.

We had a memorial for Clive in our main hall. Ivor sang a hymn in his beautiful sweet voice. It felt like he was not just singing for Clive, but for all of us, past and present. The choirmaster often said, 'Ivor's voice is made of marble, not plaster.' We were all jealous of Clive who, in his death, received a song from Ivor. Some of us jumped from the Wakeley roofs in hopes of dying, but merely ended up with broken arms and legs. The school put giant nets around the facade of Wakeley to catch us when we jumped and eventually the craze for jumping stopped, though the teachers kept the nets up and they soon seemed like they were always there.

There was one year Ivor wasn't in the class photos decorating our halls, or in the calligraphic lists which, before photographs, detailed that year's students. We wondered a lot, about this lost year. Some said he was overseas, fighting in a colonial war to which all Wakeley students were conscripted. They said that he was the only survivor, and that is where the African mask and crocodile came from. Others said he was in the Hebrides, staying with a relative who was ill and that he inherited the mask and crocodile from them.

A very senior boy told us he had run away to Europe and had a woman, but we did not believe him. Ivor was only a boy. He showed no interest in women, only sports and lessons and friendship, we said. The senior boy showed us a black-and-white photo of a woman wearing only her brassiere and said it was Ivor's wife, but that it was a secret and we mustn't tell Ivor we knew. The thought was so horrid we were sick and cried.

Occasionally boys ran away from Wakeley, and even, it was rumoured, got married and had children, but they always came back. They missed the food, their cosy dormitories, their routines, their friends and, most of all, Ivor.

They tried to find their families but could not locate their estates or anyone with the same name; we were all assigned last names similar in tone and status to our original names when we first started at Wakeley and it did not take long for us to forget what we used to be called.

Roddy, a year ahead of us, retained a clear image of his family's estate, not just the building but the surrounding trees and lakes. He missed it so much, he ran away from Wakeley and he found it, but the house was gone, torn down, replaced with multiple flats. He came back to Wakeley and said he wished he'd never left, as the house would have always existed then. He drowned himself in the school's swimming pool.

Our dorms were freezing. We filled our beds with heated bricks, hot-water bottles, stuffed toys, scarves, coats, socks. One boy even stole a teapot from the dining table over supper and lay huddled against it all night: he woke up to find his sheets all brown and the teapot cracked. Ivor never got cold. He let us huddle around him in his house common room, as if he were a fireplace, and read to us from his *Rupert Annuals*, though his body gave off no heat, which we noticed when in contact with him on the rugby field.

Once, long ago on a June celebration, the one time our families came to visit, a woman in wool stockings with a heavy, hideous face like a bundle of rusty steel wool, so unlike Ivor's, came to watch him and the other boys row on the river, their heads decorated in flower crowns. She gave him a home-made walnut cake in a large round tin before she left. None of us had asked about the woman or talked to her, we were too excited to see our own families, and spent the night after they left weeping in our beds, on a blanket of smashed carnations and roses.

Whenever a cake was eaten at Wakeley, it was tradition to scream while it was being cut, to keep the devil away, the headmaster said. You could tell, from the screams, who had hit puberty already and who was still a little boy. Ivor's scream was the highest of all, as sharp and shiny as the knife itself.

Ivor didn't eat the walnut cake himself but distributed slices to other boys, in particular the ones who wouldn't stop weeping after their families left. A few of us thought this was suspicious, others generous. Those of us who got a slice of the cake waited in anticipation for something to happen, for us to die from poisoning, our stomachs in twists of agony, for our faces to become as beautiful as Ivor's, but it was only a normal cake, not even home-made but shop-bought from Fuller's. The sweetness of it made us stop crying. The woman only came once; we never saw her again. Ivor did not seem upset, and instead charmed everyone else's parents and siblings and cousins. Our families all said they were so glad we were at school with a nice boy like Ivor.

None of the seniors became teachers or headmasters at Wakeley; our teachers came from elsewhere. Some stayed all of their lives, others only a few months. If they had families, they lived off campus and drove in, going home on the weekends. At night and on lunch breaks, we broke into their cars and pretended to drive places.

Many boys thought it unfair they could not become teachers at Wakeley, even after forty years of perfect grades in Latin, biology and Greek, their knowledge surpassing those of our teachers, but the headmaster said all the students were still boys.

Most of the seniors could only manage table tennis or chess in terms of games. Their lessons resembled those of the youngest boys: painting, reading, simple grammar, adding and subtracting. They were allowed brandy in the evening, and wine or ale with supper and lunch. They wore the same uniforms as us, with house scarves, though they also had spectacles, canes and protruding moles. When one graduated, we held a memorial for him in the main hall, his grades and prize medals placed on display for all to see and we sung the Wakeley school song in his honour. The other seniors always wept, except Ivor. He said they had all had a jolly good time together and they would see each other again some day. We had to pack up the bags and possessions of seniors from our own house who graduated. We found badly written poems about Ivor written in the backs of textbooks, and old photographs of other seniors, once young, with their arms around Ivor on the rugby pitch.

Once, we found an old brochure for Wakeley, wrinkled and yellow. It had a different font and a different year printed on it than the one we had received, but the picture was the same, a beautiful black-haired boy, Ivor, but such things were soon forgotten because the real Ivor was there among us.

On laundry day, all the boys gathered their sheets and pillowcases, their pants and their trousers, their names sewn onto the labels of each item, and threw their washing down the stairs of their houses for the cleaners to collect. The linens and uniforms billowed down like ghosts; the dirty pants fluttered onto the banisters like shot birds and all the boys laughed if the cotton was soiled. Every time, in his own house, Ivor would jump down the stairs with the laundry and float down, landing gracefully on his bottom and laughing. We all knew that if we were to do the same, we would smash our skulls. We gathered that perhaps Ivor was light as a bed sheet, made clean over and over again to comfort us in our sleep. ■

A NOTE IN THE MARGIN

Isabella Hammad

M ichel shakes the last of the peanuts into his mouth before
dusting his hands off over the grass. He grunts, swallows,
clears his throat.

'As I remember, they called it the Freedom Walk. It was only a
walk in the morning from the hotel to the conference centre, because
the organisers were worried about causing a traffic jam. But they had
renamed the conference centre – which by the way was originally
a dance hall for the Dutch colonials, no Indonesians allowed. They
called it the Freedom Centre, and they turned the walk there into a
sort of parade.'

'And he was part of it?' I ask.

'Indeed, my brother, he was. One of the main attractions. Army
fatigues, big smile.'

I register that phrase with pleasure, *my brother*. What would have
sounded natural in Arabic is touchingly stiff in Michel's English. He
holds his drink up to the light. I wonder whether he means to illustrate
something: this is how dazzling the Leader was, or that moment was,
twenty-odd years ago, when the heads of liberated or soon-to-be
liberated states, the great and the near-great, walked together between
one building and another along a flimsily barricaded path in a small,
humid Javan city, autographing children's notebooks and saluting the

crowd – how like the setting sun on a New England evening pushing its rays through a gin and tonic. Or perhaps he will segue into a new subject – and at even the thought that Michel might stop sharing his memories with me, my desire to hear them intensifies. I become shy. I try not to look at him. The clock strikes the hour.

In Arabic, he says: 'We're going to miss you, you know.'

'Oh.' I tug my jacket so it sits better over my stomach. 'Thanks.'

Our bench is directly across from the university's Science Building, where denim-clad undergraduates trail along the path. The end of semester is nigh: in a few days they will be free. For our goodbye meeting this afternoon, I've supplied the cocktail flask and glasses, while Michel has brought snacks and a farewell gift: another book, wrapped in brown paper. On Saturday, Kaitlin and I will be leaving for California.

Suddenly, Michel shouts: 'Read the sign, Bruno!'

Ahead of us, a shaggy young man with a long blond ponytail has wheeled onto the lawn.

'No *bicycles* on the *grass*.'

Standing on the pedals, Bruno directs the bike back onto the path without acknowledging his professor's rebuke. Slowed by the throng of other students, he zigzags to keep balance.

'And did you see him up close?' I ask. 'The Leader.'

'Of course.' Michel, flushed from yelling, settles back against the bench. He considers me. Then, having apparently decided, he takes me with him into the past.

First of all, he was late. The rest of his delegation, having travelled en masse, were already in situ by the time his train drew into Bandung on the Saturday night. He stepped out of the station, drenched by a quick monsoon rain, and spotted a young local uniformed man standing under an umbrella: a student helper from the Ministry of Information, watching for late arrivals. The helper chaperoned Michel to the Savoy Homann, into a marble foyer stocked with boyish soldiers in thick white socks and hard hats. Michel's English was fine by then – so he tells me in his now mellifluous American accent – but he still had trouble deciphering speech that strayed too far from a certain kind of received pronunciation, and as a result he must have misunderstood the attendant at the front desk because he took a wrong turn in the carpeted corridor and found himself by the swing doors of a conference room from which voices were emanating. One of the doors was propped open; he peered in. His wet jacket cooled in the air blown by a fan. Half the electric lights were on and a few chairs had been unstacked. And there, that figure, head of a Greek god, speaking into a switched-off microphone.

'People of Egypt!'

A seated man, narrow skull ribbed with veins, raised a finger. 'May I suggest, "People of the world"?'

'Ah. Yes.' The Leader smiled. 'A habit.'

'You must remember,' Michel tells me, 'that the coup is still fresh at this point. He's only been in power, as the head of state, for a year.'

'People of the world!' said the Leader.

A second man raised a hand, palm out. 'If I might, if I might, sir – People of the Third World? Given that, America, for example, is not invited . . .'

The Leader eyed his notes, pawing his cheek. 'Let me think.'

A small figure in a white suit and white panama hat scurried past Michel into the conference hall.

'Ah,' said the Leader. 'Why not simply say – *Mr President!*'

The white-suited man, who was Carlos Romulo, glanced around the room in confusion. It was still only 1955: Romulo would not become president of the Philippines for another seven years.

'Excellent, sir,' said the bespectacled adviser. 'That's a sensible way to go.'

'Don't look so frightened, Carlos!'

The Leader laughed to his companions, hand on his chest to help the laugh along, like a cough.

Michel's eyes are going misty with memory and gin.

'To see him so close was rare,' he says. 'Later on, of course, he became feverish about security. In Aleppo there's an Armenian joint called Hagop's, and whenever the Leader was in Aleppo, he always went to Hagop's – but don't ask me how I know this!' His smile – brows lifting, face alive with lines – feels intended for someone else, a previous interlocutor, possibly female. 'Hagop became the only person in Aleppo who knew when the Leader was coming to town.' Another sip and he reverts to a version of himself I'm more familiar with. 'Anyone who stages a coup knows the fragility of power. Anyone who overthrows the powerful – who takes power,' and he grabs the air in front of us like he is grabbing a lapel, 'becomes a paranoid maniac. And he really became diseased with secrecy, he saw conspiracy everywhere, Brutus on his doorstep, that sort of thing. But that spring, they were all puffed up in their robes and badges, and they entered the crowds like deities entering the River Ganges. Of course there was security, but . . . People came running out of restaurants when they heard the motorcades, screaming and waving like teenagers at American pop stars. Except that these were revolutionary leaders, bearing the weight of the people's hopes.'

The Leader continued practising his speech, in which he denounced the shenanigans of the imperial powers, the colonisation of Palestine, commended the valiance of the Algerians, tiptoeing around the Americans, the CIA have some nice guys, and then he zoomed in on the mushroom cloud.

'Fear of war has been aggravated by the development of mass-destructive weapons capable of total annihilation. The stakes are high. The stakes are *the very survival of mankind.*'

'Fantastic, sir, beautifully said,' said Carlos Romulo, wiping sweat from his upper lip.

'Carlos,' said the Leader. 'Why are you here?'

'What do you mean?'

'Has someone sent you?'

'Sent me for what?' asked Romulo.

'To . . . listen?' Toothpaste smile. Laughter.

'Certainly not, sir, no, sir,' said Romulo, tremulous, 'I only – I, I –'

'That's all right!' said the Leader. He looked down at the

representative of the Philippines with a threateningly benevolent smile.

'The Philippines,' says Michel, 'were in the small bloc of American sympathisers who were drawing a lot of suspicion. I was exhausted and needed to change out of my wet clothes, but my delegation happened to be in that bloc too, so I might have stayed there longer had I not – I mean, imagine, if the Leader had accused me of spying . . . I found another member of the hotel staff who took me straight up to my room.' He sips again and sighs. 'The heads were staying in these bungalows in the mountains, they descended in the mornings in cars. It was only the lesser delegates in the hotels, and the journalists, drinking late together in the lobby.'

'You were hardly a lesser delegate,' I say.

'Don't flatter,' says Michel. 'I was a minor delegate. I was twenty-four.'

'I only meant,' I say, but I don't persist.

The student throng before us has petered out and a wedge of sky between the Science Building and Graduate Studies is blushing with sunset. At any moment Michel might announce it's time to leave. I screw the cap off the flask and tilt it towards his glass. Distracted, he acquiesces. The liquid tinkles in the cup.

'And you mustn't be nostalgic either,' he says.

'I'm not nostalgic.'

'And also don't be romantic.'

'Okay,' I say.

'The age of greatness is over.'

I touch his glass with mine. Around the quad, the wind strikes up and starts to shake the trees.

'When was the age of greatness?' I ask.

'Well, it's an artificial question,' Michel replies, as though he had not a moment ago introduced the phrase. 'The idea of golden ages is basically romantic, it only exists in retrospect. But if pressed I'd probably say 1962, Cuba notwithstanding.'

I have lived in America for over ten years. When I first arrived in '65, I spent a week in Jersey City at the house of a second cousin and took the train each day into New York, waterlogged with jet lag, distracting myself with tourist sites. On two of those outings, I was approached by psychics. The first, a woman with wispy hair and stick legs loitering by the West Eighth entrance to the West Fourth Street subway station, informed me that I had a strong aura. I said thank you, what is an aura? She glittered with fake jewels. Putting a hand on my arm, she told me I'd come West from the East and that I would eventually go further West. This was not a difficult assumption given my face, I am obviously not from the West, and I might also have had the extra sheen of a clueless new arrival, or perhaps my clothes gave something away, but disconcerting to me was this suggestion of a *further* West, since I was at that time still imagining I'd return to Iraq after my studies, hopeful that the situation would have settled. Yet here I am, ten years later, there are the rumblings of another war in the Arab World and I am headed further West just like that woman told me. I still regret paying her those ten dollars. I'd just opened a bank account and there was hardly anything in it. She frogmarched me to a cashier's window then hugged me on the street with an ardour I tried to believe was real even though I could see her craning round and felt her arms pumping as she passed the singles between her hands, counting. When a second woman stopped me a few days later on a crowded stretch of Broadway, I wondered if there was a convention for psychics or crooks going on nearby and whether they preyed on recent immigrants. This one stopped in front of me, staring, told me I had a strong aura, and I immediately said, *No, thank you very much!* But now that I think about it, maybe I did have a strong aura; maybe auras are gathered by motion, an intensity of past and present. Maybe wars bring auras in their wake, maybe those of us who have seen death recently and up close broadcast certain kinds of light that only certain kinds of people can see. Maybe psychics are like our leaders, they discover they have a real gift and they start out truthful, idealistic, well intentioned, until they see a chance to make a little money off the back of the truth and they take it, and then truth and fiction start to blur, and they die before their time with a vague sense of having misused a gift, having abused the masses, unsure what they ought themselves to have believed.

Grief burnished me then, and no one in America besides these two women seemed to notice. I had lost a mother, a father, both sisters, in the coup. I had walked through flames, I was high on survival, and now I was in America, at the zenith of the wheel. Quickly, the East Coast and New York City in particular squashed any sense that I was special. I developed an odd relationship with my own name. No one could pronounce it, not even the woman who would become my wife. I think generally Americans can't force their palates into the right shapes but more importantly they are afraid of trying because they are afraid of failure, and it wasn't long before I not only accepted the American approximation but was repeating it when anyone asked who I was, so in effect I pre-empted their fear of failure, I deliberately made introductions easier, in order to feel digestible, as a stranger. After a while, the Americanised sequence of sounds practically became my name, so that when I first met Michel on campus for the interview and he addressed me correctly, my ears registered the pronunciation as a mistake. At the same time, it was like he had reached a hand out and plucked a string deep inside me, and a forgotten chord, intimate and strange, reverberated up my spine, like the beginning of a record your mother used to play in the mornings. Tears sprang to my eyes too fast for me to hide them, and the older professor said, Welcome, kissing me on both cheeks before slapping my arm, not unkindly.

My position here has been temporary. The salary was not stupendous and Kaitlin took some persuading: I explained to her about Michel. Michel is barely at the midpoint of his career and he's already a legend, swimming in the crème de la crème of the Ivy League while also having been physically present at several key points of our various interrelated movements. He is a walking piece of history, famously modest, famously well paid. Whenever, during

my research, I examine photographs taken at significant events over
the last twenty years I half expect to see him and often I do, a profile
constructed of newsprint dots, sometimes with and sometimes
without a heavy pair of glasses, lurking in the crowd at various
assassinations, meetings, summits. And yet, *miraculo*, the same man
now lived in an American cottage with an open-plan kitchen and
a yard full of iron furniture, while also – or so I'd heard, hanging
hungrily on to the academic grapevine from suburban New Jersey,
where I completed my doctorate – acting like an uncle to almost any
young Arab intellectual or entrepreneur or artist who turned up on
his doorstep. And while I generally remain sceptical of hagiographies,
there was something about this complex of facts that drew me to
apply for and ultimately to accept an adjunct position for which I was
frankly already overqualified. I'd once witnessed Michel thrash an
opponent at a public debate, speaking complete sentences with a neat
mid-Atlantic drawl, his hair immaculately combed, his original accent
appearing in the shape of an occasional word like a rock poking up
through parting waves. That was the only other time I'd seen him in
the flesh. When I arrived on campus, he was more haggard than I
expected. He wore a tweed jacket and his Arabic had started to break.

Idols can disappoint. Michel was sharp during meetings, charismatic
in the cafeteria, but, to my confusion, he kept me at a distance. I thought
up and threw out a thousand reasons why he only nodded politely at
me in the corridor. I attended all his public lectures. Then, in the second
week of my final semester, a note appeared in my mailbox.

> Are you free Friday? Am hosting small soirée, 7pm at
> 37 Carroll Street on the East Side. Please join and do
> bring your wife.
>
> M.

Our footsteps rang out on the cold paving stones. Lit gaps between
drapes shed glimpses of shiny wood and worn carpets and tartan

couches, the changing blur of reflected television light. Banisters, curving out of view. Number 37 was the last on the street. Beyond it stood a dark woodland, guarding the trickle of a river.

Michel opened the door wearing a woollen vest and chinos. He shook my hand and said to my wife: '*The* Kaitlin?' before kissing her on both cheeks. I experienced a brief internal commotion – I'd never even had a chance to speak to Michel about Kaitlin. My wife glowed, glancing at me. 'Oh,' she said. 'But what a *lovely* house you have, Professor.'

'*Michel!*' Michel exclaimed as we followed him down the hall, past a staircase decorated with a diagonal of framed pictures, and along a Persian runner into a dining slash living room that produced a general dark impression of brown and leather, including a piano and a big American hearth. Junior faculty members, a couple of senior ones, and a few graduate students, almost all men, sat squashed on a pair of opposed sofas, nodding and laughing, pinching finger food and paper napkins. Michel offered us a plate of smoked salmon rolls and as I pierced one with a toothpick I spied an old photograph on the wall, a portrait of the professor as a young man, floppy hair, hands in his pockets. Behind us, one of the historians had brought a box of unusual Kurdish sweets and was being accused of repurposing a gift. Someone read out the thank-you card he'd left inside and everyone was laughing.

Michel put a hand on my shoulder and rotated me to face them.

'This young man has performed brilliantly in the department this year. The students love him. It is our great loss that he's setting off for California this summer. Our loss and his gain, I'm afraid – no more bitter winters for you, sir.'

From both couches there came an expression of: 'Ah, what a shame!' They all introduced themselves, rising and nodding as we approached the dinner table, and I found myself beside a Lebanese mathematician named Jeanie who, resting her wrists on the table with an old-school delicacy, told me in a husky, smiling voice that she'd known Michel for years. I wondered immediately if they had been lovers.

Michel's first wife died young and he'd divorced the second after only two years. This was common knowledge. The way Jeanie spoke suggested a burden of secrets, the rising and falling action of passing years, heartache and loss and high temper. At the same time, I couldn't help feeling that Jeanie was asserting herself, trying to communicate how well she knew him, whereas I was a newcomer with no claim, a young upstart who hadn't made much of an impression, however warmly he had just described me. When I glanced at Jeanie's face, however, I saw that her eyes were sad.

'He was very idealistic when he was young,' she said.

'Dinner is served,' said Michel, carrying a tray piled high with rice and meat.

Snow streamed down through the street light on our walk home, thrust about by an uneven wind. Kaitlin clung tipsily to my arm.

'What a pity,' she said, 'only to meet them all when we're about to leave!'

A familiar pang of shame and longing mixed together was quickly swallowed by another of guilt. I'd brought Kaitlin all the way to this little town where she'd ended up making so few friends.

'You know what?' I said, pulling her close and touching her cold cheek. 'There'll be some *great* people in California. I'm sure of it.'

'Califorrrnia,' said Kaitlin, imitating me.

After that night, Michel began inviting me for private sessions in his office. He never acknowledged the change. Sometimes I saw what I thought was anxiety in his eyes – although anxiety about what, or whom, I didn't know. He presented me with reading lists, swivelling in his chair with his glasses perched on his nostrils, flipping papers round on the desk to say – and if you see here – tapping the margin with the broad pads of his fingertips – ignore the introduction but there's an interesting chapter on so-and-so – and he would dole out detailed advice: this is how you deal with graduate students, this is how you deal with professors emeritus, like an older warrior telling the younger, this is how you cock the gun and this is where you put your finger, this is how you fire.

The bottle, like the campus, is nearly empty. The street lights have flicked on.

'I was sharing my room with an American photojournalist,' says Michel. 'There was a mix-up – actually, an argument, and his partner from the newspaper refused to give up his single. I had no problem sharing. In fact, Tony and I became friends. The trouble was that when Tony drank to excess he tended to snore, and in those days, Tony always drank to excess.'

On the third night of the conference, following a reception in the governor's back garden, Tony fell fully clothed on his bed and the snoring commenced without Michel's usual head start on sleep. He poked Tony, he pulled his ears. The moon shimmered in the window. Michel, fed up, decided to go outside. He pulled on his trousers and his jacket, took his key and a newspaper, and stomped out of the room.

He glances at me.

'I'm listening,' I say, to reassure him.

'And there he was, in the hallway. In a suit.'

'Tony?'

'No, you fool. The Leader.'

'He was staying at the hotel?'

'No. No. That was the thing. As I said, the heads of state were in bungalows up in the mountains. Of course, it's possible that he deliberately forwent the pomp and splendour and asked, maybe for reasons of security, to stay at the Savoy Homann.'

Michel narrows his eyes, seeming to chew this possibility over, to weigh up the mess of historical, political and social forces in play.

'Or maybe the breakfast was better,' I suggest.

'Doubtful. And he was wearing a suit.'

'Oh.'

'Not even the uniform. A suit.'

'Strange. And what happened?'

Michel is silent. 'The strangest thing is that when I think about it, even though I know I saw him in the suit, I *feel* as though I saw him in his pyjamas.'

'Why's that, do you think?'

'You must remember he was still several years before forty,' Michel goes on, and although I can't see the relevance of this I understand that he is summoning the scene for himself, painting the portrait in his mind. 'His eyeballs were glowing in the dark. Like someone caught in the act, about to dash down the corridor into the shadows.'

'He saw you?'

'Yes. We nodded at each other.'

'You couldn't sleep?' said the Leader.

'No,' said Michel, startled into this simple answer. He was surprised by the dusty, disused sound of his own voice. He cleared his throat as a parade of more formal words of address ran across his mind. Finally, he asked: 'You neither?'

'Me neither,' said the Leader.

The Leader's voice, by contrast, was soft and high, and his eyes, wide, fell to the carpet. Dimly lit by a row of frosted wall lamps, he stood beside room 318, but didn't seem to want to knock. Michel drew breath to say goodnight; the Leader sharply turned his head in the other direction. Michel followed his gaze, seeing nothing but the empty hall. Faintly, the light bulbs buzzed. As though nothing had happened, the Leader reached into his jacket.

'Would you like a cigarette?'

'I . . . oh, yes,' said Michel. 'Thank you.'

The only sound was the leather of the Leader's shoes squeaking as they creased. He led Michel to the glass doors of the third-floor balcony, grasped a handle, slid a door aside, and stepped out.

The night out here was far from silent. The traffic carried on like the rag ends of a party, and the air, moist with recent rain, rustled the palm trees. They approached the edge of the balcony and the Leader passed the silver cigarette case to Michel and rummaged in his pocket again.

'What's your name?'

'Michel Odeh.'

'Michel,' he repeated. He drew out a silver lighter and looked at him, expectant. 'Where's your cigarette?'

'Ah – sorry,' said Michel. He popped the case and withdrew two.

'Oh no.' The Leader smiled. 'None for me. Just for you.'

Flick. His muscular face and sharp eyes glowed red in the brief flame. He smiled again in the returning darkness, and watched Michel inhale, then leaned on the cement wall and looked over at the conference centre: one half was visible between the buildings, the flags pitched in front of it all furled, asleep. Around them, the dark mountains bore down upon the tidy avenues. Michel tried to think of a question.

'How have you found the conference so far?' he asked.

In the silence, he wondered if he'd made a mistake by asking this, and he stepped forward, trying to appear offhand. Without looking up, the Leader answered:

'As a matter of fact, I almost didn't come.'

'Really?'

'But then, you see –' he emitted a curt *ha* of laughter – 'I went to India. And when I arrived, they showered me with rose petals. In the end I am just like a lover, being wooed. I couldn't resist.'

'He really said that?' I ask, amazed.

'Yes,' says Michel. 'But he was teasing me. He hadn't been seduced, of course. And he knew that I knew that.'

Michel falls quiet. I feel like I am listening to the whirring of his memory.

'He was putting me in my place,' he says at last.

'And then what happened?'

'You know something? I just can't remember. How funny.'

I scan Michel's face. I see that the moment has arrived: he has told me enough. I also understand that this final, quite blatant lie has not been delivered with malice, but simply as a way to say: this is the door. Goodnight, my friend.

'And what about after that?' I ask anyway, unable to stop myself. 'Did you ever see him again?'

'In Algiers, ten years later. And then came the defeat. And then, as you know, he died.'

Michel draws a deep concluding breath, ready to stand. Struck by a thought, he meets my eye.

'If you remember anything of what I've told you, remember this. He was a man of feeling. People might tell you he was dishonest but it's not true. He was not strategic, that I can agree with. But, in the final analysis, his biggest crime was his vivid imagination. Some people might just call that having vision. You seem to be cold.'

'Yes,' I reply, 'it's true, I am a bit cold.'

'We should say goodbye.'

'I suppose. Kaitlin will be cooking dinner.'

'Lucky you.'

'But I mean what about all the other . . . crimes, technically speaking – what he did to the Communists, the crackdowns, the censorship –'

'Yes, yes,' says Michel, flapping his hand. 'We all know. The history of the world is a history of slaughter. That's why I said don't be romantic. So. It's time to leave.'

'Thank you for telling me all of this, really, it's an honour –'

'No need to thank.' He upturns his glass to shake out the last drops of liquid onto the grass. 'Travel safely, and stay in touch.'

He shakes my hand and bows slightly. I watch him tramp along the path that crosses the quad, over to the other exit.

B eside me in bed, Kaitlin reads with her glasses on.
'You make me self-conscious,' she murmurs.

'No I don't. I don't think I make you self-conscious at all.'

Her eyes are dark tunnels.

'*Now* you're self-conscious. Before, you weren't.'

'How can you be sure?'

'Because you were mouthing along to the book.'

'What?'

'You were reading the different parts. At one point you looked surprised, then a moment later you looked sad.'

She pretends to hit me. I shield myself, laughing, before reaching for my own book.

'How was your meeting with the old fogey?'

'He's an important man.'

'You're in love with him.' Kaitlin's voice is sleepy and she has taken off her glasses.

I glance down at her, her pale hair greenish on the lamplit pillow, and consider how cleanly her joke misses the mark. I try to picture taking her home with me, to meet the people I left behind, and I realise, as though slowly turning to face the front, that I probably never will take her back there.

I left without even seeing their bodies. I left empty-handed. My colleague's nephew picked me up from a downtown cafe and pushed me so forcefully into his car that my first thought was that he was a turncoat and I was facing my end. He broke the news as he drove me to the airport, trying not to cry. He and his father had conspired to save my life. This, my life. This was what happens when, while someone else is describing from a distance, while someone else pronounces on history's sweep and fall, you discover you are just another speck in the battle air, a breath from not existing. The plane left the earth with a sigh.

'Turn out your lamp, mademoiselle,' I say to Kaitlin, 'or I'll have to lean over you.'

'Oh *no*,' she says, then – '*No!* You are squashing me!' Her laughter gurgles. I relent.

I say I want to read a bit longer and she groans, covering her eyes. I bend back the first page of the book Michel gave me. The title is *The Return of Consciousness*.

Our life in California is dense with Californian clichés, which, spectrally, remind me of Basra: we take the car everywhere, the sun is usually shining, and at the weekends we drive to the sea. We live near campus in a crumbling house with crooked ceilings, and Kaitlin has befriended some of my male colleagues' wives, who gather on Thursdays. I give a paper that first spring and, although I don't write to Michel, he's always in my mind. I keep pace with his research without thinking about it, scouring for his name in academic journals in the department lounge. Twice I catch him as a talking head on television, discussing strands of chaos unfolding in the distance. Then, in the fall semester of my second year, I receive this letter.

> Dear Professor,
>
> I don't know if you remember me but I took your class on methodologies and insights as a sophomore in Fall '75 and I was hoping you could write me a letter of reference because I'm applying for grad school. In case you don't remember me, I was the student who wrote the essay comparing Napoleon and Charles de Gaulle, and I'm sending you a copy here, too. Thanks very much, Professor, and hope your new life is treating you well.
>
> Yours faithfully,
>
> Bruno Scaveletes

I turn to the remaining contents of the envelope: an essay, typed up, with handwritten comments in the margin. In the top corner is the phrase:

> *Watch your spelling, Bruno*

Bruno seems to have enclosed the wrong essay. This one is not about Napoleon and Charles de Gaulle. The title is: 'The Disorientation of Gamal Abdel Nasser: A failed leadership, looking West'. I glance at the introduction and conclusion and see a familiar argument about the rise and fall of pan-Arabism.

> Gamal Abdel Nasser was the son of a postman. He is known to be the first Arab leader to challenge Western Rule in the Middle East, hailed as a leader and a hero,

he chose the Third Way and even though he failed in his mission, he enjoyes a reputation today that is only enjoyed by other world-famous, top-ranking charismatic leaders.

I confess I have a specific amnesia when it comes to former students. For the duration of a semester, their biographies and talents, or lack thereof, preoccupy me. I discuss them with Kaitlin, I fret if they struggle, I shell out extra reading and arrange extra meetings. But by the school year's end this relation is cut, and if one of them stops me in the street and says, Hello, Professor, I have to scrabble around in my memory for a name and usually wait for them to remind me, and if one writes to me with a request like this, I have to hunt through old files and reports for fragments of classroom discussions to piece together an opinion that might suffice for a recommendation. Bruno is an exception. I remember Bruno, and not because he was particularly sharp but because he was particularly bizarre: very tall, ginger beard, at once sulky and tender; occasionally, unexpectedly, moved to enthusiasm. I also remember him riding his bike onto the lawn that afternoon when I saw Michel Odeh for a farewell drink outside the Science Building. It doesn't surprise me, however, that I don't recognise my own comments in the margins of his piece about the Leader.

> Scholars cannot agree on the exact origins of Arab nationalism, nor can they agree on an exact answer to the question 'Who is an Arab?'

Beside this are three large question marks in red pen. They strike me as needlessly aggressive and I feel a retrospective shame. Then I see this marginal note:

This scholar doesn't footnote properly, don't trust him

I stare at the statement. I glance back to the first page again, and then I notice the date. One year after I had left the college. The handwriting, now that I look closely, is similar to but not the same as mine. On the second page, I see:

I can assure you that this did not happen. I was there!

I flip to the end of the paper.

The argument is well shaped with clear journey and denouement but you still need to work on your prose style. I disagree with your characterization of Abdel Nasser as enemy of the United States since in fact he was something of an Americanophile. As usual the picture is more complex. Come see me in office hours to discuss.
        M. O.

Now I know for certain that I am looking at Michel's handwriting. I fall once more into the cool darkness of his long, haggard shadow, and feel, as though recognising it for the first time, a stab of jealousy that I was never his student, only a brief lesser colleague, a hanger-on who passed him in the wings. I hear him telling me not to be romantic and like a switch the sun returns, baking my hands on my desk, and I smell the cool wood of my house, hear the creaking angles of the hall, the wind or my wife. I pick up a pen and a blank sheet of paper, and I imagine I hear the keen quiet wail of a man alone in another country, waiting for the storm to pass. ■

Hamish Hamilton congratulates
our authors **Natasha Brown** and **Sophie Mackintosh**
on their inclusion in **Granta's 2023 Best of Young British Novelists**

Canongate proudly congratulates

Derek Owusu

for being selected as one of
Granta's Best of Young British Novelists 2023

image credit: Josimar Senior

THEORIES OF CARE

Sophie Mackintosh

I spent a lot of time the summer I divorced sitting in what my family called the nervous breakdown chair, listening to what I personally called nervous breakdown music. Nervous breakdown music meant anything obnoxiously cheerful that I could picture soundtracking me in a montage where I was committing a crime spree. The details – murder, robbery – didn't matter, so long as whatever it was would be rampageous and remorseless both. Nervous breakdown music meant the Beach Boys, basically, so I sat there staring into space listening to 'Good Vibrations' on my headphones on full volume, thinking: the vibrations are bad. The vibrations are very bad indeed. And the irony of this small thought gave me enough comfort to lift myself above my pain for a second, even two, at a time. I surveyed the vista of that pain with curiosity, as if it were the surface of another planet, before returning into my body with a sick thump.

Sometimes a ladybird would land on my softly-furred bare thigh, and I would watch it move slowly about. Sometimes I would allow a horsefly to suckle tenderly from my forearm. My aunt would scold me for this, applying repellant to me as if it were sun lotion, her hands more vigorous than they needed to be as she rubbed it into my skin.

They carry disease, she would say. Have you no sense of self-preservation?

I did not.

There she was, my aunt, suddenly at the other end of the garden, waving from a distance. The tears in my eyes were almost pleasurable. Did I want a drink? She gestured again, raising her hand to her lips and tipping back her throat. I nodded, but made no move to get up.

Two minutes later she appeared next to me as if by magic, tall glass bustling with ice. I popped the lever so that I went from reclining to sitting in one exuberant motion.

You need to shower today, she told me. You stink. She passed me the ice. I took a sip – gin and tonic, strong, as if prescribed.

And please, behave, she added.

Define behave, I said, finishing the drink in one. She slapped me in the face, paused, then did it again.

Pull yourself together, she said.

And like this, the hours in the nervous breakdown chair passed.

The nervous breakdown chair was an old camping chair, khaki-green and reclining, that had belonged to my father. It was stained with sunscreen, rusted, full of holes. It was a chair of great penance and history, noble in its decay. My father had taken it on fishing trips, folding it carefully into the boot, setting it up next to body of water after body of water. As a teenager, after he left, I had tanned on this chair, dragging it behind the ragged hydrangea bushes and exposing as much skin as possible. It was my sister who anointed it in its new, recuperative purpose as the nervous breakdown chair. She would sit in it for hours sifting her thoughts, watching the insects, contemplating the clouds. I remember my aunt sitting on the grass, taking her pulse. She would write down the numbers in the notebook we were not allowed to read. Her theories of care were still in their infancy, back then. Her glasses hung, pendulous, from the diamanté chain around her neck.

My aunt had been a teacher once in a school for girls, or a paediatric nurse, or an anaesthetist – hard to keep the information straight, perhaps she had been them all. Anyway, she had been working on the aforementioned theories of care for a long period by the time I returned that summer. They included the healing power of submission, the idea that cruelty wasn't always cruelty, that the radio waves from phones made the cells of our brains glutinous, saggy. My aunt examined my phone as I sat across from her at the breakfast table, picking at my cuticles. I watched her scroll through something, my messages or my social media feed or my contacts, sucking her teeth, then I watched her put the phone in a drawer and lock it.

One walk, she told me. Forty-five minutes.

Through drizzle I marched myself along the lanes surrounding the house, alone, wearing a raincoat that came down to my knees. The air was thick and silent with water.

Tell me more about the Beach Boys and what they mean to you, my psychiatrist said from her box on the screen. The picture stuttered and froze. My laptop was propped on what had been my sister's dressing table, still wreathed in the gauzy accoutrements of girlhood. Velvet scrunchies, a scarf draped over the ornate mirror. The photo frames were empty, white and staring.

I don't wish to interrogate that, I said, which was my favourite phrase when speaking to her, I don't remember where I learned it. Whenever I said it, she flinched very slightly; I was pulling the rabbit out of the bag. She sighed, or maybe it was another flicker of the screen.

How are things with your aunt? she asked. She hated my aunt.

I could hear breathing outside the door, the barely perceptible motion of feet on deep pile carpet.

Things are very good, I said.

The attachment hypotheses of my psychiatrist did not bear out. I knew, sentimentally, that I had been loved and was loved again, adult though I was, returned here, temporarily, to a foetal and delicate state.

M y ex-husband had met my aunt only twice – once at our impulsive wedding and once after, at the house, when we sat on the lawn and ate a white sweet cake that crumbled everywhere.

Don't bring that man again, my aunt told me, privately, in the kitchen, as if he was a timid date and not the person I had so recently pledged to honour, love and obey. I leaned against the counter and shaded my eyes against a beam of sudden light.

It's true that he seemed to want to take me away. True that he had observed the mausoleum of my sister's room with a prickle of discontent, that he had been found examining the unmarked jars in the pantry, that after using the bathroom I had discovered him sifting through the drawers in my childhood bedroom.

He would not understand that there was no peace in the house, really, outside of the nervous breakdown chair. The monstrous years of my late teens lay lined up alongside the rest of my life like bullets in a gun. There, in the home where they had taken place, they could feel as present as if they were still being lived. And yet I returned, for I needed to rub my cheek against their coldness and remember that I was still alive, that I would continue to be alive, that a person could change, that a person could be changed, that the things around a person could change, that the body was broken, that the body was pure, that the body was a conduit for the good and the evil and the beautiful, that the body was nothing and the body was all.

A fter a week or so in the chair, I was able to hover, unafraid, for almost a minute over the vista of my pain. I marvelled at the blood-red seams that threaded the pockmarked, brittle earth – was able to see where the dirt had been scorched, where the terrain was torn up and resettled. There was no foliage except for a scrubby blue forest. If I stayed up there long enough, focused hard enough, I could see a tiny, other-worldly version of me in a tiny nervous breakdown chair, contemplating a new future, limply eating a sandwich cut into four small squares. I could see my aunt at the edge of the blue forest, crouched down on hands and knees, peering from behind the trees as if I was an animal not to be startled, an animal that must not be allowed to bolt, something wilder and more beautiful than anything had the right to be. From my vantage point I could see her in her entirety; curls tinted a brassy copper and tending to frizz, long skirt patterned with purple daisies, orthopaedic shoes. From such a distance she seemed fragile, as if she could be flicked away with the movement of one hand, and yet she was unmistakably vibrant, out of step with the dry textures of my pain. Oh and it was beautiful to see her watch me, to feel myself seen, to feel myself an unknown and surveyed thing upon a strange earth.

And sometimes I did not watch from a distance, but zoomed right into where I was placed upon this barren, ruined landscape. The shoddy details of the chair, the pores of my skin, the enamel of my teeth, bluely thinning and scalloped at the edges. The honeyed flecks of my eyes. I went right inside my body to the cool and pulsing workings of my blood, and saw there was a sheet of ice inside of me, wedged right up between my ribs and my stomach, and this ice was unbreakable, and it became possible to believe, then – many tall gin and tonics down, the hovering presence of my aunt there at the edge of the garden, the heat-shimmering green lawn, too green, a theoretical green – that I would survive, I would survive above all things, it was even feasible that I might one day rejoice in my capacity to live, to remain living. More, I prayed to the sun, to the sheet of ice inside of me, which might have been the proxy for a soul. Again. Please.

I tried to disentangle which had come first – the monstrous years, or the sheet of ice – but it was impossible.

Like this, too, the hours in the nervous breakdown chair passed.

That's my job, said the psychiatrist, regarding the disentangling. This time I had gone for an approved walk during my session, so there would be no padded footsteps in the hall outside my room. Instead of walking I huddled on a damp tree trunk, felled and rotten. I showed my therapist the landscape around me.

I'm not sure that you are in a safe place, she said to me, tactfully.

I think I might be a mystic, I said to her.

I think you might be in what we call an altered state, she said, also tactfully.

I don't wish to interrogate that, I said.

I talked about the pains of my stomach, the pellucidity of the light in the morning when I woke at five with the universe spiralling around me in motes of dust. I talked about how grief continued to undo me, about how it felt to sit in this wet patch of nature and talk unguarded. I talked, of course, about my sister. How it felt to be loved. How it felt to be afraid of love. How I was starting to feel the sheet of ice where it nudged against my organs, as if it were growing, or I were shrinking, the edges sharp and certain.

My aunt began to press her hands to my stomach in the morning. I'm not feeling for anything in particular, she said, but I knew she was feeling for the sheet of ice. She could not fool me. It was sharper now, solid as glass. The blade of it against my organs had a clarity like nothing else I had ever experienced. I sucked in my breath while she probed, twisted my torso gently to hide it, kept its good and fine secret for myself.

I wondered whether my aunt had her own sheet of ice; whether it was a genetic thing, or something environmental, borne from the house itself. The happy home. I wasn't sure. My sister had never spoken of one to me. I tried to look inside my aunt the next time I was in the nervous breakdown chair, but she was too guarded, too whole. I could not get further than inside the thick wool of her jumper, could only see her familiar and ageing skin, and then I was as ashamed as if I had tried to undress her.

I don't want you to die, my aunt said one evening, a rare admittance of weakness.

What makes you think I will? I said.

I saw it, she said, but she wouldn't elaborate. She went out into the garden and started tending to the potatoes even though it was dark. I followed her and put my arms around her waist.

I saw you walking down a long path, she said. I saw forests and terrible burnt earth, red, rocks and gravel. I saw you walk all the way down the path until you were gone.

The swifts shrieked overhead. It was still warm enough not to need a jumper. The sun had only just disappeared, with the finality that shocked me every evening.

It might not mean now, I said.

I know what it meant, she said. It was exhausting to love her. That is why you can't keep love, or it can't keep you.

She handed me one small potato and I held it in my fist, floured with earth.

I think you might be ready, my aunt said at the end of the summer. I think it's time for you to leave.

She went into the living room and lit the votive candles that were set in front of the photograph of my sister on the mantelpiece. They were very rarely lit, and I reacted to the smell of them flaring up with a sensation that came from deep in my unconscious; a jerk, hypnotic. I wasn't in the nervous breakdown chair, but I felt something within myself rise up and give. I felt the ice sheet shift, and was afraid it might melt.

When the room was ready she called me in and had me lie on the couch – placed a pillow on my stomach. Then she placed a pillow over my face.

Relief.

What did I see?

I don't know. I do.

I'd wanted to die many times, but when it came down to it I lost my nerve. I flailed against the pillow. There was an instinct I wasn't privy to, wasn't aware of running through my body, or maybe I had just forgotten.

I can only take you so far, the instinct told me. I can only be that beam of glowing light, can only be the fracturing kick against the ice, the hot heart of a star imploding.

Maybe I had just forgotten. Maybe I had not. The blind navigation around the monstrous years, not wanting to look, how instinct had pulled me on a string, saying fall, fall, and there is no slack, no safety, only the two of us, but fall anyway. Fall and be caught, somehow.

What next, when instinct leaves? I had not asked myself that question in a while.

Come on, now, said my aunt. You're distracted.

She pressed harder. I felt her fingers through soft down, tried to bite, was thwarted.

I do remember. There was the vista of my pain, the desert. The silted, lovely sand, studded with fist-sized rocks. There was a white horse to take me across it, moving towards me patiently, its head held high. A blue sun. Maybe I am a mystic, I thought, but then I realised I was just dying, at last. Or something approaching it.

My sister was walking across the vista. My aunt, on another plane, was sobbing. I was only dimly aware. She took my hands and pulled me to the ground. Together we sat, cross-legged.

Oh, darling, she said. She handed me a potato. She handed me a palmful of hay to feed to the white horse. It came to us and ate from my hand, just like that.

Stay, or go, she said. I'd be inclined to say go.

I suppose it's up to her, I said, meaning my aunt, still holding me down somewhere else. We looked up and the sky was cloudy with feathers.

She means well, she said.

My sister had been energetic. My sister had danced with the vigour of a whole troupe of ballerinas. Then she had not. A change came over her like a wind. She used to tell me about her own vista of pain, back when we were at the very start of the monstrous years. Hers was not a strangely coloured desert, like mine. Hers was very cold, bone-white and crystalline. In hers, small furred animals gambolled in the distance, but nothing dared come close. There were tiny blue flowers studding a mauve coastline. It upset her that she could only see, but never reach. She used to stay in the chair for hours, stay up there observing until I could almost see some integral part of her leaving, smoke or breath curling up, and then I would be afraid until she finally opened her eyes. It was very beautiful, she used to tell me when she returned. More beautiful than here.

I'm in a lot of pain, I said. I took her hand and put it on my stomach. Do you feel that?

That's a good sign, she said.

Will it save me? I asked.

It'll do something, she said.

Like I said, I'd wanted to die many times and had been in practice for dying, been entrenched in the service of dying, a student of circling the act of inducing my own death, suspicious, covetous, watching it like a carrion bird. I told my sister this. I felt she would understand.

You don't know anything. Take a long drink, she said, but kindly, holding a glass to my lips.

There was a sharp wind. The horse roared. I swallowed and it was a cool and strange water that did not quench my thirst.

Time to go back, now, she said to me, with some finality.

This is what not dying is like: I swam up as if through water. There was a flash of light. My aunt was sprawled on the floor where I must have finally pushed her, clutching the pillow. And I came out gasping. ∎

CIRCLES

Anna Metcalfe

I found the first one in a kitchen cupboard, a ring of dust where some bowls had been. The shelves were all half empty. I'd been giving away a lot of things. After that, I started seeing them in all kinds of places – circles of water, circles of shadow. I started making meanings from them. That's what happens when you get something in your head and you live on your own. All your thoughts become true.

Across the city, businesses were closing. At the end of my street, an office cleared out and stood vacant for a while. Then it became a cafe, not a real one but a makeshift place, with trestle tables and milking stools. I spent a lot of time there, sitting by the window, looking at the trees in the park. I flicked the pages of magazines and watched people talking over drinks, running hands through their hair, scratching the corners of their mouths. I read the profiles of a hundred men on the app and wondered whether it might not be preferable to spend my life alone.

One afternoon, I swiped right on a man with a large face, a swatch of dirty brown hair, small eyes and grey stubble. He looked large in the photo, broad-shouldered and muscular, though it was always hard to tell. He worked in design. He had a daughter, thirteen years old. He liked canoeing and spaghetti. His guilty pleasure was enjoying a cigarette immediately after he'd been to the gym. He was clever, I thought, to mention the gym this way – without being obvious, without seeming to brag. In one of his photos, he was wearing a grey marl vest. There was a wobbly circle tattooed on his arm. I looked at the picture for some time. I kept coming back to the tattoo. It wasn't long before he messaged me and we arranged to meet.

The first date went well. He was grumpy in a way that I enjoyed. It reassured me that he was easily displeased – he was discerning, I thought. I had been right about his body. He was tall with strong arms. I liked the heaviness he had around the middle, the way it pushed against the buttons of his shirt. He smelled good, too – a bit like cinnamon and a bit like sweat. When I arrived, he pulled me into an awkward hug – the way you might hug a cousin you hadn't seen for a long time – then he kissed my face very close to my ear. It felt completely normal, as though our bodies had met before.

We got the basic stuff out of the way quickly – jobs, divorces, holidays, the recent, unseasonable warm spell. We didn't delve too much into politics or the general state of the world. Mostly, we talked about interesting things. He told me that watching certain films had made him feel differently about his life, how when he wanted to cry he knew which songs to play on his phone. I wondered if this was an act – if he wished to appear sensitive, emotionally attuned – but in the end I didn't care because the films and songs he referenced were all pretty good. I talked about my favourite sunsets, the ones I saw from the bus on my way home from work. I showed him pictures: the pink one with the big blue clouds, the one that glowed green through the rain. I told him I hated peonies and any flower you could put in a vase, that I liked plants to be ugly and wild. Giant foxgloves, cow parsley by the motorway. He said he had taught himself the phases of the moon and could always tell if it was perfectly full or starting to wane.

I knew that he found me endearing; I suspected he found me attractive. From time to time, I saw him looking directly at my mouth or at the line of my collarbone.

'Do you have pets?' he asked towards the end of the meal.

'No, never.'

'Thank God,' he said.

He hardly mentioned his daughter, but men with children were often like that. Either they pretended that their kids didn't exist, or they presented them to me like a gift, as though I ought to be terribly grateful that they might be willing to share. He paid for dinner and I didn't protest. I told him I'd pay the next time and he mentioned some other places we could try.

The night air was fresher than usual, indigo blue instead of black. He asked me where I needed to go and if he could walk me there – he didn't mind going out of his way. We said goodbye at the top of a flight of stone steps. He was warm and my skin was cool. I felt myself reaching up towards him; my palms tingled, as if dissolving. I kept thinking that if either one of us lost our balance then we'd both come crashing down. A few days later, he sent me a picture of a sunset where the sun was a bright copper circle – ugly, like a coin.

There were many subsequent dates. We ate gnudi at a noisy Italian in the suburbs. We queued in hot weather for tom yam soup. On Sundays, we went for long walks by the river. Sometimes we brought a picnic; sometimes we walked until we were hungry then slipped off the riverside path in search of lunch. We didn't spend much time in each other's houses; we both liked our own space. When he did stay over at mine, we'd go out for breakfast the morning after. I didn't like sharing my kitchen table – I did all my thinking there.

We preferred cafes with seats outside. We liked to smoke with our coffees, though we never smoked at night. We ate eggs, fried potatoes and mushrooms that leaked their juices. We drank large carafes of water to make up for the caffeine and the salt. Afterwards, I'd be left with a burnt taste in my mouth.

Our best conversations took place while one of us was walking the other to the nearest bus stop. When our time was nearly up, we felt free to say important things. It was during one of those conversations that he told me his father had died and I told him that my mother had too. I told him that I still talked to her like I had as a teenager after school, sitting at the kitchen table. He was tender towards me;

he listened carefully. I liked looking at our reflections when we passed shop windows at night – our two shadowy figures, his large and rounded, mine slim and angular. We made each other more attractive, I thought. We made each other better in general.

His daughter stayed with him for a couple of nights a week, sometimes longer during the holidays. She was an interesting young person, he said – unusually intuitive.

'She doesn't have a lot of friends,' he told me, over tacos. 'Her mother worries about that, but I don't.'

'Why not?' I asked.

'Why doesn't she have friends?'

'Why don't you worry about it like her mother?'

'She's fussy,' he said. He drained the last of his margarita. 'She's good at being on her own. She respects herself.'

For the first few months, he had only good things to say – about me, about his daughter. He complained about his job, which was normal. He complained about his house, which was always in some state of disrepair. But with me, he was patient and kind. He laughed at my jokes and was generous about my appearance. He liked my clothes, even the ones that had belonged to my grandfather – clothes that other men I'd known had hated. He often spoke of his daughter's intelligence, her artistic pursuits. It was only later – and after he'd had an unusual amount to drink – that he explained how she could make life difficult for him. There had been other girlfriends, he said. His daughter had driven them away.

'How?' I asked. 'She's just a child.'

'It's hard to explain,' he said. 'I guess she has a manipulative streak.'

That night, I sat at the kitchen table with my mother. I'd poured her a drink, which usually made her laugh – *I'm dead!* she'd scream, as if I didn't know – but this time she was calm.

'What did he mean?' I asked her. 'Manipulative?'

He means he loves the things he loves when they don't cause him any trouble, my mother said. *That's what he wants you to understand.*

Just before it closed down, we arranged to meet at the temporary cafe at the end of my street. A new couple were running it, selling Vietnamese coffee and beer and banh mi. He'd taken a week of annual leave to redecorate the upstairs of his house. I'd hoped he would come in his scruffy jeans and grey vest. I imagined there would be splashes of paint on his arms, that he would tell me about the things he had been listening to on the radio while he worked. It was a Tuesday afternoon and the cafe was quiet. I ordered a coffee and drank it quickly. He sent a message to say he was running late so when I finished the coffee I ordered a beer. There were new pictures on the walls – bouquets of blobs and lines. A local artist had painted them. The colours were loud. I tried to remember what had been hanging there before.

When he finally arrived, he was wearing his usual clothes. A shirt and smart jeans, a reddish-brown leather belt. He did not look as if he had been painting. He looked put-upon, harassed. His posture was different. He stooped forwards, his shoulders bouldering up around his ears. I waved to him and he ignored me. A young girl appeared behind him, wearing cut-offs and a vintage T-shirt with a faded image of a bicycle wheel. She had the same dirty brown hair as her father; it fell unbrushed around her face. She was scruffy, but somehow she made it look good. Already, she understood her own beauty, how to play it one way or another.

As he introduced her, he sounded tired, impatient.

'Someone,' he said wearily, 'has been in trouble at school.'

The girl looked at me. I couldn't read her expression.

He went on in the same false tone, one eyebrow raised: 'Someone's mum didn't feel like dealing with it herself.'

The daughter's nose was neat and pretty, nothing like her dad's. Her neck was long, her shoulders narrow. When she moved her fringe out of her face, I saw that she had his eyes – small and perfectly symmetrical. She pulled a sketch pad from a tote bag, and then a selection of pencils. Without asking what she wanted, he ordered her a juice, and a beer for himself. He didn't ask if I needed anything though my beer was mostly gone.

For a while we talked as usual. He mentioned a depressing article he'd read, a disturbing exhibition he'd been to see. There was a new sushi bar on his road; he said he'd take me there soon. He wanted to pretend that this was a normal meeting, as though nothing remarkable were taking place. In an attempt to make him feel more comfortable, I played along. I told him I was seeing a new therapist – that her office was filled with enormous plants, that I thought they were fake but it was hard to tell. He winced when I said *therapist*, as if to say: this isn't something to discuss in front of a child. It started raining in sheets – the water was dirty and grey. His daughter looked up at the sudden noise. Then, as strangely as it had begun, the rain stopped, and she returned to her drawing.

His large body, which had once felt generous and capacious, now appeared selfish and mean. He took up too much space on his side of the bench. He spread his elbows out wide. He leaned forwards so that his face was too close to mine. I could see clearly the hairs of his beard that were still brown amid the mass of wiry grey. All the while, his daughter sat as far away from us as she could. Her body shrank in on itself; she didn't touch her juice. She was focused on her sketch pad – I wanted to know what she was drawing but instead I made myself concentrate on what her father had to say.

He complained about wasting his week off, about getting behind on his renovations, which seemed a rather grandiose word to use for repainting a couple of bedrooms. I offered to help and he laughed. 'You, with a paintbrush,' he said.

'I painted my flat,' I said.

'Well.'

'I went to art school.'

His daughter looked at me.

'Hardly the same thing, is it?' he said, as though painting a bedroom was a more technically demanding operation than a portrait or a still life.

I realised then how nervous he was. His daughter made him vulnerable: she knew everything about him, all the things I was yet to learn.

It's no use trying to put him at ease, my mother said quietly from the next table. *Much better to talk to the girl.*

'Gwendoline,' I said, using her whole name, though he always called her Gwenny. 'What are you drawing?'

She said nothing.

'Is it okay to call you Gwendoline?' I asked.

'It's Lina,' she said.

Her father twitched. 'Since when?'

She ignored him.

'Lina,' I said.

He rolled his eyes then scanned the room for a waiter but there was no one.

'Your dad told me you like drawing,' I said.

Lina seemed surprised. She made a noise like a snort, a dry laugh that didn't require a smile.

'It's not just that she likes it,' he said, speaking as if she wasn't there. 'It's the only thing she does.' His disdain was palpable and I wondered about his enthusiasm for art galleries when he had so little interest in children learning to draw. His tenderness was gone. He was defensive, eager to judge. 'That's when she isn't *stealing things,*' he added. Then, as if it were necessary: 'That's why she's not in school right now.'

Lina closed the sketchbook but kept her head bent low. Her father got up clumsily. Our drinks wobbled on the table, ice rattling in Lina's juice. He ordered at the till then asked about the loos, which were down the street in a different building.

'Can I see your drawing?' I tried again.

Her hands were small and perfect, the right still holding the pencil, the left resting gently on the table. I looked out of the window to the park. A circular cloud hovered over the trees. For a moment it was a perfect zero.

'Do you see that?' I said. 'Like a smoke ring.'

One corner of her mouth raised. She sipped her juice. The clouds shifted.

'It's already breaking up,' she said.

If I'd known she was coming, I would have prepared more things to say. But my own mother had never talked to me as if I were a child. When she asked me questions, they were always important, things she really wanted to know.

'What did you steal?' I asked.

Her father came back then. 'It's not so much what she stole –' he said.

A waiter followed close behind with two beers and a plate of spring rolls.

'It's not even that she stole it –'

'It was mine anyway,' she interrupted.

'It's that she won't take responsibility.' He shoved a spring roll into his mouth, as if for moral emphasis.

'Dad doesn't believe in conditional apologies,' she said, and held my gaze a beat too long as though to say: like there's any other kind.

She's a smart one, eh? my mother said.

Lina opened the sketchbook then, flicking through the pages until she found the one she wanted. She spun the book around and pushed it towards me.

I laughed loudly, involuntarily.

Despite the fantastical adornments, the comic distortions, it was a true likeness. I recognised her father's handsomeness, his charm, his pride, his stubborn brow. Strange objects floated in the background; animals gathered at his elbows. One side of his face appeared to be melting. I looked more closely at his expression and understood that he found almost all of his feelings unbearable, which I had suspected but not confirmed.

'It's incredible,' I said.

Holy shit, said my mother.

'For the love of God,' he said.

He went outside to vape – he didn't smoke cigarettes in front of her – and Lina came to sit on my side of the bench. She showed me other drawings in her sketch pad. She asked me questions about art school. Then she told me, in a whisper, what she had stolen and why.

On the way home, I took a detour through the park. The sun was shining and people were out walking their dogs. I stepped off the main path and walked among the trees. Several had been cut down and I studied their cross sections, the deep patterns, the concentric lines. When I was a child, I thought knowledge was understanding how things worked, but later it seemed it was more a matter of noticing repetitions, all the things that kept announcing their own existence again and again – *I'm here! Here I am!* As I walked back onto the green, the low sun was overwhelming. I squinted against the glare. My mother was sitting on a bench on the far side of the grass. I waved and she waved back. I walked towards her and she stood up, but before I reached her, she turned and ran out of the north gate.

I met him again the following week. I kept thinking about his daughter and the way he'd talked as if she wasn't there. My mother had turned against him. *They all seem nice at the start,* she said. I knew what she wanted me to do. I invited him for drinks, not dinner, and when I arrived he was already sitting at the bar with a half-drunk cocktail in his hand.

'I think I know what you're going to say,' he told me, right off the bat. 'And I think I agree.'

'We've had a good time,' I said.

I asked about Lina and he seemed suspicious so I changed tack. I made it seem as though I really cared about him.

'It must be really difficult, balancing everything,' I said.

His daughter had stopped stealing things, he told me. Now she was just the regular kind of sad.

'She seems like a really special kid.'

'Other people's children always seem that way,' he said.

I kept thinking about the drawing. Probably he was thinking about it too. In that moment, I felt sorry for him, or I thought I did. I ordered a bitter-orange cocktail and he said he'd have the same. He offered to pay but I told him it would be my treat.

'I meant to ask,' I said as he walked me to the bus stop, 'what's the meaning of your tattoo?'

'Nothing,' he replied. 'A stupid thing when I was young. I wish it had never happened.'

'I like it,' I told him.

'I hate it,' he replied.

When I got home, I told my mother what had happened. She didn't have very much to say. I thought she'd be impressed by my decisiveness, but instead she seemed flat. In the face of her ambivalence, I started to doubt myself.

There'll be others, she said vaguely. *Or there won't.*

'Did I do the wrong thing?' I said.

How would I know? she replied.

Our conversations were shorter now. She was always getting up to leave. I wished that I had asked her more about motherhood when she was alive: whether she liked it; whether, overall, the experience had improved her life. The mother I talked to wasn't the mother I had known as an adult, when she was ill and losing bits of herself. It wasn't the mother I'd known as a child either, when she was exhausted, caring for me then hiring babysitters to take over so she could go out and *meet someone*. It was the mother from when I was a teenager, when she could leave me at home on my own. That was when – suddenly – I became fascinating to her. She'd look at me in wonder, as if I were superhuman, as if she hardly knew me. As if she thought I could do anything.

The weather was getting stranger. Rent was becoming impossible. I'd never needed a lot of money – I never travelled by plane or bought new things. I had some cash to spare from selling the stuff I didn't need, but the future seemed bigger and darker. No one knew if they had what they needed any more.

I gave up on the app. The cafe at the end of the road closed down. It became a vintage clothing store, then a shop selling film posters.

For a while it was a co-working space and I went there every day, but then the rain began again and the roof collapsed and no one could afford the repairs.

Winter came but the temperature hardly dropped. I had no appetite and never felt like going out to eat. I started working from home. Days went by without leaving the house. My brain fogged and my body ached. When at last the rain stopped, I tried to get up before sunrise. First thing in the morning, I'd smoke and stroll through the park. Occasionally my mother was there too, but not often. Most of the time, I was fine either way.

While walking, I started to miss him. My mind would go blank and a spectre of him would appear – strong and warm, nice-smelling, a little grumpy, waiting for me to speak first. The sensation crept up on me; it took me by surprise. For several weeks, I tried to forget him and he always came back. Another version of my life was lurking there somewhere, beneath the low, peachy sun as it rose: me, him and Lina.

When I rejoined the app, he wasn't on it any more. I joined another, but he wasn't there either. Perhaps he had already met someone else. Or perhaps I'd put him off altogether. It occurred to me that I didn't know why he'd wanted things to end, only why I had. It must have been the drawing for both of us, I thought. It had made him ridiculous; it was humiliating. But now it seemed it was the picture, more than the man, I couldn't forget. The usual processes had been accelerated. I hadn't had to wait to see his true ugliness – to see how he lurched over his underwear drawer in the mornings, his greying skin, his too-big hands groping around. Instead, Lina had exposed him. She had presented me with his worst possible self which, in hindsight, didn't seem all that bad.

I sent him a text.

How's Lina? I wanted to write but didn't. Instead, I composed a long, nostalgic message about the gnudi restaurant closing down and the owners opening a pizza place in the park.

He replied quickly.

Rent's too high, he said.

Yes, I agreed.

Re. pizza – heard mixed reviews.

Me too, I lied.

Three little dots appeared in the message box, then vanished. Finally, he said: Shall we see for ourselves?

The evenings were bright and too warm for spring. The seasons were broken; it was never cold any more – it was either warm and dry, or warm and raining for days on end. That had something to do with it, too, the return of my feelings for him. The parameters were shifting.

The pizza place was a brick oven in the bandstand tended by a couple of tired-looking boys with burn marks on their arms. I ordered puttanesca, he ordered pepperoni. We sat on a bench as the sun went down. Mostly, we talked about interesting things. He told me he'd been thinking more and more about his father, the kind of man he was.

'Did you ever ask him about fatherhood?'

'No,' he said. 'How stupid is that?'

It was a relief to be near him again. He told me about his daughter before I even asked. He wanted me to know about her – once again, she was fascinating to him.

She was learning guitar. She'd taken his bass from the attic and could play it much better than he ever had. With a couple of friends, she'd started a band called Bowls, Everywhere! She wrote most of their songs – a bit surreal for his taste, he said, but they made a good sound. 'That kid,' he said, as though stunned, 'she can do anything.'

We started spending more time in each other's houses. Eating out was becoming more difficult, and not just financially – the food was getting worse. When I went to his, Lina was always there too. Her mother was having trouble with her own partner and they were doing the calculations, trying to see how each of them might survive in the event of a break-up. Meanwhile, Lina's father had been upgraded to primary parent.

Often, he worked late. I'd arrive for dinner and he would still be sitting at his computer, moving digital objects around a screen. When he wasn't working late, he went to the gym. While we waited for him, Lina and I sat at the kitchen table and talked. She told me about her band, I listened to her music, I knew the names of all her friends at school. She asked me questions in return. Lina liked the circles, too. Sometimes, she'd point them out to me. She showed me pictures on her phone, mostly worms curled up on the pavement.

One night, I was cooking dinner. He was pouring wine into my glass. There were candles on the table. Music was playing, everything smelled great. My mother – who'd been turning up more frequently again – was standing by the sink, a hand on her hip, an eyebrow raised, as if to say: *well, doesn't this look nice?*

We talked about the usual things. He was struggling with supply chains, I was struggling to pay rent, Lina's mother had no idea what she was going to do.

'What about you?' I said to Lina. 'What did you do today?'

She got out her sketch pad and placed it on the table, flicking through the pages until she found the one she wanted. Then she slid the book to me.

Despite the slime, the missing limbs, the gaping hole in the middle of the forehead, it looked just like my mother.

Wonderful! my mother said.

Her father said smugly: 'Well, look at that.'

Lina watched me carefully, awaiting my response. ∎

WALES

Thomas Morris

It's been three months since they saw each other, and Gareth wonders if his father will recognise him. He pictures his mother upstairs, sitting at her dressing table, practising her face. He wonders if his father will come into the house. He thinks: if Dad comes in, Wales will lose.

Hearing his mother on the stairs, he moves from the window and settles on the couch – the gap in the curtains the only evidence he was standing there, waiting for his father's car.

Got your phone? she asks.

Yep.

Text when you're on your way back, alright?

Yeah yeah, he says.

A car horn beeps outside: his father has arrived – and he isn't coming in.

There's a pause, then his mother smiles.

Well, have a good time, she says. And make sure you get something to eat. I've told your father, but you know what he's like.

Gareth nods, absorbs it all. If Wales win tonight, everything will turn out okay. His mother will find a wad of cash stuffed in the walls and they won't need to move out. But if Wales lose, the repo man – with his bulging muscles – will return and take Gareth's bike. Or the ceiling will cave in and fall down on him while he's watching cartoons on the couch.

Wouldn't it be mad if you see me in the crowd on the telly? he says.

His mother grins.

I'll keep an eye out for you, she says.

Outside, the March evening air is fresh on his cheeks.

Young man, his father says in greeting.

Alright? Gareth replies.

They drive up Caerphilly Mountain, Gareth secretly studying his father's head. One day he'll be able to read people's minds. He just needs to learn to focus harder.

What you looking at? his father asks.

I think you're going bald, Gareth says.

Wonderful, his father replies. Another thing for me to worry about.

They drive on. When they hit traffic, his father instructs Gareth to open the glove compartment, where he finds the two tickets, sacred and shiny: his first real match at a real stadium.

So what do we know about Northern Ireland? his father asks. Any predictions?

They've got some good defenders, Gareth says. But Wales will win. I'm gonna say . . . two-nil. Ramsey header and . . . a Gareth Bale bikey from the halfway.

His father laughs, then in a quiet voice explains that because it's only a friendly, Ramsey and Bale have been rested and won't be playing.

Oh right, Gareth says.

It'll still be a good game. Just don't get your hopes up, alright? And put those tickets back now, before you lose them.

His father refuses to pay for parking, so for twenty minutes they drive round one residential avenue after another, finally finding a spot in a street lined with trees.

Let's just hope we can remember where we're parked, his father says, as they walk past houses three storeys tall, with tiled porches and coloured glass in the doors.

They're lovely houses, Gareth says.

They'd probably cost you . . . pfft . . . a million pounds? his father says.

A million quid! Gareth says. That's insane, that is.

They walk on, Gareth taking two steps for every one of his dad's.

Slow down, will you? I'm literally only ten.

Well, hold my hand then.

Nah, you're alright, Gareth says.

On the high street, the air throbs with horns and whistles. Crowds with flags draped over their shoulders spill into the road, the cars slowing and honking. Outside a pub, a group of men in red T-shirts toot trumpets and trombones, and one man plays the sax and another bangs a drum. Arms aloft, the fans sing: *I LOVE YOU BABY!* and a woman, dressed like a daffodil, jumps up and down, her pint spilling onto the pavement.

Let's get some grub, his father says.

They eat outside the chippy, leaning against the window. The chips are hot and moist with vinegar. Inside, a girl with a red dragon stencilled on her cheek stands beside her dad, with a burger and a can of Coke. If she looks at Gareth, Wales will win.

Enjoying the chips? his father asks.

Yeah, Gareth says. They're lovely.

As they're about to leave, the girl smiles through the glass.

Onwards they go now, among the stream of fans, down sneaky avenues and busy roads, onwards towards the stadium. Wearing coats and scarves and bucket hats the fans sing, *Don't take me, please don't take me home, I just don't want to go to work.* Up above, the sky is purple black.

It's a long walk, Gareth says.

Best way to soak up the atmosphere, his father replies.

You should have parked closer to the stadium, Gareth says. This is a bloody marathon.

Football is all about opinions, his father says. And in my opinion: you can shut up.

Gareth laughs, and the crowd shoals through the dark streets until suddenly the stadium is before them, glowing like a flying saucer. His father buys a programme and Gareth holds it proudly. In the queue, a bald security guard shouts, COATS OFF! ARMS IN THE AIR! He looks like the repo man, the man who took away his mother's car.

Alright son? he asks, patting Gareth down. Any knives in your pockets?

As if! Gareth replies.

Good boy, the man says, smiling. Have a good game.

Through the beeping turnstiles now, into what feels like an underground car park. Bodies hassle past, and there's the smell of sizzling onions and hot dogs. A woman in a high-vis jacket checks their tickets and directs them up a flight of concrete steps, and then they are somehow, magically, outside again, and there it is – the pitch! It's way different to how it looks on the telly. The grass is a giant green stage; lit so bright beneath the floodlights, it seems unreal.

Their seats are behind the goals. As the players warm up, he feels the thud of each kick in his chest and he hears the coaches' echoing shouts. He pictures stepping onto the grass, striking a penalty, the net rippling.

When the anthem begins, they rise to their feet, and his father's voice is deep and rumbling. Gareth has sung it in school before, but this is completely different. The anthem is massive, it fills his chest and roars out of him as if everything – Wales, the world, his whole life – depends on it. At the end, his father claps and yells, C'MON WALES. And Gareth yells it too, then bellows the chant that's whirling around the stadium: WALES! WALES! He is screaming, he is letting something go.

The game is difficult to follow. There are no video replays, no commentators, just the players on the pitch and the sound of the crowd. For every Wales tackle, a swelling roar fills the air, and any decision against them means thousands of people howling at the referee. The crowd urge the players and the players drive the crowd, and it's electric, and it feels out of control. The match is a blur and before he knows it, it's half-time.

Nil-nil, his father says.

They leave their seats and head back out to the concourse. Gareth blows on his hands to warm them up. His father asks if he wants a hot chocolate, but Gareth says he needs a wee.

At the urinals, sandwiched between two men, nothing comes out. Beside him, a man sways and leans on the wall to steady himself. Gareth does up his zip and comes back to his dad.

Did you go?

Yeah, Gareth lies.

Wash your hands then.

At the sink, he sends his special energy to the players. When he was four years old, he got separated from his mum in WHSmith. Looking for the DVDs, he found a narrow blue corridor. He passed through alone. The floor was slanted and everything was so, so quiet and he realised he had entered a secret realm between this world and another. Years passed before he emerged beside his mum at the stationery. Later, at home, he tested his powers: with his hands above his head, he stood still in the corner of the living room. His father walked past and did not see him, and Gareth only returned to the world when his mother called him for his dinner.

As the team run out for the second half, Gareth closes his eyes and transmits messages: come on, he tells them. We can do this. And it seems to work – Wales play well, but then Northern Ireland start to attack, and the fans begin muttering. And in the 60th minute, when Northern Ireland score, all the air is sucked out of the stadium.

I bloody knew it, his father says.

The crowd falls silent, except for the few hundred cheering green shirts in the corner.

His heart is a bashed-up football. Every time Wales get possession, it's just a matter of time until Northern Ireland take it back. With every Northern Ireland attack, he pictures them scoring.

This won't do. It just won't do. He tells himself to shape up, to focus, to really try his best. With his mind, he keeps pulling the ball towards the Northern Ireland end. He focuses and focuses, and he wishes and he wishes, and he summons all the magic in his body. But it's no use: on the clock, 70 minutes becomes 75 becomes 80. There's only ten minutes left. If Wales lose, he just knows that something terrible will happen. He breathes deep, and this is it: he focuses on the ball, he wills it, insists with all his power, and with one minute to go Simon Church is in the box, and Gareth screams GO ON! and Church touches the ball away from the defender, then tumbles – and with a sharp whistle, the referee awards a penalty.

Oh my God, Gareth says.

His father turns his back.

I can't look, he says.

Please, Gareth says to himself. Please, please, please.

Hands on hips, Simon Church tries to compose himself, and Gareth is back in the blue corridor, the timeless place between worlds, where it's quiet and still, and everything is at his command.

When Church runs up and whips the ball into the net, the stadium erupts and Gareth roars YES, and his father hugs him tight, his stubble bristling Gareth's cheek.

Then the referee blows for full-time, and the game ends one-all.

They stay behind to clap the players and the manager off the pitch. Gareth waves, but Chris Coleman doesn't see him.

Exiting the stadium, the night air feels raw on his face, and his legs are aching.

And now for the marathon back to the car, Gareth says.

Don't you start now, his father says. God, we were terrible tonight. If we play like that in the Euros we've got no hope.

Neither Gareth nor his father know this, but in four months' time, on a July afternoon, they'll come back to the stadium and cheer the Wales team on their return from the European Championships. For Gareth, it will have been a summer of dizzy days and holy nights watching Wales play football on the telly. He'll watch one game with his dad, one game with his mum, and he'll even watch a game with his friends in the hall at school. And when the repo man comes –

and takes the TV, and the bank repossesses the house, and Gareth and his mum move in with Aunty Avril – they'll watch the quarter -final in Avril's living room. Gareth will wear his lucky socks, reeling around the carpet every time Wales score. And when Wales are finally knocked out in the semi-finals, he'll collapse on the bed he shares with his mother and cry. Afterwards, when she comes in and strokes his head, he'll say to her: I'm not sad. I just feel proud.

But right now, they don't know any of this. The summer is way off. It is March, the start of spring, the air still chilled with winter. But the evenings are stretching, and the days are warming, and Gareth, you can feel the change already, can't you? That feeling is coming back, the belief that your life is forever on the cusp of magic. Walking with the crowd now, watching your father's breath curl white into the dark night as the flowing fans chant and sing for Wales, you know, somehow, that everything will be okay. It's a private feeling, fizzing like a sparkler inside your chest. Thinking about it makes you laugh.

What's so funny? your father says. Share the joke.

It's nothing, you say.

No, go on, your dad says, tell me.

Well, I've just got this feeling we're gonna do amazing at the Euros.

Your father blows out his cheeks.

Look, he says. I don't want to be a downer, but I've supported Wales a *long* time now. Honestly, it's better not to expect anything. They'll only let you down in the end. Actually, that's probably not a bad life lesson: you're better off not expecting much, or you'll only be disappointed.

At that, you stop and look him in the eye.

Yeah well, you say. Football is all about opinions and in my opinion you should just shut up.

Your father smiles, then laughs, and hand in hand, together you make your way back through the city, back the way you came, back in search of the car. ∎

KWEKU

Derek Owusu

I don't think my dad ever told the truth, but to himself, I know he never told a lie. He spoke in stories, never complete, one leading into another, pulling you from distraction, and if you tried to interrupt he would raise his hand and threaten to bring it down on your cheek. If you don't let me finish, he would say. Always a slow crawl to a conclusion, his tongue flailing, as if it was drowning. But I never saw him lay his hands on a soul. Well, except for me, but then I couldn't bear witness to that. I imagine his palm coming down, the movement an image overlaid on itself, each one a cause to flinch. My dad denies any violence, and when I bring it up he explains his character, and how this memory of mine contradicts who he is. But I have many memories of him, each one the backdrop to a changing man. He lived various lives, depending on who was with him in each moment, who was observing him. And in any one of those moments, I believe, he could have laid hands on me, or my mother even, transfiguring us, our relationships, into something else. It was a change that always felt possible, even without a soul ever being touched.

If I were spiritual, or endeared to myth, I might think my dad altered my memories of him, because I don't resent him. I want to understand him, his stance and gait, why an unrequited wave would hurt so much, why he slowly stepped in so many directions away from me. My dad could layer a narrative to a point that you'd begin to doubt reality, accept indifference at the effort required for recollection. It wasn't the possibility of future savagery that kept me at a distance, no, that wasn't what sealed the outlines of my emotional memory. It was the question: why? Why had he brought his hand down on a nature like mine? Without force or jest? I believe there were two reasons: one, he was an alcoholic, who liked to think all people would change but him; and two, I had tried to kill a tiny spider in front of him. The most far-reaching, strange and enduring lie my dad ever told was that he was Kweku Anansi. And that this was the reason nothing would ever kill him.

Most days my mother walked around a playground, still unused to being called 'Miss', singing the gospel songs of her childhood in a low tone. At home, she had to choose between the radiator and the radio cassette player, and so she'd sit, cold, waiting to recognise the melody of one of the songs that was the background of her girlhood. My grandmother cooked, a world unto herself, a matriarch rolling cassava and yam with ease, no fear for her fingers though she might not have pressed them together in a while, hungry children eclipsing church, humidity casting each face. And then here was my mother, waiting to be full, arched back aching and imprinted with the plastic carpet prickling into her skin, eyes closed and patient, knowing the Call of Christ would come to her again. Listening, touching every note, ready to push down the two buttons that would capture the remote faith bestowed by the voices of her village chapel. There were many repeated gospels, but when finally a song was hers, she could rest her eyes. She would climb into bed and try to sing the song from memory; my dad, asleep beside her, would often wake with a voice sleepy and supple as silk to gift her the words she struggled to remember.

I only have one photo of my dad. My mum is in the same one. I wish I had separate images. They're sitting opposite each other on a coach to Brighton. It's a church trip. In the left corner of the photo is the waist of another one of the devoted – slightly blurred due to movement. Loud, I've always said of this image. The other corner holds an elbow, a captured clap. When we looked together, my mum found it difficult to argue against my description of abstract clamour: both my mum and dad are holding cans of Foster's, smiling and saluting the camera, a moment of farewell and of triumph. The last drink, my mum said, before she gave her life to Christ. My dad claimed to remember that day, and would describe the singing as out of tune, clashing with the prayer. My mum says she has prayed every day since, only the more she prayed, the more he consumed.

To maintain a story, many will alter ideas and truths, motifs and threads. We contort our tongues and tailor our thoughts, rehearse our lines to reshape the world in the image of our narrative.

My dad did not walk out on us. First, he was called back to the US by a brother – something Black keeping him back, a brother with no fight left in him. And he needed an escape from, or to delay, the process of immigration – the spell of his language, his stories, was already beginning to surround our family. Then his path led him back to Ghana, where he was needed to watch over his sisters – one father dead, the other ailing – those siblings on the side of myth bound him to rivers and wind, rain and sea to keep the Ashanti alive. And when I went back, he told me, that's when you saw Ghana's economy and all such things were doing even better than Nigeria. It was all prosperity, now you see?

The week after my dad arrived back in our lives, the council granted my mum accommodation, and so I associated his return with no longer having to breathe the smoke of tenants and landlords. Instead I wondered at, and tried to imitate, the lengths of condensed air my dad would exhale on cold days.

It wasn't often that I had permission to play outside with my friends, but when I did, my dad would watch me from the front door for a few minutes before he went inside. I knew he was looking, but I was never able to tell when the front door finally closed. We would walk to the kerbside and sit down, picking up stones and dropping them through the gaps in the drain grating, seeing whose had landed with the loudest splash, or else we'd kick a ball around on the grassy roundabout. But there were rare days when we'd walk towards the sweet shops, and I would slow my pace, as if unsure what was happening, as if my thoughts were distracted from the dissolving desire of sugar. I looked back and saw my dad watching. He waved for me to come inside. In the living room, he put his hand deep into the side of the sofa and pulled out a pound coin. Then he walked over to his own chair and did the same, submerged to the wrist, coming up with another coin. Take it, he said. If you need money, just put your hand inside here or there and collect the coins. Don't forget you are my son, he said, and as I turned I saw him reach back into the sofa, or perhaps beside it, and pull out a can. The sound it gave up as he opened it was like a hiss into his presence. This was a trick that, when I remembered it, enabled me to match the expenses of my friends.

A story, like deceit, or myth, is never finished. Each retelling or recalling is embellished by what came before, adorned by what could come after, fortified within the present iteration. My dad did not think I was stupid. He was always waiting for me to come to him. Every 'innit?', the touching end of his disparaging claims, were a wave into his presence, a calling to his silk woven with tricks. Remember, he said, whens the worlds is too big, break it into small ones, put them small ones onto your mind and then put them back when you need to. Like this, listen, 'together'? You see, so you say, 'To . . . get . . . her.' You understand me? Ahah. See, like me, you can break any worlds. Just like that. Don't forget you're my son.

This is how I remember him. Struggling for verisimilitude.

On Tottenham High Road, my dad and I entered a shop. He turned, holding my arm, and I thought we were passing through a wall, so unassuming the place looked. But inside, the shop was adorned with what my mum called kente cloths, hanging like flags, their underneaths gently undulating like their sights were set on the sky for escape: black and gold, black and white, blue and gold, purple and red. Clashing hues, symbols touching. A woman sat at a sewing machine, her foot rising and falling out of time with the cacophony of colours. Eiii, bra Nancy, she said. Named, a satisfying lie will catch on. Oheme, he replied, as we walked towards the back room. My dad told me we were there to collect his money. We had been there before, I remembered. The table they sat at held Foster's and Super SKOL, waiting like an offering. That day there was a bottle of Castle Bridge too, and a game – a broken bough split in half, six depressions either side to hold the stones they carry. I felt part of it all, proud, inducted, watching drops of water on the bottles hang like crystalline stars, but still I turned away from the offering that smelled like gasoline. Hey hey, he's too small, mfa mano. Eiiii, he has come! Who has come? Bra Nancy! Whan? Obarina wei? Wɔ ferɛ, ana? Heh, Gyae saa, wo nkanfo no too much. Kojo, find space, let him sit. C'mon, my dad said, let me correct my money and go. Around the table were Uncle Dave, Uncle K, Uncle Charlie, Uncle Kojo, Uncle Sammy, Uncle Kwabena, Uncle Kofi, Uncle Tito, Uncle Ata one, Uncle Brobby and Uncle Wofaa. Uncle Dave and Uncle K sat opposite each other, heads down, watching the beads of the game. They looked up to greet and click with my dad – I saw so many hands reaching for him at the same time, and he satisfied them all. I had not become my dad yet, so the truth of my fingers, still young and soft, slid off my indexes and thumbs without a sound. My dad put me onto a stool in the corner, where I stood and stretched to see him over everyone's shoulders. I couldn't see much, so I gave up, closed my eyes and listened. Tried to pick up words I'd heard before, and draw new ones from their proximity to the ones I knew. The last time we came to the shop I had picked up the word koromfou. This was the day I'd learn its meaning.

When my dad replaced Uncle Dave at the table, immediately there were shouts in Ga, insults in Twi, capitulations in Fante, heard as if spoken from beneath the uneven legs of the table, as if the syllables struck the floor with their shifting weight. But the game demanded silence, and with a raised hand and closed fist, my dad held their voices, the passage of time marked by the drops of pebbles into grooves as the game progressed. Dad stood and the room turned, and I knew it was time to go. He was quiet, and we walked quickly. Outside, he removed a thread, or silk, from his coat, part of his transformation inside having followed him out. Before we got to our route, he stopped and asked me which I'd prefer: this chicken shop here, or Kentucky?

We're raised in what would be a body of lies to someone else, truths expressed in a language that sings false to those of a different church, a different culture. All meaning is myth. But we can be convinced that our falsehoods are universal lore. In that sense my dad did not drink too much. We never really saw him act drunk, because being drunk meant no life was left in him. I never saw anyone offer him coffee or water. The only thing we could do to sober him up was let him talk. The lost moments and hangovers that followed were not his but ours, because he walked into each new day without the words that had come before him. My mum gave in one night, she sat with him and drank, and laughed, took a path that seemed to lead to the sky. Awurade, what was she doing? He sipped as she gulped. This wasn't her. He leaned over, touched her, slid a hand from her chest to her shoulder, and said, No, me do wo, it's enough. She didn't blink. His hand sobering her, she got to her feet and left the living room, climbed into bed, pulled the cover over her head. Every now and then, to confront the heat, she'd move her cheek along the patches of sheet left damp by the tears she had cried.

My mum would leave tubs of Marmite on the glass side table by my dad's bed, beneath, not next to, the bottle of Castle Bridge he kept there in case he woke during the night. Sometimes there was a fingerprint denting the spread, sometimes there wasn't. They didn't share a bed. My mum allowed him a room to himself, though frequently we'd find him sleeping on the floor, curled up in corners of the kitchen or at the foot of his bed. I saw him being woken by the Underground staff on my way back from work one morning, the attendant trying to explain to him that he wasn't allowed to sleep on the seats along the platform. Helping him to his feet was the only time I ever touched him. Eventually he told us what the doctor had told him months before, that he was living with a fatty liver. He said this as if it were just something to pass on, wrapped it in a story of the disease being brought over, not of our culture, closing the facts in the grasp of his storytelling. He laughed as he spoke, his low cackle full of bass, a rising drum that was soon a roar, as if immortality was all he'd ever know, all we'd ever know. Yes, the fools of modern medicine could not touch the permanence of my father.

I did not visit my father when he was in hospital. But I felt he visited me a few times, managing to reach in and out of the life he was leaving. 'One body for another' is a phrase I remember from these night-time visitations, waking and looking out the window, mistaking multiple stars for the distance between our eyes, a distortion I wasn't used to, but a confusion he knew so well. I would stand and walk around my room, sip a glass of water to rouse myself, when his voice got too close. Touched by something like anxiety that left no real impression – no sore eyes, no tremors, nothing behind my chest. Was I waiting for air? I closed my eyes to listen for him one last time, and there was a sense of him fading, a tone being hushed by a lowering hand, and then silence.

My father drank himself to death.

I don't remember his face, nor him as a whole. Pieces here and there, features and parts, the edges of memories, fingerprints spoiling images too often held and raised to the light. The afternoon he died was the evening I had my first drink. What did he feel? What did this give him? My eyes kept searching, passing empty stools, holding the corners and shadows of the pub, probing for something to hold on to. I could close my eyes, feel the weight, but never dream. What once disgusted me now filled me with nostalgia, and I doubled up on the gasoline-tinged drinks that kept my father going. Or killed him. Between every drink there was the hope he would visit me again. That this time I would have the chance to speak, his story finally coming to an end, this time there would be enough space for me to say I was sorry. Sorry I smiled back at him sometimes, sorry I repeated his questions, sorry I nodded or raised my head, sorry I greeted him, sorry I let him believe I cared that he left.

It was evening, and I was too drunk to walk home. I waited for someone to pick me up. I had my head resting on the bar when he touched my shoulder and gently squeezed. Let's go, he said. I put my arms around his neck, he removed one arm and turned me to the side. The limp arm glided over the counter as we left, my fingers skimming empty seats, someone's head, a bald patch, a collar, the tiny bumps on someone else's neck, the back of another body. I seemed to touch them all at once. My partner held me straight and steady before he sat me in the car, looking down at me. I could taste the perfume coming off his chest. I told you I hate this one, I said. I lifted my head as many times as I could to hold his eyes, and each look with another fall adjusted the distance between us. He seemed to be looking at the side of my head, like he couldn't face me directly. This wasn't me. I'll be fine in the morning, I said. I wiped my mouth. 'I just need a bath.' 'I know,' he said, opening the car door.

I lay in the bath, lifting my hand up and out the water, submerging it again, up and out the water. There was always a tiny puddle left in my palm. Deep enough to drown a small spider.

I did not put my hand on you, he used to say. How could I do such a thing? ■

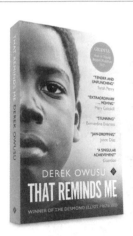

MRS S

K Patrick

Once again she wears a white shirt. This time hers, not his. I didn't know what to wear. In the end I pulled the crumpled shirt, his, from the bottom of my laundry basket. To smooth the creases I stood in the steam of the bathroom. The collar damp against my neck. She is too polite to say she recognises it. Are you excited? Yeh. Good, I think you'll like it. The car is small, old. Red paint rusted above the tyres' curves. A crack in the windscreen slowly growing larger. Inside it is spotless.

Her hand on the gearstick. No nail varnish, no bracelet. Earrings, gold studs. I notice a second hole, grown over. She touches her earlobe. Always on my lookout. Ah yes, from my younger days. When you were a painter? She laughs, avoids the question. Nothing is given away easily. She hands me a stout Ordnance Survey, a biro star, her biro star, drawn next to a particular square. OK, you need to read this, you're the co-pilot. Course, have you been before? Yes, but he drove us, Mr S drove. I let the air hang. Anyway it's there, you can see, where the river goes through the campsite. It is there, the thickened blue bend, a patch of criss-crossed green. I look again at her earlobe. She turns out of the driveway and onto the road. Goodness, what am I doing, the wrong way already. That sudden vulnerability. I want it to be me, to be my gaze, to be our gazes swapping in and out, one

209

replacing the other. She takes the car up to the sports field. A large car park sits behind. The Girls wander about, holding hockey sticks, gumshields plump behind their lips. She waves to a few. Screeches the tyres in a fast circle. She waves again in the rear-view mirror. They call after her.

You're so popular with them. Yes, only after a year of trying but never appearing to try. A minibus turns in beside us. The other team. She seems genuinely interested, craning her neck to see the uniforms, to guess the competing school. Did you want to stay and watch? No no. We drive away, past the pub, past the garage. I wind down the window. The tunnel whoosh. I lean out, my eyes watering, the hedgerow whipping close to my ear. We slow down at an enormous bridge. A long line of motorbikes is waiting to pull in. Ah, Devil's Bridge, have you seen? No. How have you missed so much? She indicates, following the motorbikes. There is no room for another car so she leaves the hazards on, blocking somebody else in. Quick, hurry, before we get in trouble. In the middle of the bridge, the river wide and slow beneath, she shows me two round imprints sunk into the wall. The devil's hands? The devil's hands. So tiny. Not if you have hooves. She presses her knuckles into the dents. Stone worn smooth. Is it lucky? Probably not, probably the opposite.

I see now she is wearing men's swimming shorts. A faded pink. Also guaranteed to be partly his, like the car, like the trip. What's wrong? Nothing. Always nothing with you. Her tone is unexpected. A closeness we have not yet shared. She senses it too, shifting subject, putting her hands against the sky. Such a glorious day! A van sells bright-white ice creams. Bikers in their heavy leathers lean against the bridge, licking their wrists, catching the melt. Cones are tossed half eaten into the rubbish. Wasps pearling in and out of the bin's mouth. Would you like one? Not yet, maybe later. I look too long at a group of young men, only in leather waistcoats, or shirtless entirely. Trouser buttons biting just below their belly buttons. Want a picture? Come on then take a picture pussy! one of the men calls to me. She is already by the car, lifting her head to see, unable to hear. Squinting through the glare she waves me over. I look back at the man who has already forgotten me, now shoving a friend with a similarly beautiful chest. His arms around his middle, then his ribs. Soft punches thrown into each shoulder. I feel the itch of skin beneath my binder. Inevitable. I notice things I want to steal.

I go back to her. How would he be, sitting in this passenger seat, watching her hand on a gearstick, watching her hands against the sky, watching her hands made into hooves. He would have a beautiful chest. He would be less astonished. Everything OK? Always. I change tune for her. She raises that eyebrow. Well then let's get going. I hope there aren't crowds like this everywhere. Don't you worry, this is a secret spot. She taps the page open across my lap, finger just wide of her biro star. Well then, I say, parroting her catchphrase, I won't tell. Oh I see, it's like that. Familiarity again. This time easier.

Sheep, fields, sheep. Slow pace of stone walls. Today the blue has heft, has a building heat. I didn't know you could have weather like this here, I didn't know. With one hand on the wheel she takes a pair of sunglasses from the door. Yes of course, honestly what do you think of us. Us. She never mentions a different home to this one. Wild flowers begin as we climb higher. The car struggles on the hill bends. Up, up, up. Tall weeds, but maybe not weeds, with starred white flowers. I am not concentrating on the map. Here! Ah, OK. She reverses down the narrow lane. A sign for the campsite appears. She pulls into a passing place. I'm sure this counts as parking. From the boot she hands me a bag. Lunch! She puts on a green backpack, worn, straps frayed. Without worry she jumps up onto the low wall, spinning over her legs, landing safely on the other side. I follow, slower, more careful with my skin, not wanting a scrape, or nick.

Each movement she makes is positive, whole. This is a body at peace. She thinks of nobody else. Are we trespassing? Only sort of. To our right a few tents have been set up. In the distance is a line of caravans and an office. I see the tall not-weeds with white flowers up close. Don't touch, don't touch those. Hogweed, it will burn. I worry now, walking even slower, the space between us lengthening. We drop along a bank, following another wall, moving through a spot where the stones have been displaced. Downhill she marches towards a thin wood. Her calves are arrows through the grass.

In the broken shade she puts things in her mouth and calls out their names. Lovage, water mint. More, there's more, but she's too far ahead for me to hear. I round a corner and find her bent over a patch of pink faces, petals uptight. She frowns. This, I can't remember what it's called. Like the roses, the information is recently learned. There have been other books, other garish covers. This is one way of belonging. I understand. She struggles, combing through the images she's stored, books stacked somewhere in that grand house. No, I can't remember, how disappointing. A plane rips overhead. Seconds later an apocalyptic boom sounds off the rocks. We are in the middle of a valley. As if a glacier had only just finished moving through. She places her hands over her ears. There's another one. Sure enough another dot appears, expanding. Not a plane but a jet. Something harder, faster. The military prefer these secret corners of English countryside. The sound is dragged behind. I don't bring my hands to my ears. She watches. How can you stand it? I don't know, I don't mind.

We come out of the trees and stagger further down. The slope is steeper now. A sound of water increases. She crouches, picks a clover and bites behind its head. She doesn't offer, or ask, me to do the same. Instead the flavour is announced. Sweet, something like honey. Wonderful! she confirms. Her personalities catch, like loose thread on a branch. The old-fashioned headmaster's wife and this person, setting her teeth to a stem's nape. Stood tall in her pink shorts.

Almost there. Scree is loose under my feet. Water appears. A clear river. Heather makes soft mounds. She whips through the bracken. Points to a distant fell and suggests climbing it, not today, but one day. I am hopeful. We drop down onto a track. There is nothing but the rhythm of our shoes on the dusty surface. Birdsong. Breath, focused in the heat. I want to ask her how she, how they, found this place, but the quiet is too lovely. Familiarity, a new familiarity, this time bodily. Little clutches of fabric. The swipe of our thighs.

This is it! At first I can't see anything, only slabs of grey stone. She moves towards a copse of only five or six trees. Slender, silver bark. Green leaves. I watch her first, standing at an edge, peering down, pleased. It needed to be as good as she remembered. Without waiting for me she removes her white shirt. Each button a piece of my own spine, undone. Her swimming costume is an athlete's. Black, streamlined. I am surprised by her strength. She adjusts the fit, a finger slid underneath the short straps, then the place where the suit meets her hips. Catches me watching her, I blush. She calls to me. My anxiety has its own heartbeat. Desperate for the cool across my sticky face. I wear a sleeveless T-shirt, the binder hidden underneath. Underpants, too, the T-shirt's hem past my hips, stopping mid-thigh. You'll go in wearing that? Yeh, no costume, didn't bring one with me, never thought it would be warm enough to swim. Little did you know. She accepts my lie. My costume balled up in my underwear drawer. I no longer know how to wear it. I reach her at the edge. She has waited for my reaction. Below is a large waterfall. A pool eroded beneath it. Bigger than I imagined, enough to spend time swimming to either side. Jewelled surface. A fish, brown trout she explains, is visible deep on the stony bed. It's beautiful. It is. She clambers down and dives. Muscle, water. Her back is a swimmer's back. All arch and grace.

For a moment I can't move. She doesn't hurry me. Treads water, calm. I grip the edge with my toes. Promise myself I'll jump at the count of five. But only manage on ten, hopping forward, I can't make the same shape as her. Rush of rock at my back. Relief of vanishing beneath the bright surface. T-shirt ballooning around me. I open my mouth to drink, to taste the cold. Reappear to her face a few feet from mine. She smiles. There you are. We haul up to the waterfall. A large, flat rock partially submerged, able to be clambered onto. Matching flex of our forearms, she admires my brawn, I pretend not to hear. We sit side by side underneath. She draws up her legs. The crease at her knee. Here she does not know, does not mind, what she gives away. Water hammering our heads, necks. Without warning she slips back in, completes a few lengths at speed. Front crawl. I float. If I could choose a different chest I would choose this water. If I could choose a different body I would choose this water. I say the last line aloud, river slipping on my tongue. What? She swims towards me. Slowly. Breaststroke now. What did you say? Nothing. But of course, nothing. She rolls her eyes. I roll mine back.

I'll buy us ice creams on the way home. Don't worry, your company is plenty. The line is well used, has been said to other people, she is sociable, she entertains. I want it for myself. It would be nice to be plenty. To be plenty the way she says it, the key change between the e and n. We eat. Olives, artichokes from the posh supermarket. She laughs when I call it that. Hummus, smoky crackers. Two kiwi fruit and two matching teaspoons. She pulls an artichoke heart from the jar and eats it whole. We swim again, rinsing the oil from the corners of our mouths, from our fingers. Afterwards we arrange our towels on the rocks and lie still. Birdsong. Insects, the river's full throat. A weightlessness arrives. I doze, waking up to her backpack zipping and unzipping. My God, the time. What? The time, it's past five. Her watch left in the front pocket. Is there a rush? She sits next to me, cramping the left side of her body into mine. It is the most we have ever touched. I feel it, I feel the moment she realises, a tightening of her torso. Too late to move away we are left in this encounter, unprepared. We inhale, we are drawn closer together. I try to control my breath.

After seconds, maybe ten, she stands and stretches. Now I'm all dried off I want to go back in. The temperature has not changed. If anything, a particular warmth now rises from the ground, the rocks. Even the trees radiate. Do it! No, no, really I should be getting back. He needs his dinner? It is an unfair thing for me to say. She is gracious, letting it go, sticking to the facts. Yes actually, we have people coming over. What people, I don't ask. I picture it instead. Him, her, a second him, a second her. Something sophisticated, fish, a whole fish. A whole fish and its special matching cutlery.

Here, come here, check me for ticks. Ticks? Yes, ticks! I approach her back. She reaches around an arm, her arm, sharp elbow skywards, and stretches her fingers, indicating an area to be investigated. There's nothing. I look closely. Are you sure? A few moles. Those shoulder blades previously in flight through the water. She raises both arms. Shoulder blades in flight again. And here? She twists side to side. I am surprised by the dark hair of her armpits. Her smell. Nothing, there's nothing. Good. The shirt is pulled back over her head. It is over. Now you. I turn, reluctantly. Her hands pause. May I? Yes. She uses her fingers, reaching inside my T-shirt without lifting it, feeling along the curves of my armpits, double-checking the moles. The touch is practical, careful. I know she will look at herself again in the mirror, after her shower, making sure I did not mistake a freckle, did not mistake a well-known moment of skin, and leave behind a determined nymph, those tiny legs, those tiny heads. She swaps a forefinger for a thumb, sweeping it down my sides. I didn't understand I was supposed to use my hands. Now there will never be a second chance. ∎

BEST LAST MINUTE SPA DEAL FOR UNDER £40

Yara Rodrigues Fowler

It's hot girl summer.

That's what Jess was saying. She was right: this morning she had showered at the house of a guy she met on the 333 bus the night before outside Elephant and Castle station. You! she had said, pointing to him as he appeared on the top deck of the 333. And they had gone back to his.

Jess, I have to go meet someone else. My friend Anita is taking me to a spa.

What station are you going to? I'll walk you there.

Don't you have to be anywhere?

Jess shrugs. Not right now. I'm just doing errands.

At the station, she says, Text me later, let me know you're okay.

I will.

I worry about you.

If you get there first go in without me, okay?

That was what Anita had said. So, when you get off the Tube at Latimer Road, you follow Anita's instructions. You walk out of the small station and down the street, past the off-licence where you and she had ended up one carnival when you were kids. You look at the yellow-and-purple shopfront. Ten years ago, you had waited outside this shop in the sound and heat, the street spilling people, while the boys from school had got their beers.

You look around yourself and the tower block is there. So much closer than you have seen it yet, since you had last seen it, since the fire. The large writing on the canvas is green on grey. You stand still and living children move past you on the street. A little Black girl with her hair in puffs wearing pink trainers goes by on a scooter. A small South Asian kid, running. Their mothers, walking slowly, hips almost touching, move past you. You take a breath.

The leisure centre building is large and next to a school. At the reception a woman with threaded eyebrows tells you to go upstairs. That's where the spa is, hon, she says. She hands you a white bathrobe and white slippers. As you walk up the stairs, you hear a basketball hit against a wall and echo. You walk past the sign that says GYM and the sign that says POOL. You press against the door with the sign that says SPA and then the door with the sign that says CHANGING ROOM.

The changing room is white like heaven in movies. No mirrors. It makes you think of the scene at the end of the seventh Harry Potter film. You stand between the rows of white benches and take off your trousers and your shirt and your underwear without going into a stall.

You get changed into the bikini you bought earlier with Jess. As you bought it you had said, I know – fast fashion – but I need a bikini for later and I forgot to bring one. And Jess had said, That's fine babe.

Your breasts don't sit in the bikini-cup scoop properly. They spread at the bottom. You touch your legs. You put on the spa robe and the spa slippers and lock your phone and bag away into a locker.

Anita's email had said that there would be an ice fountain, a hydrotherapy pool, a sauna, a steam room and a monsoon shower in the spa. You know what two of those things are. Hydrotherapy pool will mean jacuzzi, Anita had said. She booked you both head massages too. Two days ago Anita had messaged you: I'm booking us a spa, what can you afford? £40? you had texted back. This is the best last minute spa deal in London for under £40, Anita had replied, sending you a screenshot.

The main room of the spa is light but without windows. It smells like eucalyptus and lime and there is music playing, a piano without a tune or melody. You hang up your robe and sit in the sauna, the hot wood hurting your thighs. It's dark. There is a man in the sauna. He doesn't talk to you. You lie back.

Anita arrives. She is wearing a flowery bikini and the white spa bathrobe. She waves at you through the sauna door. You wave at her. I'm taking my glasses off! she mouths.

Anita steps into the sauna. How was your day?

It was good. I saw my friend Jess, you don't know her.

Anita nods.

She had just stayed the night with a man she met on the bus.

Anita opens her mouth. I love it.

Yes.

Great energy.

Yes.

Hot girl summer.

Yes.

Anita rubs her legs. All my dead skin is coming off.

Yes.

Anita says, How was your day?

Fine.

Yeah.

I'm too hot.

Me too. Should we get out?

Yes.

You walk out of the sauna into the main room. You walk in your spa bathrobe and spa slippers to the ice fountain. It has a silver funnel that spews small ice cubes, like a high-tech fridge, into a square metal sink.

Anita says, We rub these on our bodies.

You take off your spa robe and rub the ice cubes on your legs, bellies, collars, breasts and arms, shoulders and back. The ice cubes melt.

It's not even that cold.

Anita shakes her head.

Monsoon shower?

Yes.

Next to the ice fountain is a cuboid shower nook in the wall. You stand together in the cuboid shower nook in the wall. It has dark tiles and three buttons: Caribbean Mist, Monsoon Shower and Tropical Storm.

Look at these names.

Anita laughs, Caribbean Mist?

Yes.

The shower cuboid fills with a veil of misted water. The mist is very cold and tastes like orange. After twenty seconds the lights turn off and water begins to fall in two heavy streams. You put your fingers on the top of your head, on your wet hair. You close your eyes. The water stops.

You and Anita sit in the steam room. Small filtered ceiling lights turn the white plastic walls and white steam to green. White plastic seats come out of the walls like urinals, facing the middle of the room.

Anita says, This is like a spaceship.

Yeah.

Reminds me of those fairground rides, you know the ones where they strap in you before lifting you up and spinning you around.

Yes.

The lights turn from green to yellow. No one else is in the steam room. You breathe in a breath of steam. It wets your throat and makes it hot.

Anita says, Only a leisure centre in Kensington would have a spa.

I know right.

Kensington Leisure Centre.

Yes.

Leisure centres must have been a GLA thing.

Yeah they must have been.

So much better than the fancy new gyms with mirrors and scales.

Yes.

Like the one we went to for that spin class. You know near Bank or maybe Shoreditch?

Yes. So individualist.

Yes.

No adult swimming lessons or kids playing badminton.

Exactly! Whereas – Anita gestures – there's something utopian about leisure centres, don't you think?

Yes!

Every community should have a place where kids can play badminton and their mums can drink cucumber water.

Yes!

Yes.

Did you see the Grenfell stuff on the way here?

No – I got an Uber because I was late.

The tower is right here.

Fuck.

Yeah.

Anita closes her eyes. She opens her mouth.

The lights change to the colour blue. Let's get in the hydrotherapy pool.

I think it's just a jacuzzi.

Yes.

You stand up. The hydrotherapy pool has a diameter of about 1.5 metres. There is a man inside it. You climb into the other side from him. The pool bubbles.

Oh it's cold.

Cold.

I like it though.

Yeah I like it.

The man turns his back to you, leaning against the edges of the hydrotherapy pool.

Anita says, How has your week been?
Quite bad.
You float your feet in the rising water.
Anita says, Did you hurt yourself?
No.
And the suicidal thoughts?
They've come.
I'm sorry.
Yeah.
Are you keeping safe?
What do you mean?
You're not making plans?
This week?
Yeah.
No.
You float your feet in the rising water.
Anita says, I'm glad you called me last time.
Yeah.
You can call me any time, you know? No big deal.
I know.
You float your feet in the rising water.
How was your week?
You float your feet in the rising water.
Good.
What happened?
I found a new job.
That's great. Where?
A union.
You know, in theory, a union could be a really exciting place to be right now.
Exactly.
You close your eyes.
I like this temperature actually.
Yes.

The cold pool water moves and somebody says – Anita?

You turn your body.

Two women wearing grey spa uniforms call for Anita from the door of the room where the hydrotherapy pool is. The head massages will happen in another part of the spa. The women both have light brown skin. They ask you and Anita to follow them. All four of you are about the same age. One of the women in the grey spa uniforms has a British accent, the other doesn't. The one with the British accent takes Anita into a room on the left.

You follow the woman who doesn't have a British accent through a white corridor into a room with a glass wall. She pulls a purple curtain with several layers across the glass wall: one thick layer to block out the city and the light, another made of tulle. The room smells like rose, jasmine and tamarind. There is a massage table in the middle, made with thick towels and sheets like a bed. The woman who doesn't have a British accent speaks to you. She says, You can get into the bed. I will give you a minute and come back.

You don't know whether this means you should remove your bikini. You don't remove your bikini. You sit on the bed. You push your feet under the cover, which is tight and has been tucked under the sides of the table. You push your legs underneath it. You extend your body flat under the cover until your feet emerge on the other side. The cover is tight and heavy over your chest. It is like a good bed. You do not know whether to remove your bikini.

She re-enters the room. She says, touching you for the first time, Can you lower these?

Should I take the top off?

No, that's fine, just lower the straps.

Okay.

The woman's accent reminds you of your mother's.

What's your name?

I am Eliane.

Eliane.

Eliane says, You can close your eyes.

The massage begins. There is music playing. It has piano-key sounds but no tune or melody. It sounds almost like the theme from a film but then it isn't. Eliane has some oil on her hands that smells like jasmine. She touches your feet, pressing them. She pulls your arms from under the cover and touches your hands, pressing them. She makes your hands damp with the oil that smells like jasmine.

In the dark Eliane presses with her fingers into your collarbone, the breast fat and skin below it. The oil has some kind of scrub in it. She presses with two fingers into your shoulder. She turns your face to one side and touches and presses into your eyebrows, your neck, your cheek, your nose. She turns your face to the other side and touches and presses into your eyebrows, your neck, your cheek, your nose. She puts her thumb on your chin. She pulls rose-smelling shampoo through your hair. She pulls shea butter through your hair. The room is dark with the smell of roses and tamarind and piano sounds. The cover is tight over your body.

Eliane steps back.

She rings a tiny cymbal over your body.

She says, The experience is finished now.

Thank you. I feel very relaxed.

I am happy for you, Eliane says.

When you see her Anita's hair is thick with butter. She is in her spa robe and slippers. You wash off in the monsoon shower, Tropical Storm. A man and a woman are kissing in the hydrotherapy pool.

I wonder if this is a first or second date, Anita says. Or if they do this all the time.

Leaving Kensington Leisure Centre, in your outside clothes again, you hear the sound of a basketball hitting the court wall; you hear the basketball echo. Living children walk past holding badminton rackets.

Thanks Anita, you say.

Anita says, Which Tube are you going to? I'll walk you there. ∎

CRΛFTS

Discover the new era of *Crafts*

Join us as we shape the future of making
Sign-up to receive our new-look magazine, access exclusive digital editorial and attend crafts-led live events.

Become a member today
craftsmagazine.org
@craftsmagazine

PHOTO: JULIAN WATTS CARVING MAPLE
WOOD FOR UNTITLED, 2021

 Crafts Council

 Supported using public funding by
**ARTS COUNCIL
ENGLAND**

GUNK

Saba Sams

The first time Leon cheated on me, we'd been married eight months. His affair was with a woman I knew. Long before, we'd gone to school together. We'd been friends. *Small world, huh?* read her Facebook message. Her name was Megan Blake, and she'd joined my primary school in Year Five. At nine years old, she'd already worn kitten heels as school shoes and had a mini tube of lip gloss attached to her key ring. I didn't even own house keys.

Megan Blake had such bad nits that sometimes, when I looked closely, I could see her hair crawling. Her father was dead, her mother an alcoholic. I'd been a meek child: pasty and slow, with parents who still cut the crusts off my sandwiches. Megan picked me out seemingly at random and decided we were best friends. She spent break time chewing Juicy Fruit gum and calling out to pedestrians through the playground railings. Whenever a dog walked by, she'd stick her arm through the iron bars and pet it. She talked to adults like she was an adult herself. Still in the slammer, she'd say.

The adults would laugh nervously, then pull their dog's lead and hurry away. You fancy smuggling us in a KitKat? she'd shout after. There's a newsagent on the corner.

My mother said that Megan was outrageous. She'd come over after school and eat the entire contents of our fridge. When my mother called Megan's mother to come and collect her, she'd get no answer, and Megan would end up staying for entire weekends. We'd cut all the hair off my Barbies and draw biro tattoos on their arms.

At night Megan and I would lie in my single bed, straddling and kissing each other with open mouths. I was always the boyfriend, Megan the girlfriend. She'd give me tips on how to use my tongue, and I'd follow her advice religiously. She refused to brush her teeth before bed, so her mouth always tasted of Juicy Fruit. She lost a tooth in the playground once, and there was a big grey hole in it.

After Megan and I stopped being friends, I sent her a bath bomb in the post and never got a reply. Nothing dramatic had happened between us. We just ended up in different secondary schools, where Megan met new people and drifted away. By the time we were reunited at sixth form, she had white highlights striping her dark hair and a diamanté piercing in her upper lip. She didn't recognise me in the corridor, and I had to give my full name to remind her.

Fuck me, she said. Fran, it's been ages.

I nodded. I guess it has.

After that we didn't have anything left to talk about. I wanted to ask her if she remembered the punk Barbies, the ice pops we stole from the newsagent. I wanted to ask her if she remembered the kissing. Instead we were silent for a minute, and then Megan's eyes slid from mine and looked off down the corridor.

Well, she said. If you ever need a fake ID, you know where to come.

She gave me a little nod, that same wisdom in her eyes that she'd always had. I felt breathless. Yeah, I said. Definitely.

The next time I saw Megan was in the cafeteria, when I stopped her to say that I'd received some money for my birthday and would like to buy an ID, and after that in the car park, where she sold it to me. Both times I found myself incapable of coming up with anything entertaining or meaningful to say to her. It was like trying to make conversation with a crush. I don't know if I did fancy Megan, or if I fancied the person I was sure I could have evolved into if I'd stayed friends with her.

After I gave her the money, she told me about a club night that was happening that weekend. It's garage, she said.

I like garage, I lied.

She smirked. See you there then.

Megan probably knew that I had no idea what garage was, other than the place my father liked to disappear to on the weekends. Maybe she gave that tip to everyone she sold an ID to, as customer service. Still, I took the information as a direct invite. I spent hours getting ready. I wore a halterneck top, my hair scraped back with gel. I sprayed myself with air freshener, since I owned no perfume. Before I left, I announced to my parents that I was going clubbing with Megan Blake, my best friend from primary school.

Oh Lord, my mother said, shaking her head. That girl was always trouble.

When I got to the club I couldn't see Megan out front. I stood in the queue, running my fingers over the curved corners of the ID in my pocket. Every few seconds, I spun my head around and scanned the line for Megan.

What's your star sign? the bouncer said, once I got to the front.

It was over before it had even begun. I'd memorised the name on my fake ID as well as the birthday, but the star sign was a detail that hadn't crossed my mind. I walked up into town and called my father for a lift home. I went to the chip shop to meet him. I sat on a red metal chair in the shop window with the taxi drivers, my face warming over the vinegar steam, and waited.

Fifteen years passed before I heard from Megan Blake again. In that time I went to university, I taught English in three different secondary schools, I moved out of my parents' house and then I moved back in again. I had a string of uninspiring boyfriends, I saved some money which I hoped to put towards buying a house, then finally I met Leon and I married him. I thought of Megan Blake only fleetingly. The first time I kissed Leon, I remembered her advice – to flick the tongue like a snake, but slowly – and I utilised it.

A year or so later, after Leon and I were married, I thought I saw Megan from the top deck of the bus, pushing a buggy down the street. A year after that, when she added me on Facebook, I realised that it couldn't have been her with the buggy, as there were no photographs of kids on her profile. No one could resist posting their offspring on social media. People wore their children like a badge.

Megan's friend request gave me a little pulse of exhilaration. I was standing in Sainsbury's, and I scrolled her profile with curiosity. Her message came in a few minutes after I accepted the request. I was still standing around in the cereal aisle. Initially I thought Megan Blake would be reaching out, wanting to see me. The idea was flattering. I wondered if she'd seen that I was married now, that my husband and I were behind one of the most popular student clubs in the city. Recently, there'd been a write-up in the university paper, with a photograph of Leon and me looking pensive behind the bar. Sometimes we put on garage nights. The students, who'd been born just shy of the millennium, loved a nineties throwback. How the tables have turned, I thought. Then I opened the damn thing.

I'm sorry, Fran. If I'd known it was you he was married to, I would have called it off months ago. Small world, huh?

Megan Blake was online. She and I had a bit of back and forth. All the time, my heart was spasming in the base of my throat. She told me she'd met Leon two months before, that she'd known he was married but she hadn't known to who. A week ago, when she found out his wife was me, she'd updated him on the fact we were childhood friends, and he'd promised to come clean. The next day he'd told Megan, not expecting her to get in touch with me herself, that he'd confessed the affair to me. He'd also told her he was in love with her, later that night, after he'd taken some MDMA. I didn't think that counted. Still, I was angry. I got hot under my coat. I took it off and threw it in my shopping trolley. After that I bought some Weetabix, seizing the box from the shelf and slamming it down at the tills.

I didn't buy anything else. I couldn't think, by then, about what we did or didn't have in the cupboards. I even forgot that we were out of milk, so the next day I ate the cereal with water. It was gross, but that grossness was fitting. I was feeling sorry for myself. After I'd got back from Sainsbury's, I'd called Leon a cunt and a fuckhead. I'd picked up the beer bottle he was drinking from and thrown it right at his face. It had nicked the top of his cheek, the highest part of the bone, and a slow trickle of blood had moved down his jaw. He'd freaked out and gone to A & E, where the paramedics had essentially called him a pussy and sent him away with no stitches.

Back at the flat he'd begged my forgiveness, the blood oxidised now on his knuckles, and I'd told him to go fuck himself. The next day he'd begged my forgiveness again, after I'd finished the Weetabix, and I'd said OK. I liked my life with Leon: the club and the flat and the whir of the city. There was no excuse, other than that.

After I agreed to forgive him, he came over and put his palms on my cheeks. He gave me a kiss on the forehead. I was still sitting over the empty bowl. Fran, he said, I love you like a love song.

I thought I recognised that line, so later I looked it up. It was a lyric from a Selena Gomez song that had come out that same year. It was all over the radio.

The second time Leon cheated on me, eleven months had passed since the Megan Blake episode. This time, it was with a girl we'd hired for the club. She was twenty-one years old and studying History of Art. Her name was Aaliyah, blue hair washed out to the colour of sea foam. This time, I'd seen it coming. There'd been a few nights when Leon had failed to come home after work, claiming he'd fallen asleep in one of the leather booths in the club. Aaliyah had a lighter with Betty Boop on it, and always refused to look me in the eye.

Her housemate had messaged me on Instagram and asked to meet in a Starbucks around the corner from the club. All the younger people had moved over to that platform by then, after Facebook. At that time,

I didn't know why she'd chosen to track me down and tell me. Maybe her father had cheated on her mother, and the betrayal had defined her whole childhood. I figured it was something like that.

For fuck's sake, I said, in Starbucks.

The friend pulled a miniature of whisky from her coat pocket, added a glug to my hot chocolate. You can do better, she said.

Later, when I confronted Leon about his affair, he tried very hard to lie. Aaliyah? he said. I don't know an Aaliyah.

Yes you do, Leon. Even I know Aaliyah. She works in the club.

Oh, her? I thought her name was Alicia or something, I don't know. Yeah, OK. We might have kissed once or twice.

Some days later, I found out he wasn't sleeping with only Aaliyah, but also with her housemate, the same girl I'd met up with in Starbucks. Aaliyah showed up at the club one night, having just found out herself, and swung a punch at Leon in the smoking area. She had a strong arm. I was impressed. His nose bled all over his jeans, and when he looked up there were tears on his cheeks. I felt a sense of justice at that. Afterwards I went over to Aaliyah carrying two shots of tequila, one for her and one for myself. We clinked the tiny plastic glasses before knocking them back. The bouncers looked over and cheered.

When I got back to our flat in the early hours of the morning, just off from my shift, Leon was still awake and seething. She ruined my fucking jeans, he said.

I didn't tell him the trick I knew about cold water. I'd bled through more of my clothes than he could even imagine. Still, Leon always felt the world was out to get him.

Shame, I said, my voice filled with irony.

Oh Jesus. You hate me too, is that it?

Yes, Leon. I never want to see your goblin face again. I'm leaving you.

I did as I'd promised, and moved back in with my parents in the suburbs. I'd been living with them when I first met Leon two and a

half years before, trying to save some money to buy a house. Now I'd
invested all that money into Leon's nightclub, and my marriage was in
scraps. I wasn't sad so much as embarrassed. I didn't want to tell my
parents about Leon's affairs, so instead I told them we were having the
kitchen redone in the flat. I don't know if they believed me, but they
played along all the same. My mother kept suggesting colour schemes.

For six weeks, I spent the evenings sitting inside with my parents.
We ate my mother's potato-heavy dishes before retiring to the living
room, where my father would flick on David Attenborough and
sigh at the beauty of places so far off they might have been another
planet. My parents had never left the country, had not once
been on a plane.

Some nights I offered to cook dinner and was declined. Other
nights I popped one of my mother's diazepam, drank a glass of red
wine, and fell into a cramped, lucid sleep. Repeatedly I dreamed of
my teeth going soft enough that I could pull them out, like kernels
of boiled corn.

Some weeks later, when I told Dana of those dreams, she nodded
knowingly. Fear of ageing, she said. Fear of life passing you by.

Dana was the woman we employed in the nightclub to scrub
the toilets. She was easily seventy, with a thick Scottish accent and
black-grey hair that she wore in a fishtail plait. She ringed her eyes
with turquoise liner, and she could read tarot. She was always laying
out cards on the bar, trying to tell me my future.

He'll fall for one of these lassies, she said to me once. It's only a
matter of time.

Tell me something I don't know, I'd replied.

I'd returned to my marriage. Of course I had.

The day I arrived back, I breezed into the flat with my suitcase
and announced that from then on our marriage would be open.
Who knew: maybe he'd fall for someone else and run off with them,
leaving the flat and the club to me alone. What a triumph that would
be. A clean sweep.

Initially, Leon was baffled by my suggestion. But we can't,
he said. I'd be jealous.

I'd laughed, before I realised he was serious. He was on the sofa,
playing on the Game Boy he'd had since he was a kid. His stubble
had grown to an unattractive fuzz, and there was a tube of Pringles
upended on the floor. A couple of the crisps had been crushed into
the carpet. I'd been away six weeks, and the flat was a hellhole.
The whole place smelled like bins.

It stinks in here, I said.

I've been a wreck without you.

You're always a wreck, Leon.

From then on I went about my days like a street dog. I looked
out only for myself. I did my own laundry and if even a sock of
Leon's worked its way into the machine, I'd toss it out the window
when I was hanging my things out to dry. He and I kept separate
shelves in the fridge: mine full of salad vegetables and Tupperware-d
soups, his a bunch of scraped-out, mouldy jars and a single, rolling
lager.

At the club, word of our open marriage spread fast. Carlos, one
of the bouncers, invited me out for a drink. I agreed to go. We sat in
a dark bar and drank tequila sunrises with dinky umbrellas in them.
Carlos was a big man, and seeing him with that drink was comical.
Afterwards he tried to kiss me, and I was so surprised I accidentally
burned him with the end of my cigarette.

I went home after that, but I did fuck Carlos maybe two weeks
later, one afternoon when Leon was out. The burn on his hand had
healed, the skin baby pink as a carnation. The sex was fumbly and
awkward. Carlos didn't have Leon's confidence, and I didn't either.
I remember that the condom split, and the next one had dried up
inside the packet. He must have been using some shitty brand. In
the end neither of us could reach orgasm, and I just gave up and
asked him to leave. The next day when I saw him at work, he was
the same old Carlos, standing at the entrance with his security badge

blinking in the light of passing traffic. He gave me his signature nod when I arrived, stepped aside to let me in.

I went to the bar and dried a few glasses with a dishcloth. I checked there was a sufficient amount of change in the till. I did the lion's share of the work at the club: I'd spend all day on my phone or laptop approaching DJs, advertising events, looking after our accounts. Mostly we hired students, since we could get away with paying them low wages. We'd offer them free entry to any nights they wanted, so they felt like they were getting a good deal. The students' youth meant they were attractive, which meant they sold a lot of drinks. Hiring attractive people was a point that Leon and I agreed upon. The downside of the students was that they were flaky. They were always returning to their parents' houses for the holidays, or else calling in sick because they were hungover. This meant I worked the bar a lot. Leon almost never helped me out. I guess he thought it was bad for his reputation to be seen cracking the lids off beer bottles.

For the first two hours of that particular night, I barely saw Leon. He was in the smoking area the whole time. When I finally went out there for a smoke myself, I caught him offering a bump of coke to some student he fancied. I heard him tell her he could hire her at the club whenever she needed the money, that if there wasn't a role going he'd make one. Leon was always trying to give work to girls he liked. It was his way of keeping them around.

Thanks, she'd said. But I've got to focus on my studies.

After you graduate then, said Leon. He tapped the side of his head with a finger. He was so high he looked crazed. It wasn't yet midnight. You've got to get thinking about your future, he said.

I want to be a lawyer, replied the girl.

I looked hard at her, trying to ascertain if she and my husband had any kind of a future. Probably, her mummy and daddy were loaded. It was hilarious to me, how much the rich kids loved our grotty little venue. I knew that girl's sort; the university brought more and more of them to the city. I was always overhearing students talk left-wing politics in the smoking area, only to find out months later that their fathers were Tory MPs. I loved getting gossip on the students, listening in on their drunken conversations. Over their three years of university, I'd watch them transform. I noticed when they got their braces off, when they coupled up for the first time. Sometimes they'd celebrate their birthdays in the club, wearing a tiara made of plastic candles or a sash that read *21 and hot, buy me a shot!* Of course I was no one to them but the lady who worked the bar.

Now, Leon was telling the girl who wanted to be a lawyer about the hole in his heart that had nearly killed him as a four-month-old baby. He spoke with such feeling it was as if he could actually remember the surgery. Leon always told that same story when he took cocaine. In the smoking area, I watched the girl's eyes well up. She appeared genuinely moved. Her hand hovered over her own heart, as if to protect it. I had to admit it was impressive, the hold Leon could have over people. I decided the girl was ultimately too smart for Leon, too driven to stick around.

Hubby, I called over. You're up.

He sucked down the last of his cigarette, then threw the butt on the ground. Duty calls, he said to the girl, before sloping into the club.

I stood in the cold and breathed for a while. I could see Carlos through the railings of the smoking area, standing at the entrance with his eyes on the traffic, his breath white and solid around his big, meaty face. I wondered how my life would have been if I'd married a man like that. When I first met Leon I'd been tragically bored, so desperate for something to happen to me that I'd thrown all caution to the wind. Now, I was done with happenings.

That night Leon spilled a two-litre bottle of lemonade behind the bar and didn't bother cleaning it up, so that for the rest of the shift the soles of my shoes kept sticking to the rubber floor. He went off gallivanting again, and I didn't bother calling him back. It was easier just to get on with the work alone.

After close, I realised Leon had left the club completely. I scanned the crowd of kids on their way out for the girl who wanted to be a lawyer. I couldn't see her. Back at the flat, I slept alone.

L eon wasn't a straightforwardly handsome man, but he had a certain presence. The hole in his heart had stunted his growth, so he was just under five foot six and sinewy. When he lay naked in our bedroom, little more than a mattress on the floor, his hip bones stuck up out his skin like the fins of a shark. His soft, wide-set mouth was undeniably beautiful. That mouth was more than he deserved.

Once our marriage opened, there was a new girl every two or three months. I got familiar with the process. Leon was always in a better mood when there was someone else on the scene. He'd do the food shop, get up early in the morning and make Eggs Benny. Even the eggs got a nickname when Leon was in a good mood. Our flat would start to smell like coffee grounds. I always gained a little weight when he was in love with someone else. He fed me up not because he was sorry, but because he liked to cook when he was happy, and I was there to eat.

There'd be six weeks or so of the cooked breakfasts, the sneaking around, and then Leon's affair would be over. I could tell when that happened too. His mood would crash immediately. It was always the girls who ended it. Either they'd cotton on to the fact that Leon was a loser, or else they'd move over to someone half his age. Most of the time, it was both.

The flat became an oppressive place when Leon was low. After he'd been dumped, he'd flinch every time I turned a light on. He'd barely leave our bed. I'd never known anyone who could sleep like that. He'd do a fifteen-, sixteen-hour stretch, then get up for a few hours and do it over. I once told him he was sleeping his life away; he told me it was a gift.

Soon enough Leon would get over whoever it was, emerge revived, and stalk straight down to the club for someone new. Leon wouldn't have been able to pick up girls anywhere else, or at least not with the same frequency. That place gave him credibility, and he knew that better than anyone. He couldn't resist the status it gave him, to be someone's boss as well as her lover.

I was civil to all his girls. It was hard not to engage in small talk, given we all worked in the same club. There was a single occasion when I spoke my mind. I was drunk, and I got it into my head that I was lecturing my younger self. I told Leon's latest squeeze that he was a narcissist and a misogynist, that he'd been babied all his life by his doting mother and much of his adult life by me, so now he was spoiled and acting out. He's capable only of receiving, I remember I said. He won't give you a thing. Listen, honey. I never wanted children, and then I married one.

I was proud of that line, in the moment. I was proud of all those lines. They came out of me fast, in a rush of air, and afterwards I felt lithe and easy, as if I'd been bloated for a long time. The girl only frowned. God, she said. That's fucking depressing.

Her pity washed over me, and I bristled. Of course I'd made a fool of myself, when I'd intended to make a fool of Leon. That man was so jammy, I swear.

The club was officially named Gunk, though mostly we just called it The Club, as if there weren't almost one hundred others across the city. The venue was an old mansion with all the internal walls smashed through. The floors were gummy with tar-like dirt, and there was a row of graffitied Portaloos in the smoking area. Two of the huge ground-floor windows had been smashed through and boarded over with cardboard, so in the winter the whole place was freezing. Inside students bobbed in their puffer jackets, undulating from the centre of the dance floor to the edges like penguins. Sometimes stray cats slipped in through the hole in the fence, and I'd find them curled up against the generator, trying to keep warm.

The first occasion I set foot in the club, I was on a hen do. That was the night I met Leon. I was thirty-three, he was thirty-four. Christine, the music teacher in the school where I worked, was getting married. She was cooler than me, always playing drum and bass to the kids. I'd been flattered to be invited, until I got to the club and found that practically everyone there knew Christine. She must have invited over one hundred people. The entire smoking area was talking about her.

Inside, Christine was snogging another woman on the dance floor. Christine's fiancé, who I'd never met, offered me some shrooms from a blue plastic bag, and when I asked him what they were for he looked embarrassed and folded them back into the pocket of his jeans.

You must be Fran, he said. Fran from work?

I guess people saw me as a square back then, which isn't so far off what I was.

Christine's hen do was one of the few nights I ever saw at the club at which most of the punters were over the age of twenty-five. I remember the maid of honour telling me that she'd chosen the venue because they all used to go there as students. In fact it was the place where Christine and her fiancé had first exchanged numbers. The mood was relatively calm that night, far less raucous than I became accustomed to later. I think if it had been a usual event at the club, I wouldn't have lasted five minutes. As well as that, Leon would've had a younger crowd to flirt with, and most likely would never have gotten around to me.

As it was, he and I got chatting in the smoking area. Leon was smoking hash, and he gave me a little. I knew better than to ask him what it was, after the incident with Christine's fiancé. I just put my mouth on the end as he lit it for me, let the smoke fill my lungs. Afterwards my eyes began to water, and I found it very hard not to cough. Leon noticed this and smirked. He was wearing a T-shirt with a squiggly graphic that rippled against his skinny frame, and there was a fine ring of white dust around his left nostril. I asked him what he did for a living, once the tickle in my throat had passed. I couldn't think of anything cooler to say.

I run this club, he said. This place is mine.

I narrowed my eyes at him. I don't believe you, I said.

He took me inside and told the person behind the bar to make

me a drink. There was a queue, but we pushed in front. What you
having, then? said the student.

Leon ordered a Jägerbomb. I'll have the same, I said.

Yup, said the student. They didn't ask for any money.

The Jägerbomb tasted like cough syrup. Immediately afterwards
I was drunk. I'd read somewhere that Jägerbombs could kill you;
apparently the alcohol slowed your heart while the energy drink
sped it up, until your body got so confused it just gave out. I told
Leon this, right after he'd knocked his back. He put his fist to his
chest and spread his fingers wide, to demonstrate an explosion.
Ouch, he said.

I started laughing and found I couldn't stop. He leaned in and
kissed me. I wasn't expecting that. Hiccups of laughter kept coming
up from the bottom of my throat into his mouth. I was worried he
thought that they were burps. Eventually I calmed down and the
kissing got better. His mouth tasted sweet and hot, with an edge of
something rancid.

How's your heart? he said afterwards. That would have been
cheesy from anyone else, but Leon had a way of pulling things off.
He told me the story about the hole in his heart, and of course I
lapped it up.

I followed him onto the dance floor and he put his hands on
my hips as if he'd known me for at least an hour. I turned around
so I was facing away from him and started grinding on his crotch.
I don't know where that move came from, somewhere very deep
within me.

The hash and the Jägermeister had a great effect on me; I could
feel a tingling in the backs of my eyelids, and every time I closed
them I saw millions of pink sparks. After a while we went back to
the bar. He got me a tequila shot, which again he didn't pay for.
The lime wedge was dull at its edges and had obviously been cut
long ago. When he invited me up to his flat, I nodded so vigorously
I thought I might have pulled a muscle in my neck. He burrowed
his face into my hair and clamped his teeth down on my earlobe.

He was a little shorter than me, and I could feel him straining to get it.

L eon and I held hands while we walked. His flat was in a tower block just five minutes away. I'd grown up in the suburbs, where every night was pitch black and empty, the only sound the occasional hooting of an owl. In the city, the difference between night and day could be almost imperceptible: still cars cruised the roads, pedestrians walked the pavements. At night the dim, muggy light came from street lamps, rather than a smogged-over sun.

The sex was first-rate. Leon knelt between my legs and circled his tongue on my clit until the orgasm rose within me like a flare. I wrote my number down for him on a Rizla. His phone was dead. I realised I hadn't told him my name. It's Fran, I said.

Leon called me the day after. I was stunned. For our first date, we went to the cinema. He bought a six-pack of beers en route and hid the cans inside the pockets of my puffer, as well as two in the hood. At the pick 'n' mix stand, Leon shoved far more scoops of gummy peaches into a paper bag than we could reasonably eat in the time it took to watch a film.

It's all about the peaches, he said. These other ones are pointless.

I peered at the little plastic troughs. What about Jazzles?

Leon stuck a scoop in. You're right, he said. Jazzles have style.

Little compliments like that could bowl me over, coming from him. I'd have to bite my lip to stop myself from smiling.

Once we were in the screening, I don't think Leon ate a single sweet. He passed out and missed the first half of the film, snoring loudly. When he finally woke up, he was horny. He kept nibbling my neck and running his hands across my breasts. In the end we went into the disabled toilets to have sex. I couldn't get wet at first – it was cold in there and it smelt like bleach – but I got into it eventually. The handrails made for good places to hold on to.

Afterwards we stood around naked and sucked down a couple of the beers. I felt exhilarated, and the alcohol went straight to my head. Eventually someone knocked, and we pulled our clothes on and opened the door to find a boy of nine or ten in a wheelchair and a middle-aged woman wearing a lanyard. We walked sheepishly out into the brightly lit hallway, and she looked at us with disgust. I still had the sweets in a paper bag, and I placed it on the disabled boy's lap, out of guilt.

Leon kissed me hard outside the cinema, his hand cupping the back of my neck, as the passing traffic scanned its lights over us. I think I might love you, he said.

He was laughing, like it was a joke. I thought it probably was a joke, since we'd only just met. Still I let it hang in the air between us, warming me up. It was winter then, there was black ice on the roads.

Of course it had been Leon's idea to get married. By that point we'd been a couple for just under six months, living together for three. That's how Leon was: everything was *now* with him. Later I saw that was selfish, but in the beginning I found it refreshing. Before Leon, my life had been overpopulated with people whose main focus was being responsible.

He was drunk when he asked me, leaning against the outside wall of the club, one of his mucky trainers kicked out over the other. He booked the registry office right there, on his phone, his voice full of laughter. Course I'm serious, he said. Have you met me?

There was a six-week wait for our appointment. To my surprise when the date arrived, we showed up to the registry office. We caught the bus, Leon in his leather jacket and me in a cheetah-print dress. Our witnesses were the two bouncers who worked at the club, Carlos and Stevie. I remember that Carlos in particular had a sad look on his face, almost apologetic.

Does a bear shit in the woods? said Leon, when the registrar asked him if he wanted to take me as his wife.

I thought that was romantic, honestly I did.

Afterwards we went to the pub and each ordered a pint of Guinness. I sat across from him in the beer garden. He was holding a supermarket bouquet, pink roses that had already browned at the edges, and smoking a cigar. His jaw was so sharp you could have cut the stems on it. I couldn't stop looking at him. When we left the pub, I hung on to his arm in disbelief, worried that otherwise he'd float away. ∎

THE TERMITE QUEEN

Olivia Sudjic

In the late afternoon, the wind picked up and drove the bank of cloud apart, letting midwinter sun surge through at last. It flared at the horizon, insistent as it died, and the road towards it shone, blinding the approaching taxi's sole passenger. Further along the road, it illuminated the roof of her new home, still some miles away, where the sky became a more saturated blue above the waiting house. Pale smoke from its nearest neighbour floated over and quickly vanished on the breeze. At the back, the agave plant began to flail its arms beside the empty pool, one sawing anxiously against another, leaving fresh wounds among dried-out scars, and the whorl of its base littered with brown needles from the pines. In front, a chain-link curtain, recently installed, dragged against the open doorway as the local cleaning woman prepared to leave, removing rubber clogs, replacing them with outdoor pumps, donning a baseball cap and securing her loose red hair through the back as the wind grew stronger still.

It was the last house she had to clean. Just as well. She had reached that terminal point of the year when it seemed impossible to begin another job, or anything at all. Not a personal project, a new health regimen, nor even a conversation with someone she didn't know. She was done. But the year had been marked by what seemed impossible and the mood among the townspeople remained vigilant. Squinting into the low glare as if tasting a tart apple, she shut the door, double-locked, then slid a key beneath a large, flat stone beside the disused water trough. Straightening up, she felt a cold breath at her neck as the sun disappeared and the sky turned grey once more. This darkening overhead made her feel as though she were descending to an underworld. The woman shivered, shouldered her large backpack, put headphones in and hurried off.

All day, all week, all year in fact, she, like the rest of them, had noticed it: the feeling of being watched. If they had felt it before, living in a small town, then the sensation had intensified as plague restrictions came. Even now that these had mostly lifted, stepping outside again, cautiously resuming their old routines, the town's inhabitants were uneasy. They were more aware than usual of who might be observing them about their daily errands, or found themselves coming to their own balconies so as to investigate hushed conversations in the street. Gradually strangers had begun to appear, occupying the houses the mayor was offering via the scheme. As the town became populated with new faces, the existing fear, namely that some unwitting infraction could result in ostracism, had grown alongside them. Someone had taken it upon themselves to cut out a pair of cartoonish evil eyes and stick them to a boulder on the road the cleaning woman was now walking down, just as the taxi bearing the house's new occupant approached from the opposite direction. When she heard the sound of its engine in the distance, she kept her eyes low beneath her baseball cap and continued walking.

The house had stood empty, gathering dust for months before it was renovated and then put up for sale. When it failed to sell, it was reallocated via the mayor's scheme, and yet its former owner was still present to her mind. As soon as she'd arrived and begun cleaning earlier that day, she'd felt convinced she was not alone, conscious of another presence stalking hers, following her from one room to the next. She had been sure of this, though less so of what it wanted – for her to stay or to leave. The house number had been repainted on the rusting mailbox at the end of the drive, blue-grey and fixed to a stake that tilted towards the ground. House numbers in the area were not sequential, nor did they seem to conform to any rules, at least at first. This peculiarity would soon come to the aid of the new occupant, Justine; an olive branch she could extend across awkward silences. The topic was irresistible, even to the more mistrustful locals, and so Justine would have the logic revealed to her several times. The numbers described how many metres along a road a property stood in relation to the town hall. It would become clear the older residents took pride in this system, and she would make sure to compare it favourably to systems elsewhere, but on that first afternoon, arriving from the station as daylight began to fade, locating the correct house took Justine some time.

The driver had never heard of the town, no matter which way she tried pronouncing it – a series of sounds her throat could not quite produce. Most newcomers soon gave up trying, tired of being corrected by locals who each seemed to pronounce it differently and never to say it the same way twice themselves. This was if they used the name at all, rather than referring to it simply as 'the town', as if there were no other. Outsiders in the know referred to it as 'the ghost town', so its real name was rarely spoken aloud, and to do so felt strange to its inhabitants, like calling a parent by their full name. An online translation told Justine that the medieval settlement, where she was bound, meant *zenith*, or an archaic version of that word, while the more modern settlement at the base of the ridge meant *nadir*. When the taxi's navigation system refused to recognise the destination, she'd begun to panic, wondering if the scheme really was too good to be true, just as everyone back home had warned her. What if she were the victim of an elaborate lockdown scam, and had upended her life not for a town on the verge of extinction but a fictional one that had never existed at all? But then the driver entered an approximate location and the car estimated an arrival time two hours hence. As they fell into conversation, mainly sustained by Justine, her fear receded again.

At the start of the journey the driver had warned there would be a hefty surcharge, but she hadn't blinked. Her concept of money, its stranglehold on all of the decisions she made, had altered, beyond adjusting to the foreign currency. Here she no longer felt the need to watch the meter, and instead watched the scenery change outside. First the modern blocks of social housing around the station, then the pale bones of empty fields streaming past. She saw a small shrine dedicated to the town's patron saint, followed by a signpost in the lay-by where climbers parked their vehicles before setting off into the ravine. One arm pointed east to limestone cliffs, with a name meaning 'Devil's Cave'. There were actually two caves situated next to one another, each with openings at either end, so that as the sun rose the caves appeared to be looking towards the town accusingly, glowing like two red eyes. A second arm pointed almost in the same direction, to the ridge on the other side, bearing symbols which promised historic sites and panoramic views. A third pointed onwards, with the fading letters of the town's unsayable, unspoken name.

By the time the map suggested they were getting close to the house, Justine had told the driver all about the slow death of the town and the resurrection efforts of its mayor, who, in addition to bestowing grants and empty homes on people like her, was now offering them free Viagra. At first the driver didn't think his passenger was being serious, or that he hadn't heard her right. Neither was a native speaker. If what she said were true, it was surely some kind of gimmick, and yet the context was familiar, making some of what she told him plausible. He heard versions of it every day, now that his work had more or less returned to how it was before, save for the plastic membrane behind his seat that sealed the back half from the front half of the car. People were leaving cities in large numbers now, whether lured away or driven out. The part about birth rates was often debated on the radio station he listened to. Experts worried about how many people would exist in the future, some warning that growth was unsustainable, incompatible with other forms of life. Others feared the opposite – warning that a shrinking population would be worse.

As they passed a third woman sitting on a white plastic chair beside the road, each one evenly spaced but within earshot of the next, Justine remarked how nice it was to see these young, glamorous women, warming themselves by stamping their legs, find inventive ways to socialise again, not realising they were sex workers. Again he had assumed she was joking, before realising she was serious. She looked young herself. Not that young, actually. Perhaps in her mid-thirties, he would guess. She seemed younger, maybe, because she dressed like a teenage boy, and because of her childish enthusiasm for this foreign place, as though she'd never been abroad before, or had never travelled abroad alone. That was it, he realised – how exhilarated she seemed by the whole experience, an attitude that he felt inexplicably embarrassed to witness, as if she were enjoying her first taste of adult independence. She had been overawed by the scenery in a way that was initially charming, but grew irritating once she asked him to pull over so that she could take a photo of the sign for some prehistoric caves. It was only once they came to the erratic house numbers, when she fell silent and could not direct him to her own house – one she claimed only to have seen in pictures – that it occurred to him she might be mentally unstable. For who else would move, sight unseen, to this isolated ghost town?

On the last stretch of road before the house, Justine noticed how the tarmac was covered in syrupy black lines. 'It must get hot here in summer,' she said, assuming the driver had also noticed them, how they thinned and dribbled in places, as though a nouvelle cuisine chef and not a local road crew had made them. The sight thrilled her – for here was a trace of it, the kind of unseen, elemental force that could crack things open. The driver was too busy studying the strange house numbers to respond, but he noted the change in her voice. She sounded triumphant, as if she'd found what they had been looking for all this time. Her tone annoyed him, and he sighed and stopped the car abruptly in the empty road. 'We'll have to wait for someone to come by and ask them for directions,' he told her, frowning. Justine felt herself tense again as they waited, returning to the worry that it would turn out to be a scam after all. She felt oppressed by the silence of the place, which had slowly entered the car. With the engine off, she could clearly hear her companion's heavy breathing, the wheeze and rattle from deep inside his chest. When a cyclist appeared on the horizon, the driver wound his window down and waved his arm. She heard the wind in the trees, the rip of racing tyres coming towards them, a hum of electric fencing and distant gunshots from the woods. The cyclist came level with the windscreen. He did not unclip his feet but leant his hand against their roof for balance.

'Do you live here?' the driver asked. The cyclist shook his head. 'Visiting,' he said. He explained that all the buildings were numbered according to the Cartesian system, and that he had been visiting his mother for Christmas – as though an explanation were necessary here too – which he felt was the right thing to do, on balance, because she lived alone. She was old, as everyone here was, or, and he glanced at Justine as he said this, as they used to be. Justine held out her phone and showed him photos of the house they were looking for. The cyclist said he knew the one. The day was burning down to its embers. The driver tapped the wheel. He wanted to get going. He wanted to get home. People seemed so mortifyingly hungry for chance encounters these days. They followed the cyclist's instructions, continuing in the direction from which he had emerged, passing the red-haired woman who stood still against the treeline as they drove slowly by. At the mailbox, the driver unlocked the trunk and helped Justine with her bags. At last he would be free of her, free to listen to the radio hosts argue with their callers again. He closed the trunk and heard it echo across the gorge. He found the place eerie but she seemed undaunted. 'Good luck,' he said. 'You too,' she answered, bravely. In his memory of her, eyes fixed on the rear-view mirror, Justine's small figure is rooted to the spot in the descending darkness as the car speeds away. He can see her receding, red in the path of his tail lights, standing alone before the vanishing point.

Justine arrived the week Alma, the mayor's wife, turned forty, which was the week after Christmas and before New Year. In the limbo between these two holidays, birthdays tended to slide over without leaving an impression. As Alma had aged, accumulating lines, her birthdays had grown smooth and featureless, each one blurring into the one before, routines performed as if under hypnosis. On that birthday, however, and in the months which followed, Alma felt wide awake. Her sight appeared magnified, so that the familiar surfaces of her carefully ordered, small-town world grew unfamiliar, transformed by how clearly she could see their texture. The morning after Alma met Justine, her husband, Vincent, found her lying on the floor, studying the high-contrast black-and-white patterns hanging from the baby gym while the baby cried and flailed its arms in the air beside her. The longer she stared at these things, the more starkly they revealed how each element of her life had been assembled according to a set of austere instructions, and how they might now, just as reasonably, be taken apart again. It was a revelation she could not unsee, and acting on it, or allowing its force to act upon her, began to feel inevitable.

The evening Justine arrived, Alma watched her for some time – the young woman standing with a wine glass and phone as if waiting for someone, though Alma knew she had moved to town alone. She recognised the neat, close-cropped head from the passport scan in her husband's file, and then the spooky, pinched face as she removed her mask on seeing no one else was wearing one. Her body was concealed by an oversized dark coat and heavy boots, a look Alma recognised from some of the other urban émigrés who'd come to cosplay nineteenth-century villagers. The town offered the perfect retreat – a place to escape the versions of themselves who'd spent the last few years permanently online. Renouncing the cynicism of their previous lives, they talked of their arrival as being like travelling back in time. This was the romantic notion they expressed to Alma, anyway, even if their reasons for coming, or succumbing to the fantasy, varied by individual circumstance.

Though Alma had spent time away, to study and then to work as a planning consultant for a few years before returning to have children, she'd been born in the town, unlike her husband. She was never surprised by its remoteness, its out-of-nowhereness, which was the way newcomers described it. They would tell her it appeared to them as a mirage, a glitch, shimmering like the heat above the road as they approached by car. Immediately the sight disappeared again from view. Then, at the next bend, it reappeared: a town from folklore, or its outline, as if superimposed there on top of the ridge. A ridge was what Alma called it, since it was not strictly the right shape to be called a mountain, though outsiders often referred to it as one. The locals said ridge, or sometimes a bluff, albeit in their own dialect. It rose three hundred and sixty-two metres above sea level, the town balanced at the edge of a deep gorge. From the opposite side you could look back and see the town and the elegant ruins of the feudal castle with its defensive wall. Behind it, the town square, where Alma now stood, hanging back from the rest of the crowd, swaying rhythmically from side to side as if holding an infant in her arms.

The plan to hold a drinks party under the new propane heaters had been Vincent's idea. Alma had agreed, as long as nobody mentioned her turning forty. Christmas had exhausted her. Before that, the incident with the woman and her baby. She did not feel up to playing hostess that evening. Vincent had given his word he would take care of things, but she could see now, as she had already known, that it would again fall to her, and she would have her work cut out trying to persuade the guests to integrate. The recent arrivals kept to their own, presumably establishing who was who within their nascent social hierarchy. It was understandable that they stood apart from the locals, Alma thought, noting the way the latter sat in their usual formation – the forbidding line of folding chairs around the edges, following the architectural plan of the square. It reminded her of the little drawings at Vincent's clinic that encouraged expecting mothers to get their vaccinations, with the antibodies mobilising against invasion. Of course no outsiders felt able to approach them when they sat that way together.

Supposedly it was an off-duty event, billed in Vincent's email as an informal 'not-quite New Year's party', and crucially not a mayoral function. But Alma knew it had chiefly been arranged so that her husband could monitor his latest intake. Based on his reports, she had generally assumed the assimilation process was going well, but for the first time that evening, looking round at those assembled, she doubted Vincent's confidence. Teething problems were to be expected with the scheme. Even some resentment from the long-standing, majority elderly, inhabitants towards those who'd been imported. Heralded as saviours of the town simply for being under forty. But her husband had always worried more about pleasing the newcomers than the local reaction to his scheme. Many of them came from cities, he cautioned Alma frequently, and so they were used to the conveniences of urban life. These people needed constant looking after. A task which, once Vincent had the paperwork signed, usually fell to Alma. It was Alma, for example, who made sure the pregnant women could find all the relevant items they needed, long after Vincent's clinic had discharged them, Alma who set up a lending library of slings and cribs, and who came to them when their milk ducts were blocked and sore with hot compresses to relieve them. This, Alma thought to herself, was the mythical village people talked about once inducted into parenthood. It was her. Alma was the village. And yet it was also the case that Alma believed her husband was doing something truly progressive in combining his role as mayor with his work at the fertility clinic. How could it be reactionary, as some critics of the scheme had claimed, to welcome outsiders and help women afford children they otherwise wouldn't have had? In that sense, the pronatalist policies were not really about restoring the population of the town, she insisted, or at least not only that. Together she and Vincent were restoring something much more profound, that was their real motive.

Of course the recent tragedy had shaken her. Of course she kept it secret from the other expecting mothers. The poor woman, whose name Alma wanted to forget, the due date that had come and gone, the skin on the woman's belly shining as it distended. Still she had insisted on labouring at home with only Alma present, and Alma had encouraged her. It was strange, she thought now, how desperate the woman – the mother – had been to submit herself to all the interventions at Vincent's clinic, given her subsequent refusal of anything 'unnatural'. She was lonely, she had said. And she was lonely because she felt disconnected from the innate wisdom women had. That she, as a woman, presumably still had access to, somewhere deep down inside her. Located in her womb, she suspected. Ready to rise up from sleep, from suppression, through the primal process of natural labour. What could Alma do but go along with it? Her personal account promoted natural-everything, which was how the woman had found her. It was how she had heard about the scheme in the first place.

Alma flinched, and pushed the woman's shining belly away to the edge of her mind where she could ignore it, at least until it was time to sleep. She caught Vincent's eye as he listened to the local pharmacist. The man was new in the job and struggling without an assistant. Alma had recruited him. They hadn't had a full-time pharmacist in town since 1975, just longer than her lifetime. Vincent held Alma's gaze without changing his expression. The private look stretched between them, like a beam of light from an edged-open door. The image made her think of their children, who were sleeping in their rooms above the square, the youngest of whom she had finally managed to put down before arriving at the party. She should probably check on them, the connection to the monitor might be down again, but at once Vincent raised an eyebrow, forbidding her departure, as if he'd read her mind.

Before becoming parents, this kind of steady look led to other doorways. But after seven children, if she did sense Vincent's attention narrowing on her, it was most often a signal that some diagnosis or prescription would soon befall her, as though she were being subjected to his clinical evaluation. Possibly this was in her imagination, but the effect of that look nowadays, its sudden directed scrutiny, had an effect that was exposing rather than intimate. She tilted her head in Justine's direction, indicating that his new recruit was still standing alone, waiting awkwardly. Alma observed his gaze track towards Justine, noting simultaneously that the shift in focus did not stir her jealousy, as it could with other young women he'd taken in, installing them in the vacant homes that had stood empty since her childhood, driving them back and forth to the clinic for their treatments. Justine was more androgynous than the others had been. Certainly compared to how Vincent preferred women to style themselves. Perhaps that was why Alma did not feel threatened. In fact, there was something about Justine's disregard for the femininity Alma had learned to prize that she found compelling. It dawned on her, the fact sliding ice-cold into her body; now that she had crossed the border into her forties, Alma herself was no longer eligible for the scheme.

She continued observing from afar as Justine pocketed her phone, put down her wine, then busied her right hand by fiddling with a clip on one of her belt loops before kneeling to pull up a pair of thick socks from inside her boots. Perhaps she was one of those women, Alma thought, the kind always protesting one thing or another in the name of feminism, who nevertheless despised women. Particularly if they found contentment in feminine service, or spoke of it as a calling, as Alma herself did. Standing upright again, Justine headed to another table, reaching for the neck of a bottle submerged in a silver cooler. The glow under the heaters was fierce, despite the freezing night sky above. The guests would be parched by now, and drinking fast, Alma realised, watching as Justine gently shook melting ice from the bottle before refilling her empty glass. Alma turned back to her husband and signalled again, but Vincent only jerked his head in a way that communicated it was her duty to look after Justine now. Alma pushed her hair back from her face. She widened her eyes and fixed her mouth into a smile. Thinking back to this moment, she would tell herself that it was Vincent who'd wanted her to take over. By obeying his instructions, assimilating this stranger, she was only being a good wife. ∎

4th Estate proudly congratulates

K Patrick and Eley Williams

for being selected as

Granta's Best of Young British Novelists 2023

K Patrick

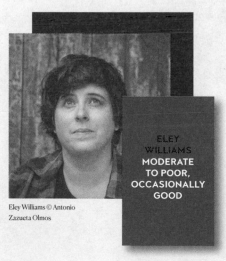

Eley Williams © Antonio Zazueta Olmos

June 2023

Spring 2024

www.4thEstate.co.uk
@4thEstateBooks

4th
ESTATE

ROSTRUM

Eley Williams

A pparently Sue would have to endure the cold morning air of her commute a little longer: the entrance to her office building did not work. *How can an* entrance *not work? Try again, Sue.* The usually-automatic, usually-sliding doors to Sue's office building appeared to be functioning irregularly, refusing to acknowledge her approach. Sue laughed for no one's benefit and advanced, ready to be greeted by the doors' normal hiss and welcoming split, but once again she came up close against the glass of the door and watched her reflection stiffen.

Sue ran through various second-guessings as she regrouped. It was definitely a working day and she hadn't accidentally misread her calendar. This was definitely the right building, the same one as always, and these were the same doors she had sluiced through for nigh on seven years. She was awake. She was almost certain she was awake.

Sue planted her feet a little further apart so that her body might become a slightly more assertive shape. During a training day at work some months ago, a bright-eyed external consultant had breezed into the building and made all of Sue's colleagues line up and one by one strike different poses. This was meant to inform or improve office culture, or customer support, or business skills. Something along those lines. He promised that after an hour with him they would all not only be able to physically impress a room but ensure that 'clients, onlookers and interlocutors from this moment on will experience value-added comportment denoting frank and open dynamism'. She watched each of her colleagues attempt frank and dynamic standing, sitting down, handshakes, and she patiently listened to the consultant outline how they might improve. When it was Sue's turn, by which time everyone was bored and fidgety, the consultant instructed her to stand as if she were addressing a room full of hostile negotiators. She did so, earnestly. The consultant tutted, then came right up next to her and ducked down, and Sue felt a hand tugging at her ankle chivvying her leg and foot into a new configuration. She kept her smile fixed for the imagined hostile patrons, and allowed her leg to be redirected. 'Far better,' Sue heard the consultant say, his grip still around her ankle, his bowed head at the level of her hip. There was a warmth in his voice that made Sue dart a glance downward, to see if he was proud of her, but he did not meet her gaze. Sue craned frankly, dynamically, earnestly at the top of the consultant's head. The parting in his hair was so neat that long after the exercise was over, after the training day was finished, and over the course of the following weeks, Sue found herself compulsively thinking about it: that neat, clean parting in his hair. It intruded on her thoughts as she rode home on the bus, smoothing a seam into a bus ticket with the edge of her thumb. It occupied her as she took a shortcut through the park, following the desire lines that communally hemmed and stitched the official design of its squares of grass. She thought of the parting in that bowed consultant's hair every time she passed a framing shop, or saw vapour trails carving across the sky. She couldn't recall what the consultant's face looked like, or what clothes he was wearing, or whether he spoke with any particular accent or what his name might be, but for whatever reason she knew the quality and definition of that parting in his hair would be with her until her dying day.

She daydreamed about the consultant's bedside table. She could envisage such a table quite clearly. It would be neatly arranged with a variety of obscure tools dedicated to precision which he would apply to his body every morning. Some kind of emery board or sandpaper to buff any creasing traces of sleep from his eyelids; a burin to finesse every pore; he might floss his teeth and between his toes with a fine wire gauge. The parting put her in mind of awls and chisels.

This morning, confronted with the closed doors, Sue thought of the parting in the consultant's hair, his clean hands clasped around her ankle, and marshalled her body into action. She shifted her balance, lifted her chin, and advanced towards the doors once more. They did not respond. Her shoulders drooped as she looked, hurt, at the speckled grey matting of the prohibited floor beyond.

It must be the case of some unseen, unknowable sensor misfiring, Sue thought, or perhaps something as simple as dust or other occluded gubbins jamming the doors' mechanism. Certainly this kind of thing just happened sometimes – it was a glitch, an unfortunate error, and could happen to anyone. Sue tried again and this time she performed a pantomime swing of her arms, as if the problem lay in a lack of momentum rather than perceived conviction, but there was no corresponding twitch of recognition from the office doors, no elegant glide of metal and glass permitting her through. This was dreadful and obscene – a complete joke. Sue looked around. She hoped to lock eyes with a passer-by and establish the whole business as daft and forgivable or gently unforgettable rather than monstrous, but no one along the busy city street seemed to be facing her direction. It felt like she was being watched, and the uneasy heat or pressure that surveillance brings to the surface of one's skin lay taut and coiling at her nape and ears, but as far as she could see nobody seemed to be giving her any mind. If anything all the commuters around her seemed to be pointedly *not* looking at Sue, hurrying past and pulling their coats more closely about their bodies. Sue returned to the doors and gnawed her lip, looking them up and down. Not even a CCTV camera to wave towards, hopefully, apologetically.

Sue pictured her desk upstairs beyond these unbudging doors, beyond the lobby, beyond the elevator's familiar wrenching hiss and the carpet-cladded corridors. She imagined the boring, necessary details awaiting her there: her overwatered plant in its glum yellow pot, the faux rose-gold stapler that she bought in order to cheer up the place. She imagined the Post-it notes on her desk that had lost their gumminess and accrued a fluffy kind of silt along their edges. Another line delivered by the visiting consultant returned to her: *The key to manifesting what you desire is to cultivate the feeling you want to experience.* Sue shut her eyes and tried to conceive herself at her desk. The iambs and dactyls of the franking machine sounding down the hallway, the air-conditioned air brittling the surface of her tea – Sue felt her breath steady and, newly galvanised, she stepped again towards the sliding doors. They didn't even flinch.

Sue brushed something invisible from her coat sleeve, extended a hand to the glass of the door as if to rap upon it and then, with a snarl, clamped her arm to her side and tried to take the doors by surprise, shivering forwards once more with an angled shoulder and a grim, set jaw. She made contact with the door and burred its surface with mustered force, but – *and* – that was all. It would not be bested.

Sue juddered back on an italicised heel, Sue-in-reflection shaking her head like a stunned, dispirited cartoon of a person.

She approached the doors again, no longer clear about anything, and allowed her forehead and the tip of her nose to press against the cool of their unyielding, unsliding glass. That feeling again of being watched. Sue's reflection squinted at her, then she slid her eyes across the glass to the view of the street over her shoulder.

Opposite Sue's office building, across a featurelessly busy rat race of a road, there stood a seafood restaurant. She was used to looking out at the restaurant from her office window. Used to it being there, that is, rather than properly taking an interest in it – just one of the unremarkable facts that upholster a working day. Sue had never considered the restaurant closely and she had never been inside – it was very overlookable, and after all she preferred to eat lunch at her desk. Recently the office had bought everyone little plastic sheaths bearing the company logo that you could slot beneath your monitor so that crumbs wouldn't fall into the keyboard. Sue had never really thought about it, but now she felt quite strongly that a seafood restaurant in the middle of this non-coastal town was vaguely embarrassing. Looking at her reflection in her awful, clarifying, firmly closed office doors, Sue saw the salmon-coloured swags of the restaurant's curtains hitched up about its windows. She imagined they were once white but had been stained by years of steam and kitchen-stink. If she stared in the reflection and really concentrated, Sue believed she could see movement from inside the restaurant. The white tablecloths, the dull shine of cutlery arranged on tables. *Who went to a seafood restaurant for breakfast?* Sue thought, disgusted at everything. Sue glared at her reflection. Sue glared at the reflection of the restaurant across the street. Sue saw there was a woman at a table in the restaurant's window, or the shape and movement of a woman. The woman appeared to be waving, and Sue felt that she needed to be certain, so she pitched away from the unmoved doors and pivoted on her heel.

Although buses and cars and people streamed past it was clear that the woman in the restaurant across the street *was* waving at Sue – staring, and waving very slowly and deliberately. By the looks of things, even at this distance and at this early hour, the woman was obviously enjoying a huge meal – she had a table to herself in the window, and it was laden with plates and dishes. Although Sue could not pretend to guess exactly what the woman was eating it had all the fresh pinks and whites and greens and chrome-sheened levels that implied some kind of seafood platter. Sue imagined oysters, langoustine; she felt the sensation of the sting and spritz of squeezed lemon wedges along the crest of her tongue.

Without thinking about it, Sue waved back.

The woman's hand stopped, hesitated, then she was waving again but in a slightly different way. Rather than tracing an arc back and forth, Sue watched as the woman across the street in the restaurant window rippled her fingers one by one through the air. If the hand had been placed flat on a table, it would have caused a drumming sound. It was a summoning gesture, camp and delicate, unnerving and beguiling. Without thinking about it, Sue returned the wave in kind, modulating her own hand movement to match the stranger's rippling gesture. She took a step towards the seafood restaurant, glad to have a reason not to further shame herself in front of the closed office doors, and as Sue lifted her foot off the kerb she noticed details about the seafood restaurant that she had never appreciated before: the grey fuzz of smudged chalk on its menu board, the dust clogging in its window boxes' artificial plants. By the time Sue reached the traffic lights in the centre of the road, she was close enough to see that the woman was about her age, with a similar build and colouring. Her shoulders were slightly more rounded, perhaps, and that was surely fair enough as the woman was hunched over her far-too-early lunch. Sue could now clearly see that the woman did indeed have a luxurious and indulgent spread all across her table. The remnants of a meal, rather, as now she could see that there were piles and piles of discarded bones and scales and shells strewn across the plates and scattered cutlery.

Grunts and squeaks of traffic and the sound of distant horns tuned the air all around her as Sue kept walking across the road, waving and waving. She forgot all about the automatic doors just as they had forgotten about her, and with her head held unnaturally high so that she would be able to meet the eyes of the woman sitting in the approaching restaurant window Sue kept walking, waving at her advancing reflection. She was close enough now to see that the woman at the table had shelled all the prawns on her plate; in fact, as she drew closer Sue noticed that the woman had slotted each of their bright orange heads onto the fingertips of her waving, waving hand. ∎

London Review
OF BOOKS

Claim Your FREE Copy Today

Explore a world of ideas with the *London Review of Books*. Covering politics, history, literature, poetry and the arts, the LRB provides a platform for the world's best writers to explore their ideas in more depth.

Try the LRB today FREE
lrb.me/granta

The British Museum

Give the gift of Membership

Set someone special on a journey through human history. They'll enjoy 12 months of extraordinary exhibitions as well as an exclusive programme of Membership events.

Buy now

Ways to buy
britishmuseum.org/membership
+44 (0)20 7323 8195

The British Museum Friends is a registered charity and company limited by guarantee which exists to support the British Museum.

Registered charity number 1086080
Company registration number 04133346

Large vase, tin-glazed earthenware (maiolica), from the workshop of Orazio Fontana, made in Urbino, Italy, about 1565–1571, with gilt-metal mounts made in Paris, France, about 1765. Part of the Waddesdon Bequest.

THE PARIS REVIEW

America's preeminent literary magazine, since 1953.

CONTRIBUTORS

Graeme Armstrong is from Airdrie, Scotland. His debut novel, *The Young Team*, was published in 2020 and became a *Sunday Times* bestseller. It received the Somerset Maugham and Betty Trask Awards and was Scots Book of the Year in 2021. He is currently undertaking a PhD at the University of Strathclyde.

Jennifer Atkins was born in London, where she is currently based. Her fiction has been published by the *White Review* and she has written for the *World of Interiors* magazine. Her debut novel, *The Cellist*, was published in 2022.

Sara Baume is the author of three novels, *Spill Simmer Falter Wither*, *A Line Made by Walking* and *Seven Steeples*, and one book of non-fiction, *Handiwork*. She lives and works on the south coast of Ireland.

Sarah Bernstein is from Montreal, Canada, and lives in the Northwest Highlands. She is the author of *The Coming Bad Days* and *Now Comes the Lightning*. 'A Dying Tongue' is an excerpt from her novel, *Study for Obedience*, forthcoming from Granta Books in 2023.

Natasha Brown's debut novel *Assembly* was published in 2021.

Eleanor Catton is the author of *The Luminaries*, winner of the 2013 Man Booker Prize, and *The Rehearsal*. As a screenwriter, she has adapted *The Luminaries* for television, and Jane Austen's *Emma* for feature film. Born in Canada and raised in New Zealand, she now lives in Cambridge, England.

Eliza Clark was born in Newcastle upon Tyne and now lives in London. Her first novel, *Boy Parts*, was written after she received a place on New Writing North's Young Writers' Talent Fund and was published by Influx Press in 2020. Her second novel, *Penance*, will be published in 2023. 'She's Always Hungry' is an excerpt from her story collection of the same title, forthcoming from Faber & Faber in 2024.

Tom Crewe was born in Middlesbrough in 1989. He has a PhD in nineteenth-century British history from the University of Cambridge. Since 2015 he has been an editor at the *London Review of Books*, to which he has contributed more than thirty essays on politics, art, history and fiction. *The New Life*, his first novel, was published in 2023.

Lauren Aimee Curtis was born in Sydney, Australia, in 1988. She is the author of *Dolores*, which was shortlisted for the Readings Prize, the UTS Glenda Adams Award for New Writing, and selected as a *New Statesman* Book of the Year. 'Strangers at the Port' is an excerpt from her novel of the same title, forthcoming from Weidenfeld & Nicolson in 2023.

Camilla Grudova is the author of *The Doll's Alphabet* and *Children of Paradise*. She was born in Canada and lives in Edinburgh.

Isabella Hammad is the author of *The Parisian* and *Enter Ghost*. She was awarded the Plimpton Prize for Fiction, the Sue Kaufman Prize from the American Academy of Arts and Letters, the Palestine Book Award and a Betty Trask Award. She has received fellowships from the Rockefeller Foundation, the Lannan Foundation and the Columbia University Institute for Ideas and Imagination.

Sophie Mackintosh was born in South Wales in 1988, and is currently based in London. She is the author of novels *The Water Cure*, *Blue Ticket* and *Cursed Bread*, and her work has been published

by the *New York Times*, *Granta*, the *Stinging Fly* and others. *The Water Cure* was longlisted for the 2018 Man Booker Prize.

Anna Metcalfe is a writer and lecturer in creative writing at the University of Birmingham. Her story collection *Blind Water Pass* was published in 2016. Her first novel, *Chrysalis*, will be published in 2023.

Thomas Morris was born and raised in Caerphilly, South Wales. His debut story collection, *We Don't Know What We're Doing*, won Wales Book of the Year, the Rhys Davies Trust Fiction Award and a Somerset Maugham Award. His second book of stories, *Open Up*, will be published in 2023.

Derek Owusu is a writer and poet. He is the editor of *SAFE: On Black British Men Reclaiming Space*, and his debut novel, *That Reminds Me*, was awarded the 2020 Desmond Elliott Prize. His second novel, *Losing the Plot*, was published in 2022.

K Patrick is a poet and fiction writer based on the Isle of Lewis. In 2021 they were shortlisted for both the *White Review* Poet's Prize and Short Story Prize, and in 2020 they were runner-up in the Ivan Juritz Prize and the Laura Kinsella Fellowship. 'Mrs S' is an excerpt from their debut novel of the same title, forthcoming from Fourth Estate in 2023.

Yara Rodrigues Fowler grew up in South London. She is the author of two novels, *Stubborn Archivist* and *there are more things*. *Stubborn Archivist* was longlisted for the Dylan Thomas Prize, the Desmond Elliott Prize and the *Sunday Times* Young Writer of the Year Award. As a work in progress, *there are more things* received the 2018 Society of Authors' John C Lawrence Award and was shortlisted for the 2020 Eccles Centre and Hay Festival Writer's Award, and after publication was shortlisted for the 2022 Orwell Prize for Political Fiction and the 2022 Goldsmiths Prize.

Saba Sams is a writer based in London. Her story 'Blue 4eva' won the 2022 BBC National Short Story Award. *Send Nudes*, her debut collection, won the 2022 Edge Hill Prize. Her fiction and non-fiction has appeared in *Granta*, the *Stinging Fly* and the *White Review*, among other publications.

Olivia Sudjic's debut novel, *Sympathy*, was a finalist for the Salerno European Book Award and the Collyer Bristow Prize in 2017. Her second novel, *Asylum Road*, was shortlisted for the Encore Award and the Gordon Bowker Volcano Prize in 2021. Her non-fiction work, *Exposure*, was named an *Irish Times*, Evening Standard and *White Review* Book of the Year. 'The Termite Queen' is an excerpt from her novel of the same title, forthcoming from Bloomsbury in 2024.

Eley Williams works at Royal Holloway, University of London. Alongside her novel, *The Liar's Dictionary*, and collection of short fiction, *Attrib.*, her writing has been published in journals and anthologies including *Modern Queer Poets*, *The Penguin Book of the Contemporary British Short Story* and *Liberating the Canon*. Her stories and serialised fiction have also been commissioned by Radio 4. She is a Fellow of the Royal Society of Literature.

Alice Zoo is a photographer and writer. Her work has been commissioned by publications including *National Geographic*, the *New York Times* and the *New Yorker*, and has been exhibited internationally. She lives in London.